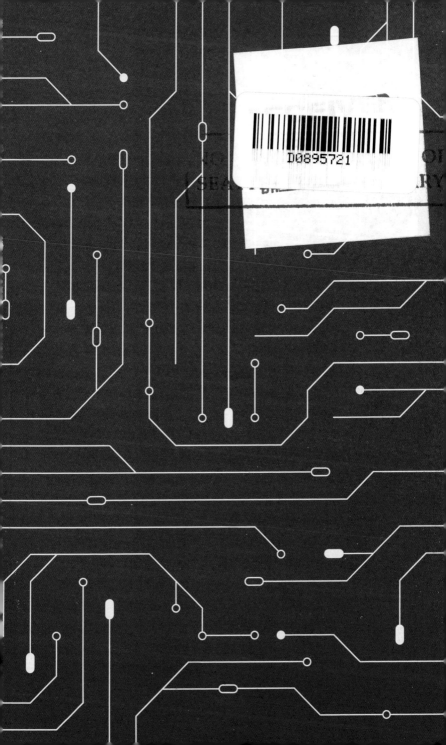

CLOCK TOWER PUBLISHING

GAME OVER

PRESS ◇ TO START

Clock Tower Publishing, an imprint of
Sweet Cherry Publishing Limited
Unit 36, Vulcan House,
Vulcan Road,
Leicester, LE5 3EF
United Kingdom

Small Press of the Year 2021

First published in the UK in 2022
2022 edition

2 4 6 8 10 9 7 5 3 1

ISBN: 978-1-78226-959-5

© M. J. Sullivan

Game Over: Rise of the Raid Mob

Cover design and illustrations by Sophie Jones

www.clocktowerpublishing.com

Printed and bound in Turkey

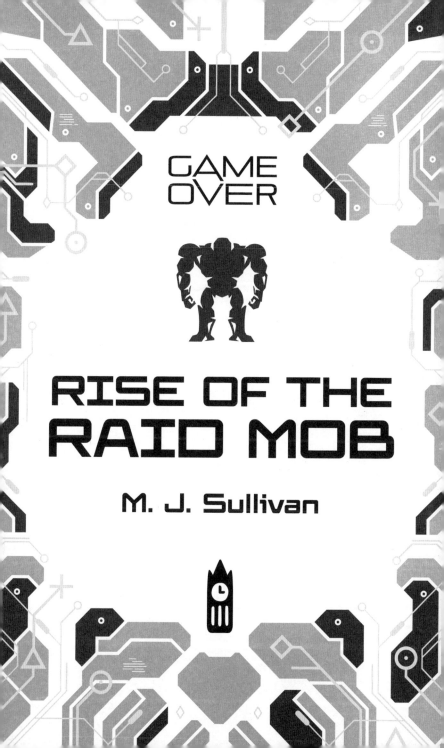

GAME
OVER

RISE OF THE
RAID MOB

M. J. Sullivan

For Claire

The Zelda to my Link
The Princess Peach to my Mario
The S Tetromino to my L

Level 1:
Distant Dawn

Liquid light dripped from the largest moon in the sky, trickling through gaps in crimson clouds and splashing across the robot's armour. The metal plates that formed the WarMech's chest distorted the reflection of Colaxia – the fifth and largest of the moons orbiting Rotec. Smaller sections of armour cut the light into silver slithers that danced like the shifting shards inside a kaleidoscope. The only parts of the metal being that didn't reflect the light were its eyes: cold black orbs that snuffed out the moon's radiance.

The WarMech stood dead still.

It was waiting for something.

'YO! Are you doing the broody robot thing on purpose? Or are you in the bathroom? AGAIN?'

A thunderous crack tore across the barren landscape, ripping through boulders and throwing up coils of violet sand. When the debris eventually cleared, a second, massive machine was revealed. It was nothing like the first. The moonlight could not dance across its armour, because every panel was either scarred from battle, plastered with blue camo print, or covered with retro console and cartoon logos. The red-and-black *ThunderCats* icon adorned its chest like a badge of honour, and *Konami*, *Atari* and *Sega* stickers were pasted all over its limbs.

As the giant robot dusted off chunks of broken purple rock, a line of holographic characters appeared above its head.

Zuul

In response to this dramatic drop-in, the first robot turned, slowly, until it faced the graffitied machine. A group of letters materialised above its head.

ForgeFire666

Then it spoke.

'S-sorry, Zuuly! Too many Sh-ShockSodas.'

The voice didn't suit the menacing mech one bit.

It was too whiny; too soft. By contrast, the reply it got was sharp, scolding, and matched the character of the grungy mech perfectly.

'*Jeez*, Forge! Your toilet bowl must take more enemy fire in a day than your WarMech sees in a week! Your bladder deserves its own ShockSoda sponsorship.'

'Actually, they did, err, offer me a c-contract. Well, I mean, they offered F-F-FForgeFire666 one.'

'Which, as a loyal member of the group, and a ... semi-sensible human being, you didn't take,' said another voice.

This rasping speech was the only sound that betrayed the arrival of a third mech. For its size, it moved with unnerving agility and control. Following its near-silent landing, it took a few final, barely-audible steps towards the other two mechs, and the holographic text above its angular grey head instantly became the most eye-catching thing about it.

Hephaestus

'Oh goody! Doctor Buzzkill has arrived!' said Zuul. 'Just in time to make sure we all get our daily dose of back-down-to-Earth.'

The matte grey stealth mech stood absolutely still, regarding Zuul with simulated scorn.

'*I'm* looking out for our best interests. Anonymity is our ally. You've seen what happens. Publicity and exposure bring–'

'Fame? Adoration? *A butt ton of money*?'

'... Trouble.'

Those two clipped syllables signalled the end of that discussion. Hephaestus quickly moved on to a more pressing concern.

'What's delaying him this time? The mission starts soon.'

'What *is* the mission, anyway?' Zuul asked.

Hephaestus barely bothered to stifle its frustration. 'Did you not watch the General's briefing?'

'Mate – those cutscenes go on *forever!* I know Hailstorm probably paid top dollar for Tom Hanks to do the voice, but honestly ... he goes on a bit, don't you think? It's like watching paint dry. In a doctor's waiting room. With no Wi-Fi, and only a tiny TV showing vegetable slicers and vacuums with faces on the shopping channel ...'

Hephaestus was about to begin a lengthy recap of the mission briefing when ForgeFire666's mech interrupted him with a sound that made the stealthy robot wince: the sound of crisps being munched.

'It's another *CRUNCH* mining protection op. The Nograki scouts have found the *CRUNCH CRUNCH* teslate deposits. They're sending in kill squads to take out the miners and–'

'And-we-must-take-them-out-first-and-secure-the-mines,' spat Hephaestus, cutting through Forge's snack-soaked explanation. 'Now, where is–'

'*Sorry!* Sorry I'm late, everyone. Well, not late, really. Technically bang on time. Ready to go. *Totally* in the zone. Sooo … what's the mission?'

A weighty sigh swelled across the violet terrain. This fourth, clunking WarMech looked older than the others. Its hinges creaked as it landed heavily and lumbered forwards. The panels of its armour were all severely dinted; patched-over lacerations and deep, rusted scars criss-crossed over every surface. A glowing handle appeared above its head.

tHeScOuRgE

'Paper round?' said the clipped voice of Hephaestus.

'Yup,' replied tHeScOuRgE.

'Flat tyre?'

'Second one this week.'

'*And* the second time you've nearly missed the start of an Elite Campaign. Double points, remember? There's not much separating the Top Ten; someone could quite easily take your spot. You might try avoiding the risk of disqualification every now and then …'

At this, the voice behind the battered WarMech

altered. The cheery, slightly-out-of-breath enthusiasm vanished, replaced by curt frostiness.

'Not everyone has a rich mummy and daddy to buy their upgrades, *Phaesterer*. I'm here, aren't I? I'm ready. And last I checked, I rank *above* you. So, why don't you worry about your own spot, and who might be looking to take *you* down?'

tHeScOuRgE nodded towards Zuul with a creaking flick of its head. A new block of text emerged, floating above the purple landscape.

DISTANT DAWN: MISSION 3A-56.2
THE MINES OF MAROK

ELITE MISSION COMBATANTS

POSITION	I.D.	XP
PLAYER 1	_Carbon_Shift_	78,975
PLAYER 2	BunnyQueen12	78,223
PLAYER 3	ForgeFire666	78,109
PLAYER 4	tHeScOuRgE	77,312
PLAYER 5	Hephaestus	77,144
PLAYER 6	Zuul	76,263
PLAYER 7	Th£D£V@ST@TOR	76,005
PLAYER 8	SaiboTron	75,768
PLAYER 9	HudsonNotHicks	75,476
PLAYER 10	Jeeroy-Lenkins	75,306

'So ...' tHeScOuRgE said, pausing to let the table punctuate his point. 'What's our mission?'

'Protect *CRUNCH* teslate mines. D-destroy the *CRUNCH* Nograki kill squad *CRUNCH*.'

'Thanks, Forge,' said the dinted robot, the cheeriness in its voice returning as quickly as it had disappeared. 'Have you completed your pre-mish bathroom checks?'

'Very funny. And yes ... y-yes I have,' came the reply, followed by the scrunching of an empty crisp packet.

Hephaestus reassumed command. 'Okay, Raid Mob. Systems check and readiness report. The mission timer is ticking. Sixty seconds 'til go-time.'

'He loves this bit, doesn't he?' said Zuul, as the camo-covered mech's panels began to whir and shift. Plates on its forearms opened up like mechanical flowers, revealing dual pulse phasers on one side and a plasma-powered railgun on the other. From the top of Zuul's shoulder armour, laser-guided cannons loaded with Nograki-piercing rounds rose on rotating turrets. A giant *Ghostbusters* logo on its back split in half, releasing two propulsion vents that fired exhaust fumes into the ground, one glowing red and the other burning bright blue. A swirling purple cloud engulfed the WarMech, and from the midst of the sand, a wild laughter grew.

Then the other WarMechs began to arrive.

SaiboTron's mech dropped first, all sleek surfaces and sharp angles. Although it was stuffed to the brim with weaponry, it had little need for any of it. The sharpened edges of its limbs allowed it to rush its opponent and slice them to pieces, like razor blades swirling in a tornado.

The mech that landed next to SaiboTron looked more likely to crush its enemies with brute force. BunnyQueen12's robot was by far the largest: a leaden bruiser able to shift its massive density on command. If it wanted to stomp a Nograki into the ground, it could transfer 80% of its weight to the sole of its giant metal foot. Or, if it wanted to send an alien soaring into orbit, it could load its fist with eight times its usual weight and swing that thing like a turbo-powered wrecking ball.

The HudsonNotHicks mech was next: pure military spec, decked out with a striped green camo skin and glinting dog tags around its thick neck, topped-off with an army helmet that had 'STATE-OF-THE-BADASS-ART' stencilled across the back. It oozed military might, and could call in weaponised satellite strikes and drone cover fire during battle.

Jeeroy-Lenkins had a medieval-knight-meets-Optimus-Prime thing going on, with a custom coat-of-arms cape and a lance that doubled as a laser sight for the stockpile of nuke-tip projectiles nestled within its chest armour.

Th£D£V@ST@TOR looked like an advert for every stick-on upgrade it was possible to purchase. But it was _Carbon_Shift_ that drew the most attention ...

The top-ranked WarMech stood at a distance from the others, as if it were a little too good to hang with the rest. Although it wasn't the largest mech in the field, it seemed to take up the most space. It was cloaked by a shimmering golden aura, which in the world of *Distant Dawn* was referred to as "The Glow".

'You know they've boosted The Glow's power-ups, right?' said Zuul. '1.5 XP, double points for tier-3 and higher kills, not to mention bigger mag capacity, quicker reload times, boosts on sprint speed *and* duration. *I* think someone's overcompensating ...'

'... For the recoil on those cannons, I'd g-guess,' replied ForgeFire666, naively. 'But it's not f-fair – he doesn't even need it. He's already f-fir, he's already f-f-fir ... he's already at the t-top of the table.'

'We wouldn't complain if one of us had The Glow,' said Hephaestus. 'The most sensible thing we could do at this juncture is to–'

Hephaestus suddenly fell silent. The aura from the golden orb mounted behind blast-shielding in _Carbon_Shift_'s chest began to change. It surged down the flanks of the giant WarMech, and panels began to shift. Weapons were revealed the likes of which the Raid Mob had never seen. Quad-barrelled pulse cannons sprung from each arm; lasergate ray shooters extended from thick metal fingertips; a recess opened below the orb mounting, and inside were *five* nuke-fuelled rocket launchers stacked like ShockSodas in a vending machine. KPS long-range rocket systems, Inciner8 heat flares, remote detonation drones on jet-powered launch mechanisms – _Carbon_Shift_ had weapons that had, until now, been the stuff of whisperings on *Distant Dawn* forums.

'Well ... I mean ... *that's* just not fair,' said Hephaestus.

'At least Golden Boy is on *our* side for this mission. Is he streaming?' Zuul asked.

'Yup – as always. And with The Glow armour and all those mods, he's getting more attention than a grumpy cat meme,' replied tHeScOuRgE. 'Have you *seen* his sub count?'

'Just passed fifty million, hasn't he? His Twitch streams are always top rated.'

'I h-heard he bought a new house with the mmm-money from his last sponsorship deal. He must be rolling in ... he must have so m-much ... he must be so *rich!*' ForgeFire666 stammered.

'Yes, but he did that because the entire internet found out where he lived. He's been doxed and swatted twice this year. *Anonymity*, my friends. It's worth more than you realise.'

Hephaestus's words of wisdom went whistling into the wind as the mission timer reached zero. The sky darkened. The WarMechs glanced upwards ...

The Nograki dropships were here.

The light of Colaxia was blotted out by three enormous vessels. Each had an arachnoid body with a shell-like exoskeleton, tapering to a sharp point at the rear. Limbs jutted out from the hull, pulsing with extra-terrestrial energy as they propelled the crafts forwards. The bow of each ship glowed red hot, still smouldering from their entry through Rotec's churning thermosphere.

The vessels came to a hovering halt a few hundred metres away. As if by instinct, Zuul's shoulder-mounted cannon popped up, and an armour-piercing round slid into the chamber ... but no shot was taken. In the early days of *Distant Dawn*, these ships had been a fraction of the size, and the Nograki invaders had abseiled from their bellies on long tentacles. Any mech with a keen aim could take them out before they even hit the ground. Now, the aliens were fired out in pods that, while susceptible to damage, travelled at such a speed that it wasn't worth wasting the ammo. Zuul knew that it was better to wait until the Nograkis crawled out into the open.

'Ugh. They never get any better looking, do they?' said tHeScOuRgE.

'Maybe that's why they're so angry all the time,' Zuul mused. 'Poor body image, social media pressures, a ravenous lust for human flesh ...'

ForgeFire666 let out a chuckle. Hephaestus didn't make a sound. A glowing red filter swept across the stealth mech's visor: a specialist upgrade for those with a sniper shot-to-kill ratio of 10:8 or higher. With it, the mech could zoom further, shrinking the rugged landscape and drawing the enemy right into its sights.

tHeScOuRgE was right. It was not a pretty picture.

Whoever – or whatever – had created the Nograki scouts hadn't been too concerned with looks. The fearsome monsters stood around four metres in height, though their elongated legs made them appear even taller. These lower limbs had joints that were hinged at all the wrong angles, with root-like tendrils for feet that made the scouts fast over any terrain, hard to knock down, and lethal at close range. Four upper limbs sprouted asymmetrically from their torsos. The top arms fired long range, focused energy blasts, the lower limbs could switch between a single shotgun-like spray of burning mucus and a machine-gun hailstorm of the same armour-melting secretion. And the closer they got, the clearer their most deadly feature became.

Two gland sacs underneath their elongated heads fed bile into four huge fangs, one in each corner of their terrifying jaws. This terrible toxin could tear through a WarMech's internals in seconds, melting it from the inside out. No combatant wanted to see a Nograki scout up close. Its six beady green eyes and dripping mandibles were the stuff of digital nightmares.

'You know what I've always wondered? Why are these things – beings from a technologically advanced predator race – totally fine with running around a battlefield completely naked?'

None of the other mechs responded, so Zuul pressed the point.

'I mean, is it a Bugs Bunny scenario? Then again, even he put a towel around himself whenever he got out of the bath. That was weird, right? And these things don't even have fur, or feathers. Do you think they *know*? Maybe we could use it against them ... harness the power of shame!'

'Zuul?' said Hephaestus.

'Yeah?'

'Shut up.'

Zuul fell uncharacteristically silent, noticing what the other mechs had already spotted. It was detaching itself from the hull of the furthest dropship, like a gigantic leech falling free after gorging itself on the blood of its host. It was at least three times as big as any of the Nograki scouts, and it stood on six, tri-hinged limbs, each covered with hundreds of spikes that throbbed with the same toxin that flowed through the scouts' deadly fangs. Its underbelly was split into thick, rough plates, with narrow gaps between each that glowed molten orange. A single green eye was set deep into its scaly forehead, and endless rows of needle-pointed fangs lined the inside of its menacing mouth.

'Oh-kay then. Never seen one of *those* before,' said Zuul, bravado faltering with each word. 'Any suggestions? Other than bowel evacuation?'

Eventually, tHeScOuRgE took a creaking step towards the Nograki invaders. The mech's thick metal fingers curled into a fist.

'Let's rumble.'

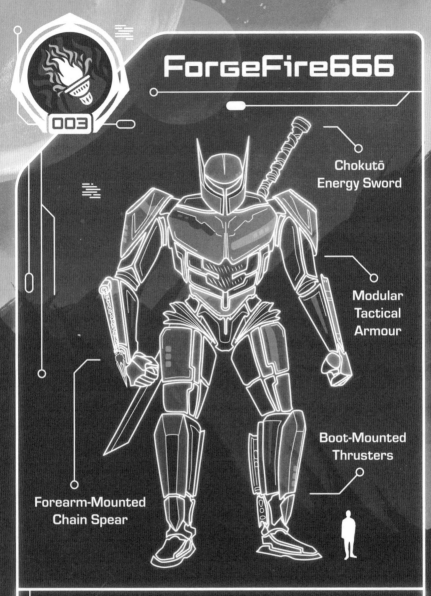

ForgeFire666

003

Chokutō Energy Sword

Modular Tactical Armour

Boot-Mounted Thrusters

Forearm-Mounted Chain Spear

ForgeFire666's shining armour and lethal add-ons strike dread and admiration in equal measure. For its elite pilot, it's certainly not a case of 'all the gear, no idea'. This mech is a heavily-customised and finely-tuned instrument of devastation, wielded with surgical precision.

tHeScOuRgE

004

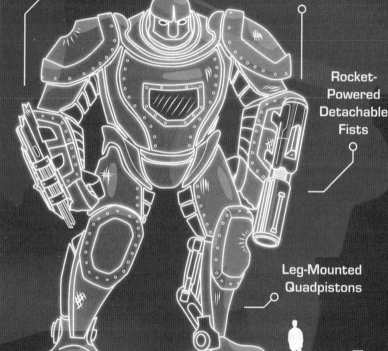

Right-Forearm-Mounted Laser Phaser

Left-Forearm-Mounted Nuke-fuelled Grenade Launcher

Rocket-Powered Detachable Fists

Leg-Mounted Quadpistons

tHeScOuRgE is a battle-scarred, bare-boned bruiser. The clunking titan had already seen better days before it was discovered in the dregs of the *Distant Dawn* marketplace. And yet, this hunk of dented metal quickly became a legendary machine of war.

Hephaestus

Nanomite Cloaking and Transformation Tech

Stealth Panelled Armour

Forearm-Mounted Grappling Hook

Sonic Sniper Rifle with Remote-Controlled Ammo

Silent and stealthy, Hephaestus grabs as much attention as a robotic shadow. This mech has developed a dual reputation as the biggest camper in the game, and the deadliest sniper. One thing's for sure: you'll never see it, or its remote-control bullets, coming.

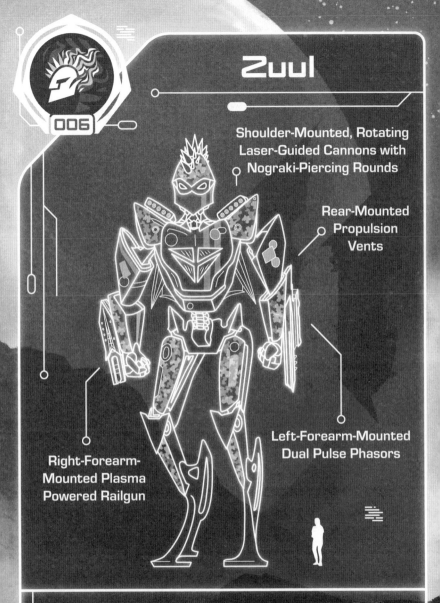

Zuul

006

Shoulder-Mounted, Rotating Laser-Guided Cannons with Nograki-Piercing Rounds

Rear-Mounted Propulsion Vents

Left-Forearm-Mounted Dual Pulse Phasors

Right-Forearm-Mounted Plasma Powered Railgun

Part ThunderTank, part Namco arcade machine, Zuul is a grungy, graffitied, butt-kicking homage to retro gaming and old-school cartoons. Its style might be unorthodox, but this WarMech never fails to earn its pilot the respect of every other *Distant Dawn* combatant.

Level 2: The Bedroom Warrior

The boy's skinny fingers turned white at the knuckles as he mirrored the curled metal fist of the robot on his grimy, fourth-hand TV. He pressed his fingertips into the palm of his right hand, grimacing at the pain in his split nails. He'd washed seven cars the day before; his skin was shrivelled and cracked. But the money he'd earned was about to come in handy. Regripping his battered game controller, he flicked through menu tabs. There was still time to grab the upgraded scope for his railgun. He'd had his eye on it for weeks. Plus, the only weaknesses he could see in the giant Nograki boss were the cracks between the plates on its underbelly. He'd need his loadout *and* his aim to be dead-on tonight.

Level 2: The Bedroom Warrior

The boy's name was Jack Delaney. He was thirteen years old. He was the gamer behind the WarMech known as tHeScOuRgE, and he also happened to be the fourth-best *Distant Dawn* player on the planet.

The moon outside Jack's window was whiter than Colaxia's; its light streamed through threadbare curtains that rippled in a draught – cold air seeping through cracks in the old, wooden window frame. Jack didn't mind, though. It kept him sharp. And if he did get chilly, he'd pull his bedcovers up around his shoulders.

His room was so small that if he stood in the middle, even with his short arms, he could stretch out and touch both opposite walls at the same time. But again, to Jack this was no bad thing. He liked to get up close and

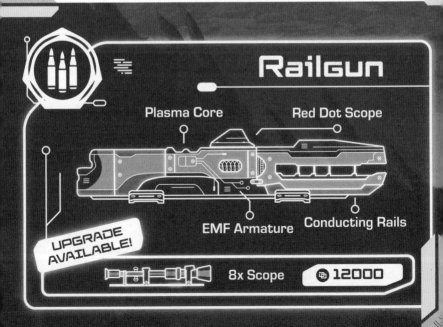

Railgun

Plasma Core

Red Dot Scope

EMF Armature

Conducting Rails

UPGRADE AVAILABLE!

8x Scope

12000

personal when he played. Sweeping a few thick black hairs from his eyes, Jack adjusted his headset and leaned closer to the TV. He forgot himself, and his cold reality, in the world of *Distant Dawn* ...

'TAKE THAT TO THE BANK AND CASH IT!'

The voice behind the Zuul mech crackled through Jack's gaming headset, along with the sound of the *Daughter of Slaughter Mix* – Zuul's battle playlist. *Through the Fire and the Flames* by Dragonforce crashed into Jack's ears as he watched the graffitied mech dive to avoid a hail of plasma fire, then pop up and let off a stream of railgun rounds that sliced an attacking Nograki alien clean in two.

A ruthless grin crossed Jack's face as he shoved the sticks on his controller forwards, hammering the shoulder buttons in time with the steps of his WarMech. Each well-timed beat boosted his pace, until the lumbering robot was within striking distance of its first target ...

But Jack held off. He'd spotted the shield generator activating on the Nograki scout's torso. A lesser gamer might have missed it, but Jack noticed the glowing "tell". In a single movement, Jack retracted his mech's cannons, slammed down all four shoulder buttons at once, and propelled his mech into a leaping, spinning somersault. Jack watched, his world inverted, as the slimy scout lowered its blocking move and attacked a target that was no longer there. When Jack's mech had reached the apex of its twisting leap, with the bewildered alien floundering below, the boy behind tHeScOuRgE unleashed two mini nuke-tip rockets from recesses in his robot's shoulder armour. The metal giant landed. An explosion erupted behind it. Pieces of Nograki scout flew across the battlefield. But Jack didn't even turn to look at the devastation his mech had wrought. Cool guys don't look back at explosions. He simply scanned the battlefield, searching for his next target.

'Here comes the b-b–, here comes the b-boo–, here comes something good!'

Jack spun the view camera around just in time to see ForgeFire666 take out two Nograki scouts with a single perfectly-placed plasma pulse. The projectile burned straight through the first scout and lodged deep in the second monster's chest. To the left, HudsonNotHicks was unloading a full mag of lightfuse rounds into an already corpsed scout. The barrels of his military Gatling gun glowed red, and Jack could see the style points racking up next to the player's name in the ranking table.

Jack had never been much of a flair player. Kill quantity over quality had earned him his place in the rankings. However, he had to admire the way certain elite gamers really went to town on their enemies. He'd seen BunnyQueen12 leap from a high-rise building and flatten two Nograki invader troops, one under each foot. He'd watched highlight reels of Jeeroy-Lenkins combo-killing his way through twenty Nograki without so much as a pause to reload. Even his teammate Zuul had a habit of setting alien remains on fire with crimson exhaust flames. Maybe it *was* time for tHeScOuRgE to earn a few style points …

Jack rolled his thumb over the D-pad and soon spotted a potential victim, about a hundred metres away, hiding behind a huddle of boulders. The Nograki scout had its root-like feet dug firmly into the ground, fighting the kickback from its own volleys as it fired mucus at SaiboTron. Jack's headset shifted as a wry smile pushed his cheeks upwards. The scout had no idea he was there.

He quickly selected a laser phasor, equipping it to his WarMech's right forearm, then set a pre-load primer running for the fire ignition on its left fist. A pressure bar appeared, the read-out rising as Jack pushed his machine into a lumbering lope. His timing had to be perfect. He hoped that the distraction of SaiboTron's shiny metal behind would give him the space he needed. *Tap, tap, tap* – Jack hit the shoulder buttons in time with his mech's heavy footsteps, building pace as the pressure gauge filled. Five more steps. Four. The gauge was almost full. Three. Jack began to squeeze the phasor trigger. Two. The Nograki turned – the element of surprise was gone – but it didn't matter. One.

A blue beam erupted as Jack pushed the trigger button all the way down. He dragged the joystick left, and the thin shaft of light ripped through the lower half of the scout's legs. But the Nograki didn't hit the ground – it never got the chance – because Jack had already unleashed the fire

fist: a one-time-only, flame-fuelled punch that crunched
into the torso of the legless scout, sending its top half
soaring into the sky. And Jack still wasn't finished. A filter
slid over his mech's visor and Jack's TV screen glowed
green, a set of shining crosshairs flashing in the centre. He
swiped over the D-pad, pulling his mech's gaze upwards
and fixing what remained of the spinning alien in his
sights. He was locked, loaded, and ready for fireworks–
and some serious style points to boot ...

That was until a second, unseen Nograki scout leaped
onto his WarMech, sinking its tendrils in.

Jack tried not to panic – even though panicking
seemed a perfectly reasonable reaction to a giant alien
tearing at your robot's armour with tendrils as tough
as steel cables. The creature clung to Jack's WarMech,
digging its powerful, twisting digits between the metal
plates, and prising them apart until it had made a gap
big enough for its fangs. As soon as the creature sank its
teeth into the mech's body, venom began to flow into its
exposed circuitry, melting its way through the WarMech's
digital veins. Jack was in trouble.

He began to vigorously shake his controller: the only
way to escape a close-up Nograki attack. Jack watched
his health bar shrinking. His mech was soon down to
half power, and the Nograki killer was still clinging on.
Through gritted teeth and watery eyes, Jack shook the
controller with all the might he could muster. It wasn't the
thought of his WarMech being eliminated that brought

tears to his eyes, but the pain in his hands – split and blistered from all the work it took to pay for a weapons upgrade that, if he didn't escape this alien's clutches, he wouldn't even get to use. He felt his arms slowing, even though he didn't want them to. His muscles burned. The health bar reached twenty percent. It started to flash red. Warning sirens sounded, but the more Jack strained, the slower his arms seemed to move. Fifteen percent. Ten. Jack began to accept his fate – this wasn't going to be his night. So much for style points ...

WHAM! The Nograki's head exploded, and Jack's screen was covered with hi-res chunks of alien brain matter. tHeScOuRgE's health bar levelled out at ten percent – critical, but still alive. Dragging his mech towards the nearest pile of rocks, Jack hit the B-button to crouch and hide, allowing the self-repair systems to activate. He pulled the camera view to the right until he spotted a rise on the far edge of the battlefield. He held in the left shoulder button and the view narrowed, zooming in on a blurry shape, only just visible on the crest of the hill. As indistinct as that shape might have been to most, Jack recognised it straight away.

'... Cheers, Phaest,' Jack mumbled into his mic. The reply came back, quick and clear.

'Always a pleasure to help a massive ranker like *you*, Scourge. May I suggest sticking to what you do best? Leave the style points to Zuul.'

'YEAAAH BOIII!' came Zuul's shout.

Jack sighed. He had, too many times to count, ripped into Hephaestus for "camping" – taking up a covered position, usually far away from the action, and picking off enemies without having to deal with much, if any, return fire. But Jack had to admit that Phaest was the best sniper in the game. As he watched his health bar creep over fifty percent, he felt relieved to be on the same team as *Distant Dawn*'s top sharpshooter ...

Not that he'd ever tell Hephaestus that.

Having made sure that he wasn't in any imminent danger of another Nograki sneak attack, Jack loosened his white-knuckled grip on the control pad and allowed his eyes to drift momentarily from the screen. It was only then that he realised, as was almost always the case during an online co-op with no pause function, that he hadn't blinked since the mission started. The first blink didn't come easy. He had to *push* his eyelids together, forcing them to scrape across his dry eyeballs like rusty wiper blades across a grimy windscreen. Jack rolled his eyes around like an athlete stretching out aching muscles. In doing so, he caught glimpses of the real world outside of *Distant Dawn*. Jack Delaney's world.

The funny thing was, Jack's world often looked far less real to him than Rotec did. While the virtual planet's atmosphere danced and churned with ruby-red dust trails in the sky, the air outside Jack's window was cold and empty. Every object in *Distant Dawn* was rendered in glorious detail; more, really, than the eye could ever truly appreciate. If a player ever thought they'd seen it all, they could simply zoom in closer, and some new and remarkable detail would be revealed to them. As far as Jack was concerned, he'd already seen all there was to see of his own world. In its drab designs, its bargain-basement construction, its leaking seals and washed-out palettes, he saw nothing to inspire the awe he felt while walking around Rotec's central citadel. Nothing here compared to the view from the TH315 carrier as it whisked him across the borderlands, where jungle met ice plain and the desert rolled into swathes of highland forest. *That* felt real to Jack. The outside world simply couldn't compete.

Flicking a glance upwards, Jack's attention paused on a shelf on the wall. Standing at the end of a stack of old computer game cases was a baby monitor. It was held together with tape and the screen for the camera feed didn't work anymore, but four of the ten lights on the front were flickering on and off in sequence. Jack recognised the rhythmic pattern: in the bedroom across the hall his brother was asleep in his cot, breathing steadily. Jack hadn't heard his mum's keys in the door yet. He knew he might not hear them until the morning. So, with his health bar at three-quarters full, Jack took hold of the controller again and re-entered *Distant Dawn*, all the while keeping a tired eye on one of the few things that actually mattered to him in the real world.

'Hope you found a doggy bag behind those rocks, Scourge!' heckled Zuul as soon as Jack raised his creaking

WarMech. 'Only a couple-a leftover strays out here!'

Zuul was right – kind of. Nograki bodies were strewn all over the place. That was one of the "real" things Jack liked about *Distant Dawn*: dead enemies didn't just disappear. If you weren't paying attention, you could be floored by a dead alien trip hazard just as easily as a toxic plasma bullet. But it seemed that Zuul had forgotten about the six-limbed behemoth waiting under the dropships. The scout forces were all but defeated, save for a few stragglers who were being dealt with by Th£D£V@ST@T0R and Jeeroy-Lenkins. The rest of the players had already turned their attention towards the new enemy.

A line of text appeared in the chat box at the bottom of Jack's screen.

SAIBOTRON: どうやってビッグママを殺すの？

The characters shimmered for a moment, then shifted in translation into an English phrase.

SAIBOTRON: HOW DO WE KILL BIG MOMMA?

Before any of the other players could respond, a reply appeared.

_CARBON_SHIFT_: YOU DON'T. I DO. ツ

Jack watched _Carbon_Shift_ take off. The number one WarMech seemed to soar rather than run, carried on a golden vapour trail of exhaust fumes. As it accelerated, a cavity in its torso slid open, and three nuke-fuelled RPG rounds burst forwards. Electric-yellow spirals lit their trail as they rocketed towards the colossal alien target. The impact was massive. The ground shook. The explosion kicked up rolling shockwaves of magenta dust.

But Big Momma didn't suffer a single scratch.

_Carbon_Shift_ didn't appear to be put off by the failed grenade attack. Quite the opposite, in fact: he was accelerating harder, preparing to unleash both KPS rockets and all four barrels of his pulse cannons. The golden mech became temporarily obscured by a cloud of detonation dust, then from the midst of the thick, fiery miasma came six separate warheads. The impact was even greater this time. Jack felt the rumble through the controller in his hands. The combined explosion of all six projectiles was enough to create a mini mushroom cloud of noxious green gas, and cut a sizeable crater into the earth. And yet, when the dust settled, the creature known as Big Momma was still standing.

A frustrated wail rang out across the chat channel as _Carbon_Shift_ launched from the ground, riding a wave of golden energy upwards with its arms spread wide. Plumes of flame surged from each outstretched arm. The golden robot became a vengeful angel; the Inciner8 heat flares forming wings of fire that carried it skywards.

Just as _Carbon_Shift_ got within striking distance, it stopped. It was struck motionless in mid-air – all its promises of great vengeance and furious anger trapped in a frozen metal form that couldn't finish what it had started. It was like someone had hit pause and left the mech stranded. But that was impossible. The figure of _Carbon_Shift_ flickered. A wave of faulty pixels washed over the glowing machine and it began to twitch, control panels all over its body flicking up and down erratically, weapons arming and disarming as glitches crept into every element of the machine. Big Momma began to close in. As if in response, the orb in the mech's chest plate began to glow brighter. _Carbon_Shift_ still couldn't break free, but the golden sphere roared with a blazing light, growing in intensity, until ...

The eruption was like nothing Jack had ever witnessed before in a game. The sound was so loud it made him rip the headphones from his head. The screen flashed a brilliant white, filling his tiny room with light and forcing him to shield his eyes.

He only dared look back once the light had faded to black. Two words blinked in the centre of the screen.

GAME

OVER

Jack sat, his mouth open and his ears ringing, until another sound snapped him from his trance: the sound of a baby crying.

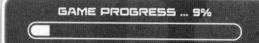

Level 3: Mob Mentality

Cameron Yates sat on the bus, his face inches from the window where a thousand raindrops were doing battle. Staring at the blurry world beyond, a single question occupied his mind.

What the hell happened last night?

The sudden clout of a speed bump brought Cameron back down to earth. His plump hand gripped a half-empty ShockSoda – only just saving it from spilling into his lap, where he'd already balanced a Double-Choc Delight bar on top of an empty crisp packet. Unlike most days, Cameron was actually looking forward to school today. Well, he was excited about form period at least, where he'd see the rest of the Raid Mob.

Before the bus had even passed the school gates, kids began piling into the centre aisle like angry tourists disembarking a flight. Cameron never understood why everyone seemed so hell-bent on being first off the bus, just so they could trudge, convict-style, towards classroom confinement. It took three attempts before he could nudge himself into a gap that still wasn't quite big enough for him, only to have a sports bag shoved into his back, pushing him straight into another boy. An older boy. A *Year Ten* boy – the last one whose attention Cameron wanted.

'*You* again?' grunted the tower of hormones and greasy hair. 'Don't you remember what happened to you last week? I thought elephants never forget?'

Cameron attempted to speak. Nothing that even half-resembled a word came out.

'Watch yourself. Shouldn't be difficult – you're hard to miss,' added the boy, smirking with self-satisfaction. He punctuated his threat by poking Cameron cruelly in the belly before turning and lumbering off the bus. Cameron stared down at his stomach as waves of dull pain radiated across it. It was only when the sports bag was jammed into his back again that Cameron began to shuffle towards the front of the bus.

'FrankenD-D-Death14 ...' he muttered under his breath.

Stepping into the rain, Cameron stopped to sling his backpack on, pulling the straps tight over both shoulders before clicking a third safety strap into place across his chest. He shivered as raindrops trickled down the back of his neck. Pulling the collar of his crumpled green windbreaker close, he slotted himself into the flood of kids surging towards the main entrance of the school, letting the rough wave of bodies pull him inside.

With one shoulder scraping along the wall of the corridor, Cameron stared at his wet shoes as he trudged towards his form room. He tried to shake off the misery of the morning by distracting himself with the events of the night before. He'd never seen something like that happen in *Distant Dawn*. Sure, he'd seen glitches, frozen players, modded mechs whose pirated upgrades had blown up mid-game ... but that stuff didn't happen to *elite* contestants. And what about the rumours? Gamers were buzzing online about what they saw, or what they *thought* they saw, on _Carbon_Shift_'s live stream. Cameron had only seen a single, blurry screengrab, but he couldn't help agreeing that it did look a bit like ...

'NAME THE PLANET WHERE THE XENOMORPHS WERE FIRST FOUND!'

The howling demand came from behind. Before Cameron could turn around, he was imprisoned in a vice-like headlock. He knew there was only one way out of it. With a strong, sinewy forearm covering his mouth, he spat and coughed out the magic words.

'LV F-FOUR TWENTY S-S-S!'

'Close enough,' said the voice, and he was released. Cameron sucked in a deep breath and turned around, finding himself eye-to-eye with his grinning attacker.

Megan Joyce was a foot taller than Cameron, and her

long arms and lanky legs emphasised the difference.
A hazel-coloured face peppered with darker freckles
framed brown eyes that looked almost too big for her
head, teeming with warmth and mischief. She had dark,
scruffy curls, cut short and left to stick out any which
way they pleased. Cameron knew that outside of school
she'd have a rolled-up red bandana tied around her
head, which she'd say was a nod to one of her favourite
kick-ass film characters. But Cameron also knew that
the bandana had a more practical function. It kept her
fringe out of her eyes when she was doing what she did
best: piloting Zuul, the sixth highest-ranking WarMech
in *Distant Dawn*.

'What's up with your face? ShockSoda hangover?
Did your toilet finally give up the good fight? Are you
grieving the loss of your porcelain pal?' Megan said,
nudging Cameron in the stomach with each guess. He
winced in pain. Megan's face darkened instantly – her
wide, playful smile folding in on itself. When she spoke
again, the warmth had vanished.

'FrankenDeath?'

Cameron nodded.

'*Again?*'

He stared at his feet.

'Well, we'll deal with that walking piece of spam
mail later, won't we, *ForgeFire* – Destroyer of Worlds
and Pwner of Noobs!' said Megan. She placed her hand
on his shoulder and waited until Cameron's gaze rose

to meet hers. A faint smile crept across his face at her assurances of digital revenge.

'Now come on,' she said. 'Ayo says he's got something we need to see ...'

And with that, Cameron saw the electric smile shoot back across Megan's face. She grabbed hold of the strap across his chest and dragged him the rest of the way down the corridor. When the pair of them got to the form room, only one pupil was inside – tucked in the back corner, on the furthest seat of Raid Mob's Row.

Ayo looked like a matchstick-man made human. He sat cross-legged, the toe of his polished shoe squeaking as it rubbed against his precisely-pressed trousers. His limbs were long and thin, but unlike Megan's powerful appendages, his looked brittle. To Ayo, the idea of physical exertion beyond carrying his own bodyweight from A to B was a waste of useful energy. It was easy to imagine that, if given the opportunity to live wholly within his own head, he would jump at the chance – figuratively, not literally. Ayo's keenness to avoid physical effort went some way towards explaining his reputation as both the biggest camper and the best sharpshooter in his favourite computer game: *Distant Dawn*.

The boy behind the Hephaestus mech was studying his phone intently. A reflected video played in the lenses of his thick glasses.

'So? Can you see anything? I'd hope so – those glasses are so thick you should be able to see into the *future*,' Megan blurted, running across the room and yanking at Ayo's hand for a better look. Ayo tutted and pulled against her, but he knew how futile his resistance was. He quickly gave up, leaving the screen hanging in the middle of a three-person huddle as Cameron caught up and joined in.

'W-what's this?' Cameron asked. He had a phone, but it had been broken – by his own mum. She was such a technophobe that she thought an iPad was something you put on your eyelids to help with wrinkles. And while she'd begrudgingly allowed him to have his own phone, she'd insisted on filling it with so many monitoring apps and parental controls that it became so slow she managed to brick it within a week. Cameron had only just been able to convince her that games consoles were okay for kids – mainly thanks to a technique he'd dubbed "the floorboard flip". This involved him wearing his gaming headset over one ear and listening out for her footsteps in the creaky hallway. The moment he heard her coming, he'd switch from *Distant Dawn* to *Highway Helper*: a road safety game where you had to guide a duck and her ducklings across busy streets.

There were some advantages to his mum's fear of all things digital, however. She was so out of touch with technology that she had no idea how huge Cameron's online persona was. If she ever discovered that her darling little duck helper was actually an elite alien-killing machine, she'd throw out his LightFire console before Cameron could even start stuttering "stop!".

'It's the end of Carbon's *Let's Play* … from last night. He was streaming when whatever happened happened,' Megan said. 'So … what happened?'

'If you'd let me examine the footage properly, without disturbance, I'd be better able to enlighten you,' Ayo huffed. 'Look – it's coming up now …'

The three faces closed in around the glowing phone. The main picture showed _Carbon_Shift_'s gaming screen, and in the bottom-right corner was a picture-in-picture view of the player's face. His hair was dyed bright green, and he wore a pair of huge mirrored sunglasses; his only visible feature was a determined grimace. Cameron, Ayo and Megan watched closely as his golden WarMech surged upwards towards the giant Nograki monster …

'PHONES AWAY! OR THEY'LL BE ON MY WALL OF SHAME UNTIL THE END OF TERM!'

Miss Barrett came rushing into the room, as she always did, as if she was late, which she never was. Her tightly scraped-back hair pulled all her facial features into an expression of permanent irritation. Cameron momentarily considered pointing out that it was still before nine o'clock, and according to school policy, Ayo was within his rights to use his phone. But he'd never known a person who hated technology more than Miss Barrett – and that included the disparager of all things digital that was his own mum. Not only that, Cameron had never been one to question authority, and they didn't come much more authoritarian than Miss Barrett. Even the crazed dictators he'd learned about in his History class seemed more lenient than his form teacher.

Cameron watched her wobble towards her desk, her slight frame hunched over a stack of papers and books so tall she had to use her chin as a top anchor. As she dropped the pile down on the desk, she looked over her shoulder to the wall behind, upon which she had fixed a row of twenty transparent pouches. Over half of them were occupied by mobile phones. These confiscated convicts had been put on display as a warning, like heads on pikes along a medieval city wall, demonstrating Miss Barrett's complete lack of technological tolerance.

The form room soon began to fill up. Cameron, Ayo and Megan continued their quiet speculation about _Carbon_Shift_'s fate, hiding their theories from both their teacher and the other students, for very different reasons.

As the wall clock flicked over to nine o'clock, Miss Barrett barked out the first name on the register.

'Deborah Adebisi?'

'Here, Miss.'

'Kevin Alvarez?

'Here, Miss.'

'Oliver Collins?'

'Hmph, Mers.'

'I beg your pardon?'

'*Here*, Miss.'

'Much better, Oliver. Enunciate. It's what separates us from the animals. Charlotte Darby?'

'Here, Miss.'

Cameron's eyes moved towards the classroom door. He gnawed at his bottom lip, darting nervous looks between his teacher's thin, sneering mouth and the doorway.

'Jack Delaney?'

Silence.

'*Jack Delaney*?'

Miss Barrett's smirk widened as she glanced up from her oversized folder. All the other teachers filled out their register on an electronic tablet; Miss Barrett preferred to mark attendance on paper with an authoritative red line. Now, her pen was hovering besides Jack's name, ready to brand him with a big fat "L" for late.

'*Jack Dela–*'

The door flew open, its rusted hinges tested to their limit. Jack all but fell into the classroom, failing dramatically to stem the speed of a mad dash down the corridor. Cameron almost began clapping at his arrival, but managed to curb this embarrassing impulse.

'Here, Miss! I'm here! Right here. Miss,' Jack spluttered, collapsing into the last seat on Raid Mob's Row. Jack did his best to steady himself, becoming motionless like prey playing dead, as if that would somehow make his teacher forget his late arrival.

It didn't.

'What time does school start, Jack?'

'Nine o'clock, Miss Barrett.'

'What time is it now, Jack?'

'Two minutes past nine, Miss.'

'Where will you be at twenty-minutes past twelve, Jack?'

'Lunchtime detention, Miss.'

'Thank you, Jack – I do enjoy our little chats. Olivia Heritage?'

Jack sank into his chair, defeated. The others looked down the row at him. They all had so much to talk about, but now they wouldn't be together again until the end of the day. It was too long to wait. A flurry of shared glances was all it took; they knew what they had to do. As they waited for their names to be called, Cameron began to sweat. A lot.

'Megan Joyce?'

'NEVER 'EARD OF 'ER! THE NAME'S MEGLAR THE UNRIPE, AND I'M HERE FOR YOUR TREASURES ... AND YOUR WOMENS!'

The class laughed. Miss Barrett did not. Megan got her detention.

After a few more names, Ayo was up.

'Ayomikun Osikoya-Arinola?'

'Well, Miss Barrett,' Ayo began, removing his glasses and wiping them on his shirt, before replacing and straightening them with painstaking care. 'The question of whether I am *here* or not is more one of existentialism than clerical administration. I mean, are any of us really *here* at all ...'

Ayo got his detention too. There was only one more member of the Mob left to complete the set.

'Cameron Yates?'

Cameron tried but faltered. He couldn't even start a stutter. He hated breaking the rules. *Especially* Miss Barrett's rules. While she was pretty terrifying, Miss Barrett was the only teacher who ever looked out for him. As strict as she was, the only thing she hated more than technology was bullies – a fact that Cameron had discovered when she'd saved him from his tormentors on more than a few occasions. This made it all the more difficult to dish out disrespect.

Beads of sweat tumbled down Cameron's temples, over his cheeks and onto his chin. He was perspiring so profusely that he worried he might start his own downpour at his desk. The rest of the Mob stared at him expectantly as he fumbled for words that just wouldn't come out.

'*Cameron Yates?*'

The stern syllables heightened the panic of an already flustered Cameron. Miss Barrett looked up from her register, eyeing him with a heady, terrifying mix of surprise and scorn. Eventually, the only words he could muster fell from the tip of his thick tongue ...

'... Bum pumps.'

The Raid Mob got their lunchtime meeting.

'So h-how does the video end?' Cameron asked.

'Forget Carbon Shift – didn't you hear the announcement? No, of course you didn't. Your mum locks your phone up like it's a national treasure. Look ...'

Megan thrust her phone in Cameron's face, squishing it against the end of his nose. This public flaunting of technology was met with no confiscation, because the warden in charge of the detention room was Mr Wilby. Mr Wilby was a fossil dressed as a teacher. The school wheeled him out to play the rickety piano during assemblies, alphabetise the library, and watch over troublemakers who got sent to lunchtime detention. Fortunately for the Raid Mob, he wasn't watching very closely.

'This is massive!' blurted Megan. 'It's huge! It's mega! This is ... MAHUGA!'

Cameron was looking at a picture posted by the Hailstorm Games account – the creators of *Distant Dawn*. It showed a VR headset and two gloves, along with a case that held ten small white discs. The design of each piece was like nothing he had seen before. Each element by itself was impressive, but as a set it looked like it had been brought back from the future. Cameron managed to tear his eyes away from the picture just long enough to read the caption underneath.

Hailstorm Games `Following`

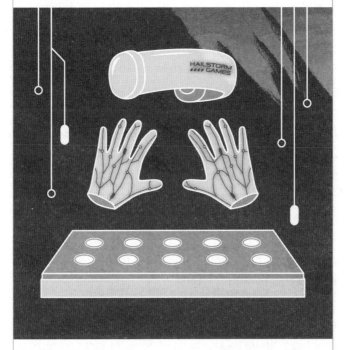

    540,349 likes

Things are about to change.
Hailstorm RealFeel control packs are on
their way to the Top Ten *Distant Dawn* players.
Tomorrow there will be an Elite Mission, the
likes of which you have never experienced.
Witness the new way to game.
Witness Fullmersion.
#DistantDawn #Fullmersion #RealFeel
#FutureOfGaming #HailstormGames
#TopTenOnly

'TOP TEN ONLY! THAT'S US!'

Megan was all but shouting. Jack and Ayo both had the same post up on their phones, pouring over every tiny detail, pinching the image to zoom in and out.

'Can we go home? Like, right now? Can we just quit school and go be pro-gamers, as is so clearly our destiny? After all, the rest of the world already thinks that the Raid Mob must be a sponsored esports team full of megastars from around the globe, all hiding behind anonymity agreements. Imagine if they knew the *real* story – that four of the legendary *Distant Dawn* Top Ten are in fact a single, ragtag gang of Year Eights from Holmes Park High School, who've been gaming together since they could wiggle a joystick! I mean, the Netflix film practically writes itself ...'

'Excuse me for cutting your grandiose and utterly reckless fantasy short, Meg,' Ayo began, his temples throbbing. 'If we bail right now, Miss Barrett will hunt us down and make sure none of us sees so much as a digital watch again. We'll wait out the afternoon – stay off the radar. If anyone finds out we're getting these new control packs ... Well, what some individuals might do to get their hands on them doesn't even bear thinking about ...'

'Fine!' Megan sighed, begrudgingly. 'But if the delay costs us that film deal, you'll be hearing from my lawyer!'

The Mob spent the next twenty minutes scouring through posts tagged #Fullmmersion. Gaming accounts were blowing up with speculation – many suggesting that it might all be a hoax. But nothing the Raid Mob read could quash the giddiness fizzing in their minds and swirling in their stomachs.

Returning to their form room for one o'clock registration, the Mob were extra careful to hide their phones and close their mouths. None of them could risk an after-school detention – especially with Miss Barrett handing them out like Skittles.

It was seventeen minutes past one when a teacher finally showed up ... and it was not Miss Barrett.

'Sorry, students,' announced Mr Beasley breathlessly, as he rushed into the classroom. 'Miss Barrett had to go home. She had an emergency call. I'll be taking your register.'

The Mob looked at each other, puzzled. Miss Barrett hadn't had a single day off in the last *ten* years – a fact she took great pleasure in announcing every time any student came back from a sick day. Cameron was particularly concerned; he always felt safer when Miss Barrett the Bully Punisher was around – especially when he had to line up for the bus at the end of the day with FrankenDeath14.

The Mob's bewilderment soon turned to smugness, however, as they all remembered Mr Beasley's relaxed attitude to technology in the classroom – and to the responsibility of being a teacher as a whole. You could get away with murder in Mr Beasley's class, as long as you did it quietly enough. Cameron shoved his end-of-day concerns to one side and leaned over to share Jack's phone screen, as he slid it out of his pocket and refreshed the feed. Only a few hours of school to get through until they could rush home and unbox their special deliveries – another look through the online hype would help tide them over. The loading wheel spun around and around, before a new image appeared at the top of the feed – an image that drained the colour from Cameron's flushed face.

The image was a screengrab taken from the end of _Carbon_Shift_'s livestream video. It showed him being dragged from his computer by something powerful, something inexplicable ... something that looked – even though it couldn't possibly be – like a *Nograki tentacle*.

Level 4:
All in Your Head

Megan stomped speed into her BMX's pedals. She was
halfway home. The text she'd received from her dad
played on repeat in her mind: a typically retro message
that read '*Tubular-lookin' package here for you, Meg-
atron!*' It made her race faster as she hopped on and off
curbs, slalomed around parked cars and got too close for
comfort to the odd, unsuspecting pedestrian.

'Sorry Mrs Browne!' she yelled as she skimmed past a
doddering old lady and her equally prehistoric dog. 'Got
a war to win!'

'Give 'em hell, Megan! Just like my Arthur did!' the
woman screeched in reply, balling up her fist and
shaking it like she was cheering on a beach assault.
Megan grinned and powered on. She'd listened to Mrs
Browne's war stories many times over copious cups
of tea at her dad's art space/café/live music venue,

ArTeaSang. Tales of proper battles always fired Megan up for an online rumble.

She yanked the back brake on and skidded around a final corner. A black tyre line burnt onto the concrete as she straightened up and sped down Foster Street, towards number twenty-five.

Megan skidded to a halt on the Indian stone driveway, chucked her bike over the wrought-iron fence and fumbled frantically for her keys, and even more frantically at the lock once she'd found them. Pushing her way into the entrance hall, she slammed the expensive front door that her mum always told her not to slam, threw her keys onto the expensive console table that her mum always told her not to scratch, and leaped over the bottom section of the expensive glass banister that her mum always told her to keep her grubby hands off. While her dad's hipster hang-out ticked over nicely, it was the income from Megan's mum's lucrative career as a private airline pilot that paid for their upmarket home – and all the things in it that Megan wasn't allowed to touch, smudge, move, or breathe on wrong.

Megan clambered up the staircase, across the first-floor landing, then up a second flight of stairs, leaving hand prints on the banister as she went. She passed her dad's study – or, as he called it, "The Shadow Gallery" – the only room where he was "allowed" to play his retro arcade collection by Megan's perpetually disapproving, exceedingly uptight mum. Between her dad's obsession with pre-millennium gaming and her mum's general disdain for anything Megan did, her parents had no real clue what a big deal she and her friends were in the contemporary gaming world. And if she was honest, she didn't mind their disinterest in the Mob's business one bit.

Continuing onwards to a final, narrower flight of stairs, Megan reached the door at the top, marked with an industrial-looking sign for the "Weyland-Yutani Corp". Scrawled in red paint underneath were the words *"El riesgo siempre vive"*.

Megan stumbled, breathless, into her bedroom, passing shelves full to bursting with a film and book collection that anyone three times her age would've been proud of – especially as most of the films were 80s and 90s classics. She stepped deftly through a sea of strewn vintage trainers, dodging Nike Vandals, Jordans, and a well-worn pair of Avia 880 high-tops. She paid no attention to the framed *Ghostbusters 2* poster on the wall, hung next to prints from *Aliens* and *Ferris Bueller's Day Off*. She didn't even glance towards her gaming rig – consisting of a 65-inch, wall-mounted HDR screen connected to a hub that allowed her to switch between six different consoles, including her LightFire Pro. Megan only had eyes for her EarthCroc gaming chair. Or, more specifically, for the black box that was sitting on it.

The one that was simply addressed ...

The box measured about a foot cubed. Its matte surfaces and sharply honed edges gave the impression that it was dense and heavy, and so when Megan picked it up, she was surprised to find that it was remarkably light. Slowly and carefully, she rotated the box, cocking her head from one side to the other. Apart from the gamer handle etched into the top, each surface was completely blank. She lifted the box above her head; the base was just the same. Megan really didn't want to start hacking at it with a pair of scissors, but there didn't seem to be any other way in. Rummaging in her desk drawer, she stopped suddenly at the sound of her LightFire console booting up. The TV screen on the wall turned on by itself. Megan looked up at the screen, then the console, then back to the black box.

The "Z" of Zuul was glowing blue.

Megan approached the black box again – slowly. The "Z" throbbed with a steady pulsing glow. As she reached out towards it, the blinking quickened, then slowed when she withdrew her hand. Without taking her eyes off the box, Megan grabbed the red bandana from the back of the chair and tied it around her head. Then she steeled herself and reached out once more. The "Z" pulsed quicker as her fingertips neared, blurring into a solid, shining beacon …

Contact.

Like creeping frost, the blue glow flooded into the other letters. Then the light spiderwebbed outwards from her gaming handle, sprawling and overlapping to form a complex circuitry. When it reached the edges of the box, a white beam tore its way across the seams and the container fell open like an origami bloom, revealing its contents.

The cube contained a head. A *human* head … and a familiar one at that.

Inside the box was an all-white replica of Megan's head. It was perfect in every detail, right down to the bandana-wrapped nest of chaotic curls. But her big eyes were obscured by an object that Megan somehow found even more fascinating than the reproduction of her own face. A white visor sat fixed to the model; a single sweeping bar curved around the face, with circular panels covering the ears, and a Hailstorm logo glowing icy blue in the centre. It seemed alien, or like some form of evolved humanity, where technology and biology had become one. Megan thought it was beautiful; so beautiful that she never stopped to ask herself how the people who made it knew *exactly* what she looked like …

At the base of the head was a small white cylinder. A light flashed blue on its curved face, then beamed a steady sapphire, signalling that a connection had been made. The words "Welcome to the RealFeel Revolution" swept across Megan's TV screen, quickly replaced by a virtual rendering of the model of her face. She watched, her eyes even wider than usual, as an avatar that looked just like her appeared. It lifted the headset from the model and slid it over its head. After a moment, the process repeated: the avatar appeared, removed the headset from the model and placed it on its own head. It was then that a few things twigged.

Megan realised that this was a demo video. She also realised that it wasn't surprising at all that both the model and the avatar looked so precisely like her. The LightFire console had an Ocular Connekt bar feeding it visual information all the time – it was used for motion control games and gesture commands. The last update even included a new feature where you signed into your gaming account using facial recognition. The Hailstorm Games company knew *exactly* what Megan looked like – and they had put that likeness to impressive use.

The hairs on Megan's forearms bristled as she reached out and gripped the headset, just as the avatar was doing on the TV screen. She closed her eyes and took a deep breath. Then she slid the headset on. In an instant, a new universe burst into life.

Megan watched the birth of light at the centre of a vast explosion, tearing across her retinas in electric hues of every imaginable colour. She watched streaks of cosmic fallout fire across empty space, moulded into countless orbs. Having burst through a shower of comet-fire, Megan's personal tour of creation itself reached a single planet: a planet with a churning red atmosphere. A planet she knew. Rotec. Then another recognisable shape started to emerge from its swirling mist. It was the Hailstorm Games logo, and with it came the realisation that this – all of this mind-bending visual insanity – was just the game's loading screen.

Megan's heart felt like it was being pummelled by a prize-fighter. Instinctively, she reached up to tear the visor off her head – but in that moment, the virtual universe dissolved. She could see her own room again. Not a digital recreation of her room, but her *actual* room. The visor had somehow become transparent. Her breathing slowed, and her heart rate followed. She looked down at her feet, grounding herself back in her own reality. Eventually, she managed to loosen her grip on the headset and allow her arms to fall at her sides.

However, Megan was no longer alone. When she eventually looked up, she was faced with her *twin*, returning her own wide-eyed gaze. Megan staggered back and gripped her chest in shock.

'Visual calibration complete,' it said. 'Please swipe right to select your assistant.'

Megan fought to assure herself that this was a trick of augmented reality. She reminded herself that she had apps on her phone that made dinosaurs come to life and run around the living room; this was no different. Apart from the fact, obviously, that this wasn't a scaled-down CGI T-Rex. She was standing in front of *herself* – a perfect copy. A copy that seemed to want a response.

'Please swipe right to select your assistant.'

Megan waved her hand from left to right. The clone avatar evaporated in a cloud of digital vapour, and in its place another figure materialised. This one was shorter, stockier, and wore army fatigues. Its skin glistened with grime and sweat, and it looked as tough as they come. Right there, in the middle of Megan's bedroom, stood none other than Private First Class Jenette Vasquez – her heroine from the film *Aliens*.

Megan beamed. Vasquez looked exactly as she should: a lean, mean, ass-kicking machine that would rip out your spleen and eat it for protein. Megan loved the idea of having "Vasky" alongside her ... but her gamer habits compelled her to keep looking and see what else was on offer. After all, you don't just select the first weapon they give you.

In total, Megan was offered ten different aides. Lion-O, the leader of the *Thundercats*, was next up. After him came Kevin Flynn, decked out in his Game Grid gear, then E.T the Extra-Terrestrial, then Son Goku and Saitama. Megan cycled through the list three times, enjoying the novelty of having these iconic characters standing in her bedroom.

In-game helpers are more annoying than the members of my mum's vegan book club, she thought to herself. *I never listen to them – but I might actually need their help this time. If any of these would be difficult to ignore, it'd have to be …*

She swung her hand through the air, creating and destroying potential helpers, until she met herself again. She flicked an approving grin at her double. In response, her avatar raised its hand.

'Great choice! Fist bump to confirm your selection.'

Megan's smile widened as she dabbed knuckles with herself. The avatar smiled back.

'Please fit the RealFeel feedback plates as demonstrated.'

The cylinder at the base of the model head opened to reveal a row of ten thin white discs. Megan picked one out. It was the size of a ten-pence piece, with no markings, buttons, logos or circuitry that she could see. She looked back at her avatar, which was repeating the process of pressing a disc onto its forearm. Tentatively, Megan did the same. The moment the disc made contact with her skin, a web of electrodes shot out, binding the plate to the inside of her arm. The disc glowed white: light pulsing from its centre to the tips of the web strands – and with it, Megan's pulse rocketed again. It felt super weird, but it didn't hurt. Megan looked up at her avatar, and felt an odd sense of reassurance. *If I can do it, I can do it too,* she told herself. Soon enough, she'd applied all ten discs to various points on her arms, legs and torso.

'Let's get you on the Game Grid. Please put on the RealFeel gloves and we'll calibrate your equipment.'

Megan frowned through her visor. She'd been so caught up that she hadn't, until now, noticed the absence of the other two items shown in the picture that the Raid Mob had been drooling over all day. She wondered briefly if there was another box, a second package that hadn't been delivered – until she heard a sharp hissing sound. From the centre of the model's forehead an opening began to appear, spreading vertically to split the face in half. When it reached the base, the head fell open, revealing a pair of pristine white gloves. A matrix of digital veins pulsed blue beneath the surface of the rubbery white skin, and the tips of each finger glowed intensely with the same sapphire shine.

There was no hesitation this time. Megan pulled on the gloves, which, although loose at first, contracted to fit her perfectly. She looked eagerly towards her clone, who ushered her towards her gaming chair.

'Entering orientation and thermal feedback calibration mode,' said the clone, and Megan's room disappeared as the visor turned opaque again.

Inside the visor, the edges of Megan's view began to glow orange. The world shifted around her. Suddenly she was no longer in her room. She found herself sitting in an old wooden cabin, reclining in a big, comfy armchair, with a glowing log fire burning away. She could hear the wood crackling and splintering. More unbelievably, she could *feel* the heat radiating in warm waves across her skin.

'User sensitivity data required. Please indicate the perceived temperature from one to ten.'

'Mmmm ... six,' she mumbled through a disbelieving smile of contented cosiness. Her tense limbs starting to relax – until her world shifted again.

Now she was in the middle of a desert, standing on the top of a huge rolling sand dune. She knew that she hadn't stood up from her gaming chair, but she could have *sworn* that she was upright, struggling to pull her suddenly heavy legs out from sand that shifted around her feet. The scorching heat prickled over her skin. She reached up and touched her face. Impossibly, she felt sweat on the tips of her fingers.

'Eight,' she said. Reaching down, she could feel coarse sand between her fingers. She could taste salty sweat on her lips. Then her world changed again.

Megan threw her arms around herself as a sudden, biting cold ripped over her skin. She was on a narrow chunk of ice that swayed and bobbed on the surface of an arctic sea. Again, Megan *knew* she was sitting down in the real world, but in this frozen place she was all but convinced that she was crouched over, struggling to stay on her feet. She started to realise that these discs – the RealFeel feedback plates – must not only be stimulating her nerves, but her muscles as well, somehow mimicking the sensation of feeling and movement. Suddenly and violently, the chunk of ice pitched to one side. Megan dropped down. The icy cold bit at her hands. With her face inches from the ice, she saw her reflection, clouded in frosty breaths. She looked up to see a dark shape moving under the surface of the water, and realised that whatever it was must have tried to knock her off the ice – and it was coming around for another attempt.

'Two. Two. TWO!' Megan shouted. Before the shape reached her, the frigid world fell away, and she was released back into darkness once more.

'Orientation and thermal feedback calibration complete,' came the voice of the assistant. 'Motion and impact calibration will take place in-game. Your friends are waiting for you on the training ground. You must agree to the terms and conditions to continue.'

A dense page of text appeared. Megan had seen so many of these before; every console and game update was fronted by one of these impenetrable walls of rules and regulations. Megan had never once read any of them, and she certainly wasn't about to start now – especially not after she'd heard that her friends were already in the game. She gestured downwards with her hand, and the page began to scroll like the opening text from the *Star Wars* films. She swiped again, quicker – the words flying by in a blur. There was no chance for Megan to spot phrases like "... global broadcast ...", "... no guarantee of personal safety ...", "... risk of serious injury ...", "... surrender all rights to ...", and "... notify next of kin ...". She raced right to the bottom where a box appeared – the text above it read "sign here". Megan waved a finger in the air in the shape of her signature, and the moment she flicked the tail onto the final "e", everything went dark.

Her virtual assistant spoke once more. 'You are now ready to play. Just remember, no matter what you see, or hear, or feel ... *it's all just a game.*'

Megan's replicated voice faded away. She scrunched her eyes closed against a sudden wash of bright light, and when she opened them again, she found herself in the middle of an alien training ground, six metres in the air, standing inside her very own WarMech.

Level 5: The New Playground

'WELCOME TO THE P-P-PARTY, PAL!'

The ForgeFire666 WarMech bounded past the stationary Zuul. Inside, Cameron Yates was experiencing a rush that even Tropical Turbo ShockSoda couldn't match. With control grips in his hands and his feet locked into robotic stirrups, Cameron propelled his mech across the training ground. He screamed with joy as his mech shot across the space, riding a trail of meteorite dust. Cameron felt the sensation of his mech's feet pounding into the ground, the dirt shifting beneath his steps, moulded by the power of his movements.

The exosuit that he found himself wearing was feeding back sensory information with every motion. Cameron had never felt more invincible. Pulling his

WarMech up and switching directions with the speed and agility of a featherweight boxer, he set off rocketing across the landscape once more.

Cameron passed the Zuul mech again, streaking by and leaving it standing in a cloud of swirling dust. He still couldn't believe it. He was in a WarMech – *his* WarMech. And he wasn't the only one.

On the other side of the training ground, another mech Cameron recognised was standing in front of a multi-level shooting gallery, built to mimic a shelled-out building and populated by mock Nograki scouts. And this war-scarred machine was giving the practice targets the business. It unleashed a hail of nuke-tip rockets that wiped out six of them simultaneously, then showered the next four hapless aliens to emerge with a swirling trail of lightfuse rounds. The WarMech only stopped when the enemies were dust – the smoking barrels of its mini gun glowing white. Inside this machine of righteous fury was Jack Delaney.

Clad from head to toe in his own exosuit, Jack had quickly managed to master the controls for his mech, which were far more intuitive than a controller pad. The targeting system was completely visual: the weapons' aim followed Jack's eye movement – like the HMD systems that fighter pilots used. No more moving the crosshairs with analog sticks while trying to crouch and crab at the same time. He had a trigger button under each finger, giving him simultaneous access to eight weapons, and he could use voice commands to outfit any of his available arsenal to any trigger he wanted. No more scrolling through weapon menus, and no limiting his selection to his two favourite weapons. They were all available, all the time. He was the Master of Blaster Disaster.

Jack had also started to get the hang of the thrust controllers under his thumbs. These were slider controls: push them to the top and the WarMech's jet boosters powered up to the max. Jack had watched Cameron getting overexcited with these to the point of flying his mech into a wall only a few minutes earlier, so he'd decided to stick to weapons practice first. But he had to smile at the sight of the ForgeFire666 mech, which was now running laps of the training ground at blistering speed.

While it looked like Cameron and Jack had their robots' controls down pat already, Megan was only just beginning to find her metal feet. Unsurprisingly, she hadn't had to think about the mechanics of walking for a *very* long time, so she got a shock when lifting one leg almost caused her mech to topple over.

'Easy ... you've got this ... total cakewalk ...' Megan told herself as she inched her robot forwards gingerly. 'As easy as the first level on *Candy Cru*– HEY!'

Megan yelped as a blast shook through the sole of her robot's foot, sending her stumbling backwards.

'What was *that*? Did someone just shoot at me!' she yelled, scanning the training ground. 'Hey! Virtual me! Look alive! What's going on?'

Megan's avatar appeared. 'I believe we are under fire, Zuul.'

'Yeah – and in other news: water is wet! *Who's* shooting at me?'

Megan shrieked as another projectile impacted at her feet. Then she heard it – *laughter*. The heckling mirth of an unseen shooter, camping out, taking potshots at the noob.

'HEPHAESTUS!' she roared, swinging her view from left to right, trying to spot Ayo's mech. 'I'm gonna kill you until you die!'

'Just a bit of target practice, Zuuly,' Ayo replied, entirely unfazed.

'I think we should send up Maverick and Goose,' said Megan's virtual assistant. Before she could ask who they were, Megan saw two sleek drone aircrafts outlined in green pixels on her weapons board. Beside the items were a variety of deployment options, including "Rocket RaccBoom", "Snoop Foggy Smog", and "Old Painless". Megan smiled a half-smile, impressed at the slick custom references. Then she swiped down to the final option – "The Full Carrie".

Two objects that looked like torpedo shells rose from apertures on each of the Zuul WarMech's shoulders, extending a set of metal wings. One was painted black with red and white stripes; the other was red with monochrome bands. With the sound of another potshot acting like a starter pistol, the two drones launched themselves into the sky.

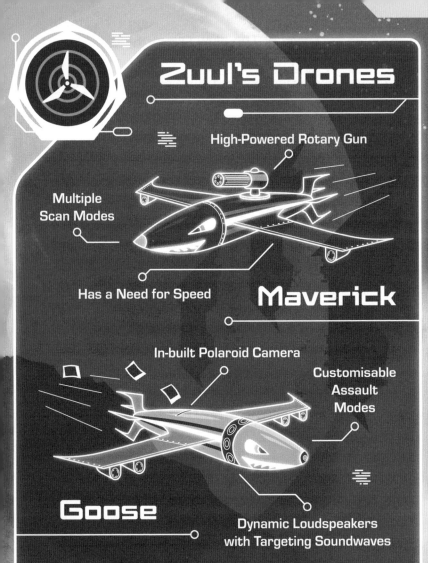

Zuul's Drones

High-Powered Rotary Gun

Multiple Scan Modes

Has a Need for Speed

Maverick

In-built Polaroid Camera

Customisable Assault Modes

Goose

Dynamic Loudspeakers with Targeting Soundwaves

These two weaponised drones are the *Distant Dawn* equivalent of Odin's ravens – only less flapping and yapping, more seek and destroy. They sit below apertures on each of Zuul's shoulders, ever-ready to soar into the sky, hunt down their targets, and deliver a hefty dose of customised pain – even when inverted.

Dual video feeds appeared inside the cockpit, and Megan watched as the drones broke through the lowest cloud layer before splitting off to canvas the training ground. Maverick and Goose scoured the entire area, doubled back and searched again – but there was no sign of Hephaestus.

'Check the outcrops, the ridges, and any pile of rocks big enough for a big, fat, camping sack of crotch rot to hide behind,' Megan barked, tracking both feeds closely. But nothing showed up; not until Megan switched the tracking mode to scan for microelectronic activity.

'Got you ...' she murmured, watching the feed from the Goose drone. She was looking at what appeared to be nothing more than a pile of jagged boulders, but the scan revealed that Ayo's mech was buried *under* this pile of rubble. He must have dug himself in as soon as he arrived.

'Is my playlist loaded up?' Megan asked through a widening grin.

'The *Daughter of Slaughter Mix* is ready to play,' replied the assistant.

Megan swiped a finger through a holographic playlist. 'Those birds can sing, right?'

'Of course,' said the avatar. 'Please select volume.'

Megan's smile reached from ear to ear.

'Turn it up to eleven,' she replied.

Above the pile of boulders, the circling drones began to scream out Daft Punk's *Robot Rock*. The sound of the pounding drums and grinding guitar was earth-shattering – in more ways than one. The Hephaestus mech erupted from beneath the rocks, sending rubble flying as it clapped its metal hands over its non-existent ears – imitating the actions of the pilot inside. Then, before Ayo could bark his usual order to turn the noise down, Megan enacted the second phase of her revenge.

'Give him *The Full Carrie*!' she yelled.

The nose cone of each drone spiralled open. Before Ayo could dig his mech out of the pit he'd made, his robot was showered with bright red paint.

'About time that dull-as-dishwater mech got a fresh coat!' Megan heckled. 'I bet the colour really brings out the redness in your face!'

By this time, Jack and Cameron had made their way towards the source of the robotic racket. tHeScOuRgE's battle-scarred shoulders were shaking, and Cameron's robot had one arm on tHeScOuRgE's back, the other resting on its knee. The two WarMechs were creased up – mirroring the laughter of their pilots. Megan also made her way over, more confident on her robot's feet now, and finally ready to call off her birds.

'We all square, Phaest? Or should I see what else this mech can do?'

'I believe I have succeeded in my goal – helping you acclimatise to your mech's control systems via a heightened-stress scenario,' Ayo replied, wiping paint from his robot's viewing window. 'You are welcome.'

'*You* are weird,' Megan replied. 'But yeah – I know what I'm doing now. So who did you guys choose as your assistants?'

'I picked *Iron Man*,' said Jack. 'Well, Tony Stark really, but in his *Iron Man* armour. So I've got a dude inside a robot suit, talking to me: a dude inside a robot suit.'

'Nice! What about you, Phaest?'

'Sun Tzu. Chinese military strategist and author of *The Art of War*. He was born in 544 BCE and lived in the Eastern Zhou period of ancient China, although Han dynasty historians believe tha–'

'Oh my God! How have you managed to make *this* boring? What about you, Forge?'

'I p-ppp-picked my m-m-mum.'

The comms fell silent. Of all the surprise reveals of the day, none of the rest of the Mob saw that one coming at all.

'... And suddenly I feel a lot better about my choice.' Megan eventually managed. 'And I picked *myself*!'

'Your *mum*?' Jack said to Cameron, incredulously. 'So she's in there right now?'

'Well it was her or the duck from that s-stupid *Highway H-Helper* game – they were the only ones with a l-l– feature to help me not get caught!'

'Dude – what you do in your own giant killing machine is your business,' said Megan, holding up her mech's hands. 'Who are we to judg– hey, what's going on?'

The sand beneath the Mob's metal feet had suddenly started to fall away. The distant landscape melted; everything was disappearing in a rapid digital drought. Then the thick red atmosphere above the training ground began to descend. Instinctively, the Mob ducked, shielding their mechs' heads as they passed *through* the falling crimson mist. When they emerged on the other side, they found themselves in a very different place altogether.

Wherever it was, it was loud and dark, aside from two rows of red emergency lights that barely illuminated walls of grey metal. And, wherever it was, it was *moving*. The mob, too, had moved – as if some invisible giant had picked them up like chess pieces and shifted them around. They were now arranged in a row, facing the far side of what seemed to be a vast metal container. Before any of them could speak, a voice erupted from the darkness.

'YOU JOKERS QUITE FINISHED TICKLING EACH OTHER'S TORPEDO TUBES? 'CAUSE LAST TIME I CHECKED, THE INFAMOUS *RAID MOB* WERE AN ELITE SQUAD OF DEATH-DEALIN' DOOM DELIVERERS HELL-BENT ON MAKING FINE MAGGOT CUISINE OUT OF THE NOGRAKI FILTH THAT INFECTS THIS PLANET. AND IF I'VE NOT MADE A MISTAKE – WHICH I HAVEN'T SINCE I TRIED SUGAR-FREE, CAFFEINE-FREE, TASTE-FREE SHOCKSODA – THE FOUR OF YOU HAVE BEEN SELECTED FOR A TOP PRIORITY MISSION.'

Inside her WarMech, Megan beamed at the familiar sound of Colonel J. Hardcastle. He was their mission commander; the only voice that Megan wouldn't skip past during the cutscenes. Projected onto the far wall of the container, at least twelve metres tall, was the colonel's face. His two-metre-wide moustache bristled as his lips drew back, revealing yellowed teeth clamped around a soggy, chewed-up cigar. His leathery skin wrinkled around his nose as he sneered, scanning his soldiers from left to right.

Jack saluted, and Megan's mech shook its metal head. 'Smooth,' she chuckled.

'JOYCE! Eyes up and ears back, or you'll find out double-quick what I can do to your mech with just a can opener and some determination.'

Megan straightened herself up – shocked by the colonel's words. He hadn't used her gamertag like he usually would. He said her surname.

'Now, I'm going to make this short and sweet, just like my pet Shih Tzu, Mr Tiddles. You are going to a hot zone – a colony outpost on the eastern ridge of the terraforming frontier. We've had an emergency communication. Nograki scouts have been spotted three clicks to the south. You get in, you protect the colonist, and you wipe every single last one of those slime-sacks off the face of our God-given, human-hijacked planet. Understood?'

'Yes, Sir!' they all chimed, even Megan – surprising herself with her readiness to play the obedient soldier.

'Good, because we're coming up on the drop zone now!'

The colonel's face disappeared and the wall upon which it had been projected fell away, allowing a sudden and thunderous gust of wind to tear through the space. It was then that the Raid Mob realised that they weren't in a container at all.

The opening was a hangar door.

The movement under their feet was turbulence.

They were inside a giant dropship, and they were about to be dumped into battle.

'Green light in ten, nine, eight ...'

The colonel's countdown continued. Inside the Zuul mech, Megan was muttering to herself – repeating her pre-game mantra.

'This is my WarMech.
There are none like it, this one is mine.
Without me, my WarMech is nothing,
Without my WarMech, I am nothing.
I must fire my weapons true.
I must shoot straighter than my enemy, who is trying to kill me.
I must shoot those slimy butt-biscuits before they shoot me.
I will ...'

'ZERO! GO! GO! GO!'

Level 5: The New Playground

And with that, the entire floor of the hangar fell open. The WarMechs, and their pilots, were sent tumbling through the ruby-red sky.

Level 6: Close Encounters

Being *inside* a cloud was something Jack could never have imagined experiencing. Actually, he *still* hadn't experienced it – yet the Fullmmersion feedback made the sensation of slipping through the rainy haze above Rotec feel as real as anything he'd ever felt. The goose bumps on his arms were quickly replaced by beads of sweat, though, as tHeScOuRgE WarMech broke through the cloud layer and Jack saw the carnage below.

Green flames had engulfed the south side of the colony settlement. Jack knew what this meant. *Shellers*. Nograki shellers were named after the impenetrable armour on their backs, and their ability to fire long-range rounds of incendiary mucus. They were the Nograki equivalent of armoured tanks. Jack could see surviving terraformers scurrying around like panicked ants in the midst of the fiery emerald onslaught. Narrowing his eyes, he flicked through booster selectors and threw his mech into a nosedive.

'DO THE SUPERHERO LANDING!'

Jack heard Megan's voice as the blue terrain came screaming up to meet him. He pulled his mech's legs under and fired the reverse thrusters just in time to let him plant one foot, one knee, and one balled fist hard into the ground – each impact sending up its own plume of blue dust.

Nailed it.

Rising up to his Mech's full height, Jack surveyed the scene. The supply store lay in blazing ruins. The living centre had taken heavy fire, with terrified terraformers still piling out of what remained of the burning structure.

A sudden beeping alerted Jack to an incoming projectile. Throwing his mech's arm towards the horizon, Jack activated the heads-up targeting display and locked on to the flaming green missile, firing two rockets of his own. Direct hit; the sheller's mucus bomb exploded like a phlegm-filled firework. For the first time, Jack noticed a score total on a display on the forearm of his exosuit. For each civilian that escaped, his total increased by 1000 points. And yet Jack wasn't pleased to see his mounting score. He'd already forgotten that this was a game, and the achievement notifications only served to remind him that none of this was real. He quickly found a way to turn them off before returning to his preferred reality.

'Phaest! Can you use your magical camping skills and do something about those shellers?' Jack shouted up, losing himself in the action once more.

'The wheels are already in motion,' Ayo replied, 'and bullets will soon follow.'

'COVER FIRE, PLEASE! BEFORE THE NEXT ICE AGE!'

Jack saw Megan's mech running to join Cameron to guard the nearby battery field. He knew that if just one mucus bomb hit a single power cell, the explosion would cause thermal runaway: a chain reaction of electrical explosions that would wipe out the entire site. Thankfully, Megan and Cameron had already turned the Rotecian sky into a shooting gallery – picking bomb after bomb clean out of the air. Jack continued to pick off any strays, hoping that none would slip through before the cavalry arrived.

'Any t-tim–, any ti-tim–, whenever you're ready!' Cameron shouted between shots.

A matte-grey silencer, attached to the end of a sniper cannon, jutted out of a distant spider hole. It was all that could be seen of the Hephaestus mech, which was hiding in a deep-cover vantage point – and its sights were already trained on the first of six shellers. Its aim would have to be perfect; the shellers only had one vulnerable spot. The Rotec winds would also have to be accounted for. The ballistic drop compensator clicked around slowly, then Ayo pulled the trigger.

Jack had to admire the camper's handiwork. One by one, the Nograki shellers exploded in detail so vivid that it might have turned his stomach if it didn't look so damned cool. Every time Ayo sank an explosive-tipped tracer round into one of his targets, the detonation caused blue plasma energy to flash through the joints of the shell plates. For a moment, the glowing hexagonal pattern looked quite beautiful – until the charge overloaded the shell and ripped it apart, sending chunks of alien soaring into the sky. Jack saw blue steam rising from the puddles of extra-terrestrial entrails, and smelled the putrid odour of cooked Nograki carried on the wind, coughing as it stung the back of his throat. He smiled; lost again in a reality realer than real.

'You can thank me individually or as a group. Either way, make it quick. My modesty won't take more than three solid minutes of applause.'

The three other mechs turned to face what they assumed was Ayo's direction, clapping in half-mock, half-genuine appreciation. Then Cameron and Megan stomped towards the remains of the living centre where Jack was ushering out the last stragglers. Everything seemed to be under control. Cameron swung his mech's head southwards.

It took him even longer to get his words out than usual. When he finally managed it, they were loud, urgent, and dripping with panic.

'WE H-HAVE I-INCOMING!'

The Zuul mech's head snapped up, and Megan saw what Cameron had seen: a swarm of Nograki scouts, *way* closer than they should've been. Both of Zuul's arms shot out instinctively. Double plasma cannons glowed with the heat of pre-ignition. They must have used the shellers' bombardment as cover for their creeping advance. The scouts would be within attack range in moments, and Jack was still clearing out survivors.

'We'll hold them off! Get those meat sacks to safety, quickly!' Megan shouted, pulling her mech into a bounding sprint, with ForgeFire666 following fast.

Jack was *still* funnelling colonists out when he heard a sudden splintering crack. The heat was too much, and the wall above the exit had fractured. The structure was failing. The final few survivors would be buried in the inevitable collapse. Unless ...

Approaching the burning doorway, Jack lowered his mech and wedged its shoulder under the arch, forming a makeshift escape tunnel. The metal beams around the door frame quickly conducted the immense heat, and inside the mech, Jack started to sweat. He grimaced as the heat seared into his shoulder and down his back. His face reddened. He puffed out his cheeks, breathing hard as the final few colonists escaped under his arm. The last one was a woman carrying a baby. She turned as if to thank the giant robot, and as she did, Jack looked down at the infant in her arms. What he saw shocked him so much that he almost dropped the building.

Jack was looking at the face of his own baby brother.

'SCOURGE! BEHIND YOU!' Megan cried.

Jack only managed to tear his eyes away because the colonist carrying the baby had bundled it into a blanket and ran. She had seen what Jack had not: a Nograki scout climbing through the wreckage. One of the limbs extending from its torso was on fire – its skin already blackened by the emerald flames – but it seemed like the creature hadn't even noticed. Its focus was singular; its target clear. Rounding the corner of what remained of the living centre, it charged at tHeScOuRgE.

Jack refocused, but didn't actually react. Even when the Nograki was close enough that he could smell its burning green flesh, he kept his mech perfectly still. He waited until the creature bared its toxic fangs and pounced. That's when he made his move.

Jack pulled his WarMech's arm out of the doorway and rolled *into* the remains of the burning building. The scout dove in after him, but not before the arch gave way completely, collapsing on top of the alien and trapping it underneath. Jack was only inside the structure for a moment, but the heat was almost unbearable. He scanned the roof for its weakest point. Crouching down, he overloaded the boosters in his robot's legs, then ignited the propulsion systems. Jack arched his back hard, threw his head towards his heels, and his mech exploded through the roof in a tumbling ball of green fire. At the apex of the backwards somersault, Jack extended his hands and loosed ten Nograki-piercing rounds from his mech's outstretched fingertips, obliterating the trapped alien below. Landing outside the wreckage, Jack scanned the area to the north. The survivors were all gone – including the woman and the baby. The southern ridge was ablaze with gunfire, soaked in Nograki blood. Ayo's tracer rounds lit up the sky, like shooting stars soaring straight into the hearts of alien attackers. Shaking off the lingering distraction, Jack pointed his mech towards the battlefield and launched into a lumbering run. It was time for the Raid Mob to reunite. And disassemble.

In the ForgeFire666 mech, Cameron was running again. He'd hurled a proximity mine into the closing space between his war machine and an oncoming swarm of attackers. Once the gap had all but disappeared, he punched his mech's foot hard into the ground, faked right, then rolled left, leaving the Nograkis no time to adjust. The mine erupted behind him, and he watched as the top halves of four scouts sailed into the air on a trail of inky-blue blood and explosive residue. Cameron smiled, but he wasn't finished. He pressed the two middle fingers of his right hand down on the weapon selector and threw out his arm. The gesture activated a plasma-powered chokutō – a straight, single-edged Japanese sword that glowed along its outer edge with burning blue energy. Springing upwards towards the spinning alien remains, he unleashed a barrage of devastatingly accurate cuts. The ground was splattered, and the edge of the chokutō steamed with blue mist as alien pieces rained from the sky.

'Nice moves, Forge! Getting a little *slice* of the action.'

'Thanks, Z-Zuul! I'm thinking of trying that one out on FrankenDeath14 next time I r-r-run into him!' Cameron replied, brimful of digital daring. 'You look b-b-busy. Need some help?'

The Zuul mech was doing something strange. It was running *away* from a group of pursuing scouts. And the weirdest thing was, it wasn't running very fast.

'I'm channelling my inner Maverick,' said Megan.

Suddenly Cameron knew what she was doing. He had watched *Top Gun* with Megan and her dad on one of their many 80s film nights. He recalled the famous scene: Maverick pulls the brakes on his F-14 jet fighter, much to the surprise of his co-pilot Merlin, and the enemy plane flies past – right into Maverick's gunsight. But Cameron didn't know how Megan would get the Nograkis to run *past* her, rather than straight into her …

Inside Zuul, Megan watched on a rear-view camera feed as the Nograki hoard closed to within striking distance. Then she gripped the weapon selector and threw her arms and legs outwards. Internal boosters fired and the graffitied WarMech split into five completely separate pieces. The legs and arms detached from the body and flew in opposite directions. The torso and head stayed intact, shooting up into the air and looking down over the pack of Nograkis below. Inside the hovering control capsule, Megan was looking down, laughing. The Nograkis scrambled and fell over each other as they realised they were chasing nothing – ending up a tangled heap of awkwardly hinged limbs and toxic fangs.

Megan pulled her knees to her chest and crossed her forearms, and her mech recombined just in time to make a solid landing. From the dust of the impact, the Zuul mech strode forwards, walking in time to an appropriate song from the *Daughter of Slaughter Mix – Danger Zone*, straight off the *Top Gun* soundtrack. The hapless Nograki hadn't even managed to unknot themselves before Megan was standing over them, aiming dual pulse phasors and a plasma-powered railgun.

'No points for second place ...' she said with a smirk that would've made Tom Cruise proud. Then she painted the ground a thick, sticky coat of indigo.

'Not bad, Zuuly,' said Ayo, from somewhere still unknown. 'Check this out ...'

Ordinarily, Ayo used silencers to help conceal his position on the battlefield. But whatever he'd just unleashed, it was far from quiet. In her rear-facing camera, Megan had seen the sonic blast from the shot warping the treeline before she'd even heard the detonation. A tracer-tailed projectile screamed its way towards the Nograki at the head of an approaching pack – and it didn't stop when it got there. It tore straight through the alien's armoured skin ... then kept going. Megan watched, her jaw dropping as the bullet *split in two*. One half veered to the right, finding a second scout to rip through, while the other half changed course in the opposite direction, piling right through the middle of a third. Then came the icing on the bullet-cake: Megan watched the two halves of the projectile come *back together*, lining up perfectly to sink straight into the heart of the final alien attacker. The four Nograki scouts fell in sequence like dead dominos.

'Remote-control bullets!' Ayo announced, smugness saturating the comms channel. 'I call them the *undodgeables*.'

'Nice! It's about time you made some noise!' Megan called back.

'Speaking of which,' Ayo replied, 'could you turn the music down? It's *in* my control capsule, and for some reason it's making my virtual helper dance.'

'No way!' Megan laughed. 'See if Sun Tzu likes a bit of this ...'

Megan scrolled through the *Daughter of Slaughter Mix* until she found *War* by Edwin Starr. She was about to hit play when something entirely unexpected flew past her mech's face.

It was tHeScOuRgE's fist.

Just the fist, that is. It wasn't attached to the machine – it was flying, by itself. The balled-up metal hand soared across the battlefield, landing square on the forked jaw of a Nograki attacker with enough force to spin the alien's head all the way around before it dropped down dead.

'Rocket-powered fists, y'all!' Jack shouted with glee, as his mech's hand soared back towards him like a boomerang, slotting neatly into the wrist joint.

'That's awesome!' came Cameron's call, as he surveyed the battlefield. It seemed that the invasion had been well and truly squashed.

'We came, we saw, we kicked their butts!' announced Megan, joining the other two. Jack extended a metal hand towards Megan's mech, ready for a congratulatory fist bump – then withdrew almost instantly. Jack's eyes were suddenly wide as dinner plates, as close-range cannons popped out of his mech's forearm. In their moment of celebration, none of them had spotted a last, hidden Nograki scout launching itself at the Zuul mech from behind ...

But the beast never reached its target. Instead, it exploded in a shower of alien guts, leaving the Zuul standing there unharmed, flicking Nograki remains off its shoulder. Behind Zuul, Jack saw the Maverick and Goose drones. Their gun barrels were still smoking. Inside the mech, Megan was smiling.

'At least *I've* got my back. Thanks, me!' she said to her clone assistant, who had sent up the drones to provide her with video feeds during combat.

'Good birdies – Polly want a cracker?' said Ayo, who had watched Megan's drones through his scope. 'What do your pets eat, Zuuly?'

'Socially stunted teenagers who've never kissed a girl ... And they're *hungry*,' Megan clapped back.

'To be fair, that c-could be any of us,' said Cameron.

'Speak for yourself ... my milkshake brings all the girls to the yard,' Megan sassed, before adding, '... in my dreams!' The whole group fell about laughing.

Inside tHeScOuRgE, in that moment, Jack felt like things were close to perfect. He was in his better world, with his best friends, doing what he was best at. Nothing could ruin this moment.

Nothing except the Nograki tendrils gripping his shoulder.

Not his mech's shoulder – *his* shoulder. Jack looked down to see an alien limb *inside* his control capsule, sliding over his body, flailing digits gripping at his chest. Then another tendril fell flat across his face. Before he knew what was going on, the view of Rotec was torn away, replaced by a blinding light. He leaped up in a disorientated panic, rubbing his eyes forcefully, trying to restore his sight. Eventually, the blurry world came back into focus.

Jack found himself in his bedroom. His mum was standing next to him. She was holding his visor in one hand and a cigarette burned almost to a nub in the other. Jack's senses took more than a moment to retune, but before he could even make out his mum's expression, he could smell where she'd been.

'One in the morning ...'

Her speech was slurred, but after repeating herself three times, Jack got the message. Her blurry figure stumbled out of his room, mumbling something about Jack's brother. At the mention of that word, Jack was all of a sudden much more awake. He got up from his bed and crossed the narrow hallway into his sibling's equally tiny, darkened room. As the real world finally came into sharp focus, he saw his brother, Alexander, sleeping soundly, peaceful and calm. Jack slowly reached out his hand, then realised he was still wearing the RealFeel gloves. Quietly, he turned to leave, glancing back one more time before he pulled the door closed.

Jack returned to his room and sat on the edge of his bed. The cold wind creeping through cracks in the window frame chilled the beaded sweat on his forehead and neck, sending a sudden chill down his spine. He pulled his duvet up around his shoulders and took a few deep breaths, trying to process the evening's extreme events. He didn't get very far before he heard familiar sounds coming from outside his window.

Keys in the door.

Heels on the pavement.

The sound of his mum leaving the house.

If it hadn't happened so many times in the past, Jack wouldn't have believed it. She was going back out. That meant she wouldn't be up on time to get Alexander ready in the morning, which meant that he'd have to do it, which meant that he'd be late for school. Again.

Jack stood up and looked out of the window. His mum had already vanished. He glanced upwards, wishing that the moon he could see high in the night sky was Colaxia – that he could take his brother and escape to Rotec. He smirked at the painful realisation that a world full of angry alien monsters still appealed more than this one did.

Removing his gloves, Jack took out his phone and set an extra-early alarm for the morning. He stabbed at the screen, taking his frustration at his so-called mum out on an already cracked display. Then he looked up to the shelf where the lights on the baby monitor tracked Alexander's rhythmic breathing. Jack matched his own breaths with the pattern on the display, calming his resentment, and reminding himself of what mattered most.

Putting down his phone and picking the visor up off the floor, Jack felt himself overcome by a sudden wash of dizzy exhaustion. He collapsed back onto his bed and fell into a deep sleep.

Level 7:
Déjà View

Ayo rubbed his temples. His head had been pounding since he was all but dragged out of bed, having slept through each of his six alarms. Usually, Ayo was up before the first one even sounded, cancelling each one exactly a minute before it was due. It was one of a laundry list of coping strategies he'd developed to get himself through the day, as he battled with autistic compulsions that might otherwise have kept him in his room, away from everyone – including the Mob. His three friends had long been Ayo's most important reason to push himself into the outside world each day. Amongst everything else they shared, they were the only ones who'd ever seemed capable of acknowledging his autism (unlike his parents), without making him feel like an outsider (unlike literally everyone else).

That morning, however, Ayo had woken up in a panicked daze – his gaming visor and gloves still on – and now he felt even less a part of the real world than usual.

As their plush Range Rover wafted Ayo towards school, his dad's thick Nigerian accent and harsh words were the only thing anchoring him to reality. While his dad yelled at some poor office technician about today's board presentation through the car's hands-free phone system, Ayo sat in the back trying to piece together last night's events.

He remembered being picked up after school by his mum; she'd nearly crashed their other Range Rover (they were a two Range Rover family) rifling through patient notes while weaving through traffic. He remembered being dropped off at an empty house. He remembered, in his excitement to get up to his room, whacking his skinny shin off the stair rail and nearly falling flat on his face. He remembered locking the bedroom door behind him. He even remembered remembering how pointless this was, as no one ever bothered to check on him. If neither of his parents had managed to pry themselves away from their work long enough to realise that their son had become one of the best gamers in the world, then he could be pretty sure that his latest online endeavour would also be completely ignored.

After he put on the visor and the gloves, that's when it all got hazy. Ayo could hardly remember a single detail after that with any real clarity. He could remember *sensations*. Smells. Sounds. Flashes of images. He remembered dirt under his feet and hands. Blue dirt. He checked his fingernails unthinkingly, then scolded himself. What was he expecting to find? Encrusted alien soil? He rubbed his temples again. He saw bursts of light … green fire … rainbow explosions … and a … flying hand? And he *swore* he could smell burning, even now. He could *taste* it, right at the back of his mouth. Burning flesh. Burning *alien* flesh …

'DAD, WATCH OUT!'

The 4x4 screeched to a tyre-torturing halt, throwing the occupants forwards against their strained seatbelts. Ayo straightened his glasses, knocked crooked by the force of the emergency stop, then he stared out of the front window. It had disappeared.

'Mr Osikoya? Hello? Are you still there?'

'… I will call you back, Carl.'

'Okay, no problem, Mr Osikoya, whatever suits yo–'

Ayo's dad hung up and glared over his shoulder. It felt like he was staring directly into Ayo's soul. The stern gaze shifted back to the street ahead, confirmed that the road was indeed empty, then returned to Ayo, burning even more intensely.

'I don't know what *that* was, but if it happens again, you will walk to school. Every day. For a month.'

It was over an hour's walk to school, and yet Ayo knew that this was no idle threat.

'S-sorry, Sir.'

The car crawled off. Ayo removed his glasses and scrunched his eyes closed, then replaced them and looked again. Still nothing – but he knew what he'd seen. A Nograki scout. Standing right in the middle of the road. One of its arms was burnt. It was standing *right there*, as real as the shops and the streetlamps. Except, of course, that it wasn't. It couldn't have been.

Ayo's dad pulled up at the school gates, and Ayo quickly swapped the awkwardness of the car for the awkwardness of school.

He always tried his best not to let it show, but this morning, as he walked into school, Ayo felt even more self-conscious than usual. His normal list of daily anxieties included issues like outgrowing his trousers for the third time that year, with his stupidly long, spindly legs making his lollipop head look even bigger. But today, for some reason, his legs felt like they had been disconnected from his body completely: like he was piloting them via remote, and he wasn't very good at it. Then there were his vision problems. Not his *actual* short-sightedness, but that whole "seeing an alien in the middle of the street" episode. He reached under his glasses and rubbed his eyes, then he looked upwards. Was it just him, or was the sky much *redder* than usual?

Ayo was almost at his form room when he was obstructed by a stuttering bundle of nerves, dressed in a green windbreaker and a triple-secured backpack.

'Everyone s-saw us!'

Cameron was shaking. His face glistened with sweat. His mouth hung slightly agape, and his head jerked around like a bird, darting paranoid glances in all directions.

'Everyone saw us A-Ayo! *Everyone!*' Cameron repeated.

Ayo held Cameron's shoulders, doing his best to focus his friend's skittish attention.

'Saw us do *what*, Cam? What are you talking about?'

But Cameron couldn't answer. And he didn't need to. Ayo looked around the corridor, now bustling with students, and began to catch snippets of excited conversations. He turned his ear to the nearest group and tuned in.

'I thought Zuul was gonna get wasted! Whoever controls that thing's got *game*.'

'What about *Hay-fess-toos*, or whatever its name is? He gives campers a *good* name!'

'ForgeFire666 was the *sickest*, man – did you see his samurai skills? He's probably in his 40s. Been gaming since the Atari days. Deffo still lives with his parents ...'

'What about Scourge's burning building backflip! I bet he's one of those pro-gamers – American, maybe, or one of those esports guys from Japan.'

'How do you know they're all *boys*? Girls play too – I'm better than all of you on *Distant Dawn*.'

'We'll find out soon enough. *Millions* of people watched that stream – you can't stay off the grid too long with that kind of shine.'

'When are the rest of the Top Ten playing?'

'Tonight. Last night was just a preview of the new team mode; obviously Hailstorm put the most famous squad in first to show off the co-op features. The Hailstorm Games account posted again this morning – look ...'

Ayo watched as the group took out their phones, all hyped over what the Raid Mob had done. But Ayo's recollections were so vague. He looked at Cameron, but there was even less recognition in his eyes – just sheer panic.

'Listen,' Ayo said, quietly but firmly. 'If anyone knew who we were, we'd have been mobbed as soon as we got here. And if our identities had been leaked, your mum wouldn't even have let you out of your room. Hailstorm Games may have streamed the mission, but they obviously didn't broadcast our comms chat.'

Ayo hoped that was true. The Mob was usually very careful about not saying anything that could give away their real-world identities, but right now, Ayo was struggling to remember even the most basic details about last night – never mind what every member of the team might or might not have said.

'Let's just get inside, away from everyone else,' said Ayo, herding the near-catatonic Cameron into the empty form room. 'Megan and Jack will be here soon – they'll help us make sense of all this.'

Ayo barely had the chance to escort Cameron to a chair before Megan came crashing into the room. Her red bandana was drenched in sweat. Her complexion was grey; the skin around her eyes was ashen. She was shaking. This wasn't the Megan that Ayo knew at all. He caught her awkwardly as she collapsed, breathless and shivering, into the nearest seat. Dragging her head up with Herculean effort, Megan looked Ayo in the eyes.

'I *saw* one of them. A *Nograki*. It's *outside* ...'

While this was more than enough to hurl Cameron back into a state of panicked stupor, Ayo tried to stay calm. He was about to explain that he, too, *thought* he saw something that morning, but before he could, the classroom door flew open, and a walking stack of paperwork entered.

'SIT DOWN, BE QUIET, PUT AWAY ALL ELECTRONIC DEVICES. THE NEXT PERSON WHO UTTERS SO MUCH AS A SINGLE SYLLABLE ABOUT THAT RIDICULOUS ONLINE GAME WILL BE IN LUNCHTIME DETENTION QUICKER THAN THEY CAN SAY "I'M WASTING MY POTENTIAL, MY TIME, AND MY EXISTENCE".'

Miss Barrett looked even angrier than usual. In the back row, Ayo was propping up Megan. His feeble, fragile frame was barely up to the task, but he didn't want her to draw the teacher's attention – not while she was spouting what he hoped was delirium about aliens on the school grounds. And where was Jack? Ayo prayed the last member of the Raid Mob wouldn't be late again. They clearly needed time together; time to work out what happened; time to get their heads straight. Ayo watched the clock tick towards nine o' clock. Miss Barrett started barking the register. Eventually, she reached Jack's name.

Silence. Ayo stared at Jack's empty seat, as if willing him to appear out of thin air.

'Jack Delaney?'

Ayo looked up at the door. Maybe Jack was off sick – maybe the nausea and delirium that the three of them were suffering with had hit him even worse. With the mood Miss Barrett was in, that was looking like a better prospect than turning up late ...

'Jack Delaney?'

Having craned her neck around the tall stack of papers to check his empty chair, Miss Barrett was just about to coil herself back up with her register when the classroom door burst open.

'Sorry I'm late, Miss! My bike got a flat tyre – two flat tyres! The front went, then I tried to wheelie my way here, then I ran the back over a broken tile that fell out of the back of a van that was driving with the doors ope–'

'Jack?'

'Yes, Miss Barrett?'

'Time?'

'Six minutes past nine, Miss Barrett.'

'Meaning?'

'Lunchtime detention, Miss Barrett.'

'Thank you, Jack. A rewarding tête-à-tête as always. Olivia Heritage?'

'Here, Miss!' said the next squeaky voice. It added wryly, 'We missed you yesterday afternoon!'

The tip of Miss Barrett's pen thudded onto the register, scoring a begrudging red tick next to Olivia's name. Her face flushed the same shade as her pen as she shot a piercing glance across the classroom.

'I had a *personal emergency*, Olivia,' seethed Miss Barrett. 'I'm sure you can forgive me a half-day's absence, once in a decade.'

'Yes, Miss. Sorry, M-Miss.'

During this exchange, Jack had made his way over to Raid Mob's Row, and upon doing so had discovered the state of the team. Ayo was looking up at him with the same dumfounded look that Jack gave the three of them – but for different reasons. While Ayo, Cameron and Megan were a collectively confused shambles, Jack looked alert and full of energy. Jack tried to whisper to Ayo; Ayo tried to whisper back. Jack asked what the matter was. Ayo told him they were all feeling ill, and that they'd seen things. He asked what Jack remembered from the night before. Jack told him that he remembered everything. Ayo told him they remembered nothing. Jack asked Ayo what they'd seen. Ayo told Jack that him and Megan had seen aliens.

Then before she'd even reached the rest of their names in the register, Miss Barrett got annoyed with the whispering and gave the whole Mob detention.

Having spent most of the morning dissecting highlight videos of himself and his friends on a phone tucked well under his desk, Ayo had raced towards the detention room as soon as he was dismissed from his last class. As he turned into the final corridor, he ran into Cameron – who was even less okay than the last time Ayo saw him. The cause was Franky McGrath, the big bullying Year Ten boy who was better known to the Mob by his gaming handle: FrankenDeath14.

Franky had been joined by his two snivelling underlings, Aaron and Callum, and together the three of them had backed Cameron into a cloakroom corner – forcing him further and further into a cluster of coats until he'd been all but swallowed by them.

'Hasn't someone put you on a diet yet?' said Franky, prodding Cameron in his stomach again. 'When people say your body is supposed to be a temple, they aren't talking about the *Large* Mahal.'

'Or the *Entire* S-S-State building!' said Callum, lisping through a gap in his front teeth.

'Or the *Eye-full* Tower!' said Franky, snorting out an obnoxious laugh.

Even though the Year Ten boys would snap Ayo like a twig, he was about to risk a beating of his own when a third member of the Mob showed up.

'Franky!' Jack shouted, striding over with what Ayo

could tell was a ton of false bravado. 'The Headteacher wants to see you – something about you breaking one of the school computers?'

'What? I haven't broken a computer!' he protested, turning away from Cameron.

'Yeah,' Jack continued, his chest puffed out as far as it would go. 'She said that just because you were told to *reboot* it, that didn't mean kick it twice, you pleb.'

Cameron gasped. So did Ayo. Franky launched himself at Jack, but Callum grabbed hold of his coat and pulled him back. Jack stood his ground, watching as Callum mumbled something to Franky. Franky looked at Jack again, and with a final scowl he stormed off in the opposite direction with his underlings in tow. Ayo watched as the trio walked past Miss Barrett, who was now storming down the corridor, heading towards the Mob members.

'Everything okay here, boys?' she said as she approached, scowling back at Franky.

Slowly and nervously, Cameron emerged from the coats, like a joey kangaroo from its mum's pouch. Ayo was doubly relieved that Jack had stepped in before he'd started his doomed peace talks with the Year Ten cavemen, and that Cameron was okay.

'Yes, M-m-miss. Everything's f-f-fine.'

Miss Barrett nodded at Cameron slowly. Then she pointed the pen in her hand towards the detention room, her scathing manner returning as surely as it had disappeared. 'Then why are you still standing here when you should be in *there*?'

'Sorry, Miss!' Jack started, herding Cameron and Ayo in the direction indicated by their teacher's brandished biro.

They shuffled towards the detention room. 'What happened? Why did Franky l-leave you a-l-lone?' Cameron breathed.

Jack shrugged. 'There aren't *many* advantages to living on my estate, but sometimes its reputation does come in handy. Come on,' he added, giving Cameron a reassuring slap on the back. 'You'll get your chance to dish out some sweet online revenge to that oxygen thief soon enough. Let's go figure out what the hell happened last night ...'

Ayo, Jack and Cameron entered the detention room. Without looking up from his book, Mr Wilby rocked his chair onto its back legs, something he'd made a career of telling kids not to do, and waved them to the back. Ayo spotted Megan hunched over her phone and looking much more herself.

'You guys feeling better?' she asked as the other Mob members sat down around her.

'I'm feeling better for having slept through the whole of my Geography lesson,' Ayo replied. 'I told the teacher I'd suffered a fairly severe derealisation episode. She told me to "put my head down". I have some concerns about the medical training of the staff at this school.'

'Same. Although you're kinda bringing my headache back,' grumbled Megan.

'I slept all the w-way through break,' Cameron said, finally finding his voice. 'M-Mrs Williams had to wake m-me up.'

'So you guys still don't remember what happened last night? I don't get that – how can you have forgotten? It was so awesome!' said Jack.

'Well, the highlight videos are certainly proving to be of some assistance,' Ayo replied, flashing a phone with a playlist of clips from the mission. 'But it feels like watching a video of something I did *years* ago. My memory is so hazy.'

'Mine's w-worse. I haven't seen any of the highlights yet – I just h-heard everyone talking about us when I g-g-got to school this morning. Can I see?'

Ayo handed his phone to Cameron as Megan looked at Jack quizzically.

'If it was so awesome, why did you bail early?' said Megan. Jack's face scrunched into a ball of confusion.

'What do you mean?'

'You left the game. You almost didn't get your points. You missed Colonel Hardcastle's debrief. He told us that mission was just the start of things ...'

'I thought the op was over!' said Jack, clearly dismayed at the idea that he'd missed out on some action. 'My mum came in and took the visor off me. At first, I thought one of the Nograkis was inside my suit, but it turned out tha–'

'You thought a Nograki was *inside* your suit?' Ayo interrupted.

'We saw scouts in the real world!' Megan started up. 'Ayo saw one this morning, and I saw one hiding behind the bike shed on the way into school. I nearly browned my pants. No one else reacted: so I just turned and legged it inside as fast as I could!'

'I saw something t-too,' said Cameron. 'When Mrs Williams woke me up – I saw it on the playing fields, through the science lab w-w-windows.'

Ayo removed his glasses and scrunched his eyes shut, as if he was trying to work out one of Miss Barrett's purposefully torturous maths problems. He rubbed them on his shirt before repositioning them on his face. Beside him, Jack had pulled the image of the VR visor up on his phone.

'So ... I'm the only one who *hasn't* seen a Nograki in the real world, right?' Jack said.

'None of us *saw* a Nograki, Jack,' Ayo replied, irritably. 'We aren't stupid. We all *thought* we saw something, but they must be hallucinations. Delusions. Figments of our imagination. Nograkis aren't real.'

'I know that!' Jack retorted. 'But the question is, why have *you* all "seen" them and I haven't? It was one in the morning by the time I stopped playing. Did you all fall asleep with the visors on?'

Silence.

And then the penny dropped.

Ayo, Cameron and Megan all started rubbing their temples simultaneously, as if they'd rehearsed it. They *had* fallen asleep with the visors on, while they were all still inside the VR version of *Distant Dawn*.

'So that scuzzy data stayed in our heads even after we left the game grid?' said Megan. 'No wonder we're having a hard time separating the game from reality! It felt so real. My muscles are aching today, as if I really did spend all night running and jumping and fighting alien scum.'

'But you didn't,' Ayo replied. 'Those discs that we stuck on ourselves – they must stimulate our nerves and our muscles while the visor feeds us the visual and auditory information. I remember feeling heat, feeling dirt under my knees. And did we ... did we *jump through a cloud?*'

'Yes! Yes!' Jack said. 'When we left the dropship. I could feel the water. I could even smell the burning wreck of the colony – I could taste it in the air. How can a game controller make you smell and taste things?'

'The cinema down the road does 4DX – the seats release smells that match what's on screen. Maybe the visor does the same?' Megan suggested.

'Maybe – but that wouldn't explain the weirdest thing I saw.'

'Weirder than aliens holding up traffic in the real world?' Ayo said.

'Maybe not – but not far off,' Jack replied. He hesitated, and for a long moment it seemed like he wasn't going to be able to find any more words. Eventually, he managed four more.

'I saw my brother.'

Ayo stared down the row at Jack. He'd almost come to terms with the explanation that the VR might be having a lingering effect on their subconscious by causing Nograki hallucinations. But Jack seeing a member of his family inside the game was something else.

'One of the colonists – the ones I was helping out of the burning building. She was carrying a baby. I *swear* it was Alexander.'

'Babies all look the same to me. Like smooth, slightly squishy potatoes.' Megan interjected, her nose wrinkled.

'I think I know my own brother,' Jack replied, determinedly. 'I get why you guys would imagine you saw Nograkis *outside* the game if you fell asleep with the visors on; mixing up the virtual world with the real world. But why would I see my brother *inside* the game?'

'Because you're the most protective big brother in the world?' Megan offered. 'And you might just have been projecting a bit?'

'If my m-m-mum can be my digital assistant, mm-maybe your brother made a virtual g-guest appearance too?' suggested Cameron.

'But how would Hailstorm know what he looks like? It's not like he's got his own gaming account!' Jack replied.

'N-neither has my mum,' said Cameron.

'Look,' Ayo interjected, 'this new tech has clearly taken its toll on our faculties. Maybe we should just avoid the game tonight; allow our cerebra the chance to recalibrate and acclimatise to the advanced visual and visceral stimuli.'

'For those who don't speak Verbosian, he's suggesting we give our brains a rest,' said Megan. 'Whether we're seeing things inside or outside the game, I think we can agree that neither is a good look. And we might – and I can't believe I'm the one saying this – but we *might* need to spend some time out here in the real world.'

Just then, an alert sounded on Ayo's phone, with Megan's and Jack's quickly following suit.

'... Or maybe not,' said Ayo, glaring fixedly at the screen. Megan and Jack gawped at their phones, while Cameron craned over Ayo's shoulder to see what had them all so utterly transfixed. On the screens there was an image, posted by the Hailstorm Games account. The Top Ten elite mechs were all there, arranged in two rows of five, with a caption underneath.

Hailstorm Games

Following

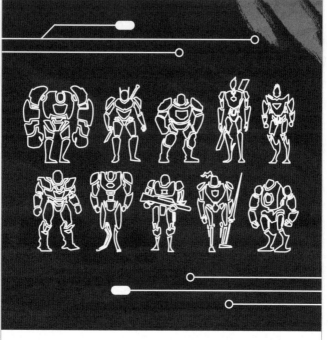

    584,335 likes

You have seen a fraction of the potential of Fullmersion gaming. What you will see next will defy all expectations. Defy what you thought possible. Defy reality itself. Ten Players. One Ultimate Prize. Witness the future of gaming. #DistantDawn #Fullmmersion #FutureOfGaming #HailstormGames #Gamers #Elite #TopTenOnly #RealerThanReal

GAME PROGRESS ... 31%

Level 8: War of the Worlds

Jack sat on the edge of his bed, turning the visor over in his gloved hands.

The Mob had agreed that it'd be safe to play that night, as long as they didn't fall asleep with the visors on again. After that Hailstorm Games post, and a resulting hype that almost broke the internet, the truth was they would've found any excuse to play – even if they knew the whole world would be watching. However, Jack had taken a few precautions. He'd set a string of alarms on his phone, which he'd stuck in his pocket. He'd fed Alexander, changed him and put him to bed. He'd even taped the baby monitor to the back of his visor, so that if his brother cried it would be loud enough for him to hear, even from inside the game.

He'd seen his mum leave – watched her walk down the street and disappear around the corner. God only knew when she'd be back, and for once, Jack hoped she'd be gone for a good long while.

Jack had all the bases covered. He was ready.

And yet, he couldn't bring himself to put the visor on. The special mission, whatever it was, started in five minutes. But Jack just couldn't shake the image of his baby brother being bundled through the flaming wreckage.

'It's just a game,' he kept telling himself. 'It's not real.'

Threadbare curtains flailed as a cold wind whistled through cracks in the window frame. Jack had to admit it, the real world really did suck – all bleak and bitter and dim. Jack gave the lights on the baby monitor one last look; the rhythmic blinking tracked Alexander's steady breathing.

'See you soon, little guy. I'll keep you safe in whichever world I find you,' he whispered. Then, slowly, he slid the visor over his head, and sank into the world of *Distant Dawn*.

Except, it wasn't *Distant Dawn*. It wasn't any part of Rotec Jack had been to before, and he'd been *everywhere*: from the Shattered Ice Forest to the varicoloured sands of the Dappled Desert, and every place in between. This wasn't Rotec.

This was Earth.

According to the original *Distant Dawn* storyline, the exoplanet colonies were formed in the late 21st Century to ease Earth's over-population crisis. The colonies appealed to people who were struggling. Opportunities for a new life and a fresh start were promised – and it worked. By 2098, half the global population lived off-world. But there was one group of people who didn't leave Earth: the rich. As the masses left, the elite redecorated – and there was no greater shrine to excess than *New York City* ... where Jack had just landed in his hulking metal machine of war.

Jack drank in the sights and sounds and smells. It all looked very different from the real New York. Even the smallest high-rise was twice as big as the old Empire State building – which itself had been housed *inside* an enormous God-poking monstrosity known as The Antiquitum Tower. Winding neon beams marked out five different levels of sky-road, all of which were oddly empty. Even the 200-metre-tall holographic billboards had been shut down. The whole violently bright and boisterous place was unusually dark and quiet, but Jack still knew that he was standing in the middle of Times Square, in what used to be known as Manhattan. The fat cats who had bought up New York's richest borough had renamed it Maximalum. And Maximalum, it seemed, was in trouble.

'MACHINES OF WAR! HARBINGERS OF BOOM! KNIGHTS OF ASS-KICKERY ONE AND ALL – STAND TO ATTENTION!'

A wireframe hologram appeared inside Jack's control pod. The fizzing green face of Colonel J. Hardcastle came into sharp focus.

'WarMech pilots! We have recalled your squad from Rotec because those scaly, slime-sucking space maggots have found a way through the Earth Orbit Defence Shield. One of their dropships – an Ex-Phase 8 class adapted for interstellar travel – slipped through the net like an oily fish … and it has just uncloaked above Maximalum. Even though an evacuation order is in place, the city is not yet clear. We can't bring the ship down over a populated area; we need to force them to retreat, then we can launch a ground-to-air assault and obliterate them over water. We need you to drive them back. Whatever comes out of that ship, you need to beat it so bad it'll wish its weird alien daddy never set one of his six beady eyes on its weird alien mummy.'

A pair of mission objectives appeared on a screen in Jack's pod.

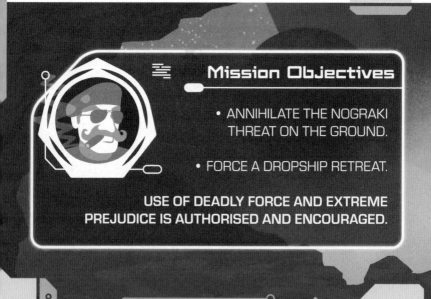

Mission Objectives

- ANNIHILATE THE NOGRAKI THREAT ON THE GROUND.

- FORCE A DROPSHIP RETREAT.

USE OF DEADLY FORCE AND EXTREME PREJUDICE IS AUTHORISED AND ENCOURAGED.

'Lucky for you kill-hungry dogs of war, we've left your old mechs on Rotec. The ones you're standing in now are more than mere replicas. You'll find them packed with new tasty treats and deadly delights,' the Colonel explained through a vindictive grin. 'Oh, and one more thing. We have identified a weak point in the ship's hull – towards the rear left of the fuselage. Tag it with as much spare fire as you can; it'll make them turn tail quicker.'

A damage bar appeared under a diagram of the alien ship, and the target area blinked deep red; another reminder that this was just a computer game. Jack swiped it away even faster than he'd turned off the score total display, then did his best to pretend that he'd never seen it in the first place.

'Look out for each other – this is a *team* exercise. I ain't got time for hotshot cowboys riding their own egos like ponies at the fair.'

The Colonel often said stuff like this, and by-and-large, everyone ignored it – for one simple reason: the Top Ten Table, which had popped up inside Jack's mech to replace the dismissed diagram of the alien ship. Jack was about to swipe away this further unwanted reminder that he wasn't *actually* standing inside a robot in the middle of New York in the distant future, when he noticed something. _Carbon_Shift_ was missing from the leader board. No one had heard from the golden boy since his mysterious disappearance during the Mines of Marok mission. But after all the abduction stuff had been dismissed as clickbait, everyone had expected to see _Carbon_Shift_ back in the game. Instead, BunnyQueen12 was now at the top spot, and a new name sat at number ten: PrincessShatterSparkles. Jack had seen this mech around. It was as deadly as it was pink – and it was *very* pink. A worthy addition, but the question remained: what happened to _Carbon_Shift_?

While Jack pondered, ten green beacons appeared on his scanner. The other WarMechs had arrived. In fact, it seemed they'd all been there the whole time, but they were only now revealed to each other. Jack saw Megan's mech first, brash as ever, leaning on a building on the corner of Broadway and West 47th. He saw three mechs lining 7th Street: Th£D£V@ST@T0R and SaiboTron, with BunnyQueen12 heading up the group looking even bigger than before thanks to the power of The Glow. HudsonNotHicks was on West 48th, and PrincessShatterSparkles was standing at the top of West 46th with Jeeroy-Lenkins. Cameron's mech appeared closest to Jack, standing at the opposite side of the square.

That was everyone, except ...

'Phaest? You on the grid?' Jack heard Megan shout up over the comms.

There was a long silence.

'I'm where I need to be, Zuuly – and I've got eyes on all of you. Would you like me to shoot that fly off your shoulder?'

Jack smirked as he watched the Zuul mech momentarily lose all its cool; swatting furiously at its own metal shoulder. Megan hated insects, and the game probably knew it.

'Well, if you didn't like that close encounter, I wouldn't recommend looking up,' said Ayo ominously.

Alongside the members of the Raid Mob, every mech from Broadway to West 46th looked up in unison. They all saw it at the same time.

The Nograki dropship brought nightfall with it as it lumbered through the sky, blocking the sunlight street by street. Maximalum's remaining glare burned brighter in this sudden darkness, and Jack felt an electrical surge tingling across his skin. The towering buildings became giant neon spectators, baying for a fight, and the Nograkis had brought their meanest heavyweight to the ring.

At the front, the ship had been fitted with an ultra-heavy-duty nose cone – an interstellar snowplough good for smashing through galaxies and brushing off burning atmospheric temperatures. The belly of the mid-section was equipped with the same torpedo-tube ports used to fire out the scout descent pods. Only this ship had *double* the usual number of ports. It also had twice as many propulsion limbs as a standard Ex-Phase 8. The only unmodified section of the vessel seemed to be the rear. There, to the left side of the ship's undercarriage, Jack could make out some minor flight damage: cracked panels, scorched armour, and what looked like a plasma leak. It wasn't much of a target, but if it was too easy, it wouldn't be half as much fun …

'INCOMING!'

The robotic yell came from SaiboTron, who'd actually shouted '来襲'. The cry had been translated in real time by the upgraded comms system in Jack's WarMech, and it heralded a hailstorm of Nograki pods. They screamed through the sky on trails of emerald vapour. Some cratered themselves right in the middle of the street. Others tore through buildings in explosions of fizzing neon. One even managed to land right on top of the Times Square Ball, obliterating the historic relic in a beautifully violent explosion of glass and light. Jack and Cameron threw their mechs' fists forwards. Quad-barrelled plasma cannons, railgun turrets and NPG launchers erupted from the robots' limbs.

Jack's index fingers hovered over triggers that would unleash a world of hurt. He saw gas hissing from the seams of the nearest pod. The shell opened, and from inside it emerged … something that neither Jack nor any of the players had ever see before.

The comms channel erupted.

'What the hell is *that*?'

'That's not a scout! It's way too big … look at its fangs!'

'That ain't a wedge, or a sheller, or a convertor, or a–'

'Anyone got a clean pair of pants in their inventory? I just sh–'

'WHAT THE HELL IS THAT?'

'I've got four over here! They're *huge!*'

'What are those things sticking out of their backs! Are those weapo–'

'It's game over, man! Game over!'

'WILL SOMEONE TELL ME WHAT THE HELL THAT IS?'

Jack said nothing. He was transfixed by the appearance of his enemy, enraptured by the gross stench, stricken by the damp heat that ebbed in waves from the creature's smouldering skin. This thing was marvellously disgusting. It stood a good third taller than the scouts, and its skin was porcelain white, arranged in thick plates that covered its entire body. The shielding extended all the way down its muscular legs, to feet which looked more like hands: there were five finger-like appendages where the toes should be, with claws as long as rolling pins sticking out of each one, tearing into the concrete as if it were candy floss. It had four arms, like the scouts did, but each one had double the number of excretion tubes, with who knew what mixture of toxic mucus behind them. At least a dozen tentacles flailed wildly at its back, and they all dripped with armour-burning secretion. But it was the monster's *mouth* that most arrested Jack's attention. It started in the middle of its chest, running upwards and splitting its whole face in half, stopping only when it reached the top of the creature's head. A row of yellowed interlocking teeth ran from the beast's sternum all the way up to its brow, each glowing with deadly venom.

Jack waited a moment to see if this extraordinary creature would open its equally extraordinary mouth. Then – as if on cue – it did. It let loose a thunderous roar, and the inside of its mouth was revealed in all its disgusting glory. It was all Jack could do to keep his microwave dinner down.

It looked like someone had filled an old, rotting hot water bottle with blood, teeth, tentacles, slime, and several eyeballs of varying sizes, shaken the whole lot up, then forced the bag inside out and shoved it inside the alien's gaping face. It was gross. *They* were gross ... and they were everywhere.

'LET'S ROCK!' Jack heard Megan scream. She let fly a barrage of cannon fire, which signalled the start of the War of the Worlds.

Level 9:
Realer Than
Real

The noise of ten elite WarMechs letting rip in a city of skyward structures was enough to tear eardrums like tissue paper. The ground shook under the weight of the combatants, and the acrid smell of burnt ignition fuel was enough to bring tears to a glass eye.

Jack was in heaven.

'Two on your six, Scourge!'

Ayo was already calling plays from his hidden vantage point, wherever it was. Jack locked his mech's feet into the ground, concrete gathering in the cracks between its curled toes. Then, with a combo of button pushing and torso twisting, he rotated the body of his mech 180 degrees and released a double dose of rocket-propelled grenades. The projectiles spiralled through the air, but Jack didn't wait to see the explosion of white armour and blue blood. Before the brutal sapphire mist had even settled, he was on the hunt for his next victim.

Kills of the craziest calibre were being made all across the urban battlefield. The Fullmmersion control system was allowing all ten elite players to do things they'd never done before. All of them were taking full advantage of this, knowing that the whole world was watching their every move.

Newcomer PrincessShatterSparkles was clearly looking to make an impact in the Top Ten. The fuchsia-skinned WarMech activated a power source in its chest, unleashing a crossbeam of burning laser the length of West 46th Street and catching a freshly hatched Nograki in its path. The piercing light slipped through the creature so cleanly that it simply froze – as if it hadn't quite caught on to the fact that it'd just been quartered where it stood. In a flurry of ferocity, PrincessShatterSparkles boosted towards the target, both arms cocked at the elbow, and delivered a devastating double blow. Four chunks of Nograki flew in opposite directions. The new kid on the block was left holding the alien's brain in one hand, and its still-beating heart in the other. Blue blood dripped through pink metal fingers that squeezed the Nograki organs until they burst. PrincessShatterSparkles had most definitely arrived.

Two streets away, HudsonNotHicks had chased down a target of its own, having scrambled halfway

up a city skyscraper using nothing more than a pair of grappling hooks. The intercept had been swift and the takedown merciless. The war machine – daubed in urban camo for the occasion – was standing on the Nograki's tentacled back as it lay beaten on the ground of one of the building's terraces. In the hunt for additional style points, the military-looking mech activated a brand-new taunt, attaching a claymore mine to the defeated alien's chest. Seconds later, an explosion that shattered the windows of the surrounding twenty floors sent both the mech and the alien crashing downwards through the building. The WarMech rode the alien like a surfboard, tearing through floor after floor on a wave of fire, the journey halted only by the building's foundations. Emerging from a giant pile of rubble, HudsonNotHicks strolled coolly back onto the street, right where SaiboTron had just executed another Nograki.

SaiboTron's sleek silver mech had flung a very special weapon at its Nograki target: a compound sword that, when launched from above, split into six separate harpoons in mid-air, encircling the enemy as they landed. With a click of SaiboTron's metal fingers, the blades snapped back together like a bear trap. HudsonNotHicks nodded in approval as SaiboTron pulled the sword from the middle of a pile of diced-up alien remains. Then they both ducked for cover as half a hover-taxi flew between them.

Th£D£V@ST@T0R had discovered the surprise ability to charge objects with plasma power. It was busy launching a barrage of car chunks and street furniture at three advancing Nograkis. Two copped incendiary projectiles before they even reached attack range: one took a spinning car bonnet to the neck, the other ended up *inside* a flying bus shelter. But the third creature managed to evade all the plasma-powered parts, coming almost close enough to strike. SaiboTron and HudsonNotHicks readied their own weapons, but neither was fast enough to steal the kill. Th£D£V@ST@T0R had already torn a street lamp from the ground; it fizzed with energy as the hulking robot wielded it like a baseball bat. The Nograki leaped. Th£D£V@ST@T0R swung. The impact sent parts of the alien back into the stratosphere, and all SaiboTron and HudsonNotHicks could do was stand there and clap – after they'd finished wiping alien entrails off their armour.

No matter how intimidating these new Nograki invaders had seemed at first, they were just no match for the elite WarMechs – especially now they were all equipped with such a bevy of devastating abilities. Across the square, BunnyQueen12 was busy stomping a Nograki *through* the ground with her new rocket-propelled spike boots. Jeeroy-Lenkins was riding his shield, skidding between alien legs while using rear-mounted guns to mow down the confused would-be attackers left in his wake. However, it was the infamous Raid Mob who were pulling off all the sickest moves …

Inside the Zuul WarMech, Megan was flicking through a list of her new abilities, getting giddier the further she scrolled. 'Guys! There's something in my special moves list called the Flux Capacitor!' Megan shouted over the Mob's private group chat. 'I have no idea what it does, but if I didn't use it, would I be ... *chicken*?'

This was met by a laugh from Cameron – who'd watched all three *Back to the Future* films with Megan.

'Nothing b-but a little ch-ch-chick–'

Megan cut Cameron off, smashing the button combo to launch herself into a sprint – heading straight towards a trio of nearby Nograkis. A white box with a red digit read-out appeared inside her cockpit. There was a crude sticker on the side.

HOLD TO 88

Megan's smile widened. The readout on the speedometer rose. Sixty miles per hour. Seventy-two. Eighty. Eighty-six. Ninety. Megan eased off. The gap was closing; she needed to maintain a steady eighty-eight miles per hour. White hot sparks began to whip around the war machine. Eighty-eight, bang on. A churning cauldron of cosmic matter formed in front of the mech. Still eighty-eight. Megan was closing in on her Nograki target. Then a sudden and blinding explosion sent the graffitied war machine tearing down Broadway, leaving behind two parallel tracks of blazing fire.

Megan pulled the breaks. Had she time travelled? Was she in the Wild West? Was she going to get her own pair of self-lacing trainers and a reflective baseball cap? She looked around. She was still in Maximalum. Still in the game. Confused about what the special move had actually accomplished, Megan turned and looked back down Broadway.

There, in the middle of the street, was a portal into space-time. It had swallowed up the Nograki invaders like fish in a cosmic net. The intergalactic gateway spat space dust all around its edges, and through this window an alternate reality revealed itself. Megan could see the three Nograkis, all stuck in a '46 Ford that was brimful of horse manure. It was Megan's favourite scene from the *Back to the Future* films. Her smile was so wide that her freckled cheeks almost touched her ears. This game was amazing. It was perfect. As she watched the Nograkis spitting manure from their awful mouths, Megan's virtual clone assistant beamed into view.

'Would you like to *destroy* this reality?'

Megan's hand suddenly felt heavy. She lifted it up and found that she was wearing the Infinity Gauntlet. It was almost too much. She was being given the chance to go full Thanos.

Megan snapped her fingers. The portal imploded in a spluttering shower of energy emanating from light years away.

'Zuul! Did you just kill a bunch of Nograkis by crushing them with the force of *space-time*?' Jack blurted. tHeScOuRgE mech had appeared just in time to see the galactic gateway collapse.

'I totally did!' Megan squealed. 'This game is INSANE!'

But her elation was short-lived. In the very next breath, Zuul had dropped to the ground, shielding itself against a hail of gunfire that tore overhead. The street was filled with dust and shrapnel, making it nearly impossible to detect the source of the attack.

'... I heard that crack about my glasses.'

The voice came as the onslaught ceased. Megan raised her mech up slowly, cautiously. She looked at the wall behind her. It was riddled with bullet holes. Bullet holes that made a pattern. A pattern that spelled out a message ...

ICU

'Very funny!' Megan grunted, dusting off shards of concrete, suddenly glad that her robot didn't have the ability to blush. 'You planning on leaving your hidey-hole and joining the *real* fight any time soon, Phaest?'

'Oh yes – about that,' Ayo began, 'I worked out how to use one of my upgrades. I don't think I'll need to dig myself any more holes ...'

Megan saw sudden movement across the street. One of the Broadway theatres seemed to be shimmering and shifting in the falling dust. Its walls swelled. The building itself was somehow spilling into the street. Then a vaguely recognisable shape began to emerge: the silhouette of a giant figure was growing out from the concrete and glass. As it came closer to Megan, the form became clearer, its edges more defined, its parts more recognisable, until finally ...

'PHAEST?'

It was the only word Megan could manage. Standing in front of her was Ayo's mech – its metal surfaces still sporting the digital disguise that had allowed him to blend perfectly into the background of the city.

'Nanomite Optical Pattern Recognition and Replication,' Ayo said as the last of the camouflage pattern disappeared, leaving his mech its usual shade of dull grey. 'NOPRAR for short. My Sun Tzu assistant told me that "all warfare is based on deception". This tech makes me invisible. I've killed *nine* of those monsters so far, and not one of them saw me coming any more than you did.'

'Man, just when I thought your mech couldn't look more boring, you get an upgrade that *literally* makes you look like nothing. Impressive.'

'It doesn't make me look like nothing,' Ayo hissed. 'It makes me look like *anything* ...'

Within seconds, a wash of tiny automatons had turned Ayo's mech into an exact replica of Megan's machine – 80s cartoon logos and all. Her reaction was equal parts impressed and revolted.

'That's really cool, man ... Now take it off. You ain't worthy of the Thundera emblem.'

'Anyone spotted Forge lately?' Jack said, emerging from the dust and scanning the destruction. Scattered piles of rubble and glass formed funeral pyres for dead aliens; burst pipes and torn cables bled water and sparks, and the air was thick with concrete dust, booster exhaust smoke, and the smell of Nograki death. Jack stared through the fog of war but could not see his friend. He was about to bring up his virtual map – and had he done so, he would have been alerted to something *extremely* unnerving – but he was stopped by a familiar stutter.

'THIS G-G-GAME IS EPIC!'

From the heart of the swirling smoke and debris, the gleaming figure of ForgeFire666 emerged. The WarMech strutted towards the group, curls of dust kicked up by each confident step, the haze framing a machine that had all the swagger of a Wild West sheriff. The confidence appeared well-founded, too, considering what Cameron's mech was carrying. An impossibly large sword rested on its shoulder. It must have been more than six metres long. Maybe ten. It might've been taller than the mech carrying it, with a blade as wide as a tree trunk. But it wasn't the sword itself that drew the Mob's attention. Skewered along the blade like hunks of kebab meat were the bodies of no less than *six* dead Nograkis. Cameron walked his mech right to the middle of the street – parading his trophies – limbs and tangled tentacles flopping with each step. When he reached the mob, Cameron drew his mech's arm up, lifting the sword high. Then he plunged it into the ground. In one single, flowing movement, he had created a Nograki totem pole.

'Anyone want to t-t-take a souvenir? I'm thinking about starting a t-trophy c-cabinet, or a belt full of b-b-bones and skulls. P-P-Predator-style.'

'Anytime!' Megan said. *Predator* was her third favourite film; she loved the idea of making a necklace out of Nograki teeth for her mech to wear in battle.

'The mission isn't over yet,' Ayo interjected, nodding towards the airship that loomed in the sky above. 'We still have our second objective, remember?'

'About that ...' Jack started as he made his way towards a pair of crashed Nograki pods. 'I've had an idea. Let's send these alien scum sacks back where they came from, along with a few souvenirs.'

Jack dragged the two empty pods out of the rubble and laid them on the ground, then he pulled one of the Nograki bodies off Cameron's blade and threw it into the nearest one. The rest of the Mob got the idea, and soon, all six dead aliens were crammed into the two pods, along with a volatile payload of grenades, mines, mini bombs, armed missiles, signal flares, and a pair of Lasonic TRC-931 boombox radios.

'Who put *those* in there?' Ayo exclaimed. 'Actually, need I ask?' He turned to face Zuul.

'Trust me,' Megan chuckled as she tapped a special code into an input pad. 'When *they* go off, it'll be the sauce on the burger!'

With that, she closed the lid on the pod and Jack closed the other, sealing both with a lightwelder.

'I'm happy that we're taking out our rubbish. It shows that we're a responsible, environmentally conscientious death squad,' said Ayo. 'One small enquiry though – how do we get *these* up *there*?'

Jack crouched down and took hold of the frames of the pods, one in each heavy metal hand.

'I'm going to need some room,' he said.

No one questioned him. The other three mechs backed away and watched as what looked like six miniaturised oil drills extended from the lower legs of Jack's mech. They plunged into the concrete, burrowing down and fixing the robot to the spot. Once he was rooted in place, Jack unlocked his mech's torso at the waist and activated a rotating mechanism that allowed him to spin the top half of his robot while keeping the legs in place. The torso began to turn, dragging the pods along, scoring the concrete in a circular pattern.

Soon enough, the pods were spinning around on a trail of sparks, gaining momentum with each rotation, revolving faster and faster until they began to lift.

Inside the mech, Jack strained to keep his grip on the capsules. The centrifugal force was pulling at them, and the faster he spun, the greater the pull became. A screen displayed the on-board computer's targeting trajectory and velocity – Jack knew that he needed to build up to the right speed and release at just the right moment. The faster he moved, the harder it was to hold on to the pods. He felt his grip begin to weaken. The muscles in his forearms burned. His fingers began to pull apart. Then he was bellowing – screaming through glorious pain. He could feel the tendons in his hands and the muscles in each one of his fingers stretching to breaking point. He could *feel* it all.

He let go – one pod a split second after the other. The war-scarred mech continued to spin as the pods soared through the air. As he slowed the rotation, stopping just in time to watch the pods sailing through the last hundred metres of their journey, Jack prepared to detonate the remote explosives. Around him, the rest of the Mob stepped forwards, doing the same. He waited for the perfect moment …

'... Now!'

The explosive power of the Mob's combined ammunition was enough to white-out the sky. It burned Jack's eyes, but as the brightness showered down on him, he forced himself to look on. His pain was rewarded by the sight of the Nograki attack ship with its rear third completely engulfed in flames. The wounded ship was already dropping out of the sky as it began its retreat. While he watched the craft floundering through the atmosphere, Jack heard a familiar song emanating from the flames: *Another One Bites the Dust* by Queen.

'Boombox Beatdown – one of my finishing moves! This song has *killer* bass!' Megan shouted over the top of the thumping track.

Jack smiled so joyously that he felt tingling goosebumps all over his body. Cameron was approaching, his mech's metal hand raised for a high five, and Megan was two-stepping to the baseline of Queen's ass-kicking anthem. Only Ayo hadn't joined the celebrations.

'Ugh – guys?' he said, with an uncharacteristic brevity. 'Guys? OI! YOU LOT!'

Hearing Ayo shout was like hearing Miss Barrett give a compliment: equal parts rare and disturbing. It was enough to snap the Mob out of their reverie.

'WHAT?' Megan shouted over.

'Where is everyone?' Ayo asked.

For a moment, there was silence.

'What d'you mean?' Megan shouted again.

'Everyone's gone. Look at your maps,' Ayo said. Jack brought up the correct display in his control pod.

'Where is e-everyone?' stuttered Cameron.

'That's what I'm asking *you*!' shot Ayo. 'My map is blank. No enemies and no mechs.'

'Mine too,' said Jack and Megan in unison. Jack furiously zoomed further and further out on his scanner, getting the same result each time. 'There's no one in the entire city!'

'Is the g-g-game over? Has the level finished?' said Cameron.

Having reached the perimeter of the level map, and with nothing to show for his searching, Jack swiped away the display and swung his mech's head around, and then up. That's when he saw them.

'LOOK!' Jack yelled, pointing upwards. From somewhere vast and unseen, huge tentacles had descended from the sky, tearing towards the mechs. They were so fast that none of the Mob had the chance to evade before the tentacles were upon them – and they did not stop when they reached the WarMechs' armour.

Jack felt the tentacles grab him. Not his mech – they had hold of *him*. Somehow, the terrifying appendages were *inside* his control pod. Within moments they surrounded Jack, sliding under his arms, wrapping around his waist, and one coiling tightly around his neck. Then they began to squeeze. Jack felt the breath being crushed out of him. Each panicked inhalation became more difficult than the last, until he felt like he was drowning in dry air. Jack clasped his hands over his eyes, feeling the faint outline of the visor back in the real world, and he pulled with all the breathless effort he could muster as the tentacles gripped him tighter.

He felt the mask come off in his hands. The control pod vanished. The world of *Distant Dawn* evaporated, and his tiny bedroom rematerialised all around him ...

But the tentacles had not disappeared. Somehow, they still had hold of him – and they were lifting him from his bed. Jack struggled, but the arms gripped him tighter. He tried to scream, but another grasping alien organ clapped over his mouth, stifling the sound and stealing away what little was left of his breath. All Jack could do was look upwards at the hole in the roof of the house – *his* house, his *real* house in the *real* world. The hole that had been created by the terrible tentacle when it broke into his bedroom.

Then, all at once, Jack was pulled through the opening, and dragged into total darkness.

Level 10: Captive

Just when Jack thought the chance to inhale would never come, the tentacles finally released him. He gulped in air as if he'd never drawn breath before. He didn't know where he was or what was happening. But in that moment he didn't care – he was just happy to be alive.

As the feeling returned to his limbs, Jack found himself curled up on a solid surface that he couldn't see. Wherever he'd been deposited, it was zero-visibility dark. He felt around on the floor tentatively, scared of what he might touch – scared it would burn, or sting, or trigger a deadly trap. After cautious rummaging, Jack discovered a wall. He backed himself up against it, drew his knees to his chest and wrapped his hands around his legs, cocooning himself against the darkness.

Ragged breaths echoed off unseen surfaces. The sound of chattering teeth rattled up his jawbone. In fact, the only sounds Jack could hear were being made by his own body. Scrunching his eyes and gritting his teeth, Jack forced himself to fight back against the fear that had taken his body hostage. He counted through each breath, focusing on his heartrate and willing it to slow. Then, as the panic began to subside, Jack tried to figure out where he was.

In the darkness, he began tracing the features of his face with his fingertips. He was searching for the visor. He *knew* this couldn't be real – none of it could. But no matter how much he probed and prodded, Jack couldn't feel anything besides his own face. He pressed one palm into the other. He couldn't feel the RealFeel gloves. Patting himself down, he felt the rolled-up sleeves of his thick, chequered shirt. He found the familiar holes in the knees of his jeans. He wasn't wearing an exosuit anymore. He was in *his* clothes – the same ones he was wearing when he'd sat on his bed to play … and if he wasn't wearing the RealFeel controller gear anymore, then he couldn't be in the game.

Jack closed his eyes, focusing in on his other senses.

Although he was dripping with sweat, he wasn't hot. He'd put his shivering down to panic, but when he really concentrated, he realised it was *cold* in the space. Jack imagined that he could've seen his breath, had he been able to see anything at all.

Next, Jack held his breath and listened. After a few seconds, he heard a new sound; a sound that suddenly

seemed to be everywhere. It was a deep, throbbing hum
– powerful, rhythmic, systematic. Jack realised that it
was the sound of a machine. Was he *inside* it?

Jack placed his hands on the floor, enduring the
cold sting in his fingertips until he felt it. A vibration.
Movement. It was a particular type of movement, too.
One that Jack recognised from a long time ago. He'd
been on a plane just once in his life, when his dad was
still around. The pilot had announced that they were
travelling at 500 miles an hour, and Jack had asked his
dad why it felt like they were hardly moving. Jack's dad
had tried his best to explain *constant velocity* – the idea
that if something is moving in the same direction at
the same speed, even if it's going really fast, you can't
feel it. But if Jack *really* concentrated, his dad had said,
he'd be able to sense the movement of the plane. Jack
remembered the sensation he'd felt as he gripped the
armrests of his plane seat, and he felt it now. Only this
time it was deeper – *way* more intense. He was flying,
and he was flying quickly.

He was also running out of senses. Short of licking
the walls, there was only his sense of smell left to
explore. Jack was soon sniffing like a bloodhound, and
on the fifth inhalation he smelled it: a scent that brought
an unexpected smile to his face. It was an odour he
recognised even though the trace of it was only faint,
and it meant that none of this could possibly be real.

He could smell Nograkis.

Jack had been up close and personal with the Nograkis twice now. He knew *exactly* what they smelled like. He'd talked about it during the Mob's post-game chats. To Jack, it was a cross between damp laundry and battery acid. The fact that he could smell the scent of a fictional alien race from a virtual world meant that somehow, even though the rest of his senses told him otherwise, he must still be in the game.

The tension began to ebb from Jack's shoulders. He slumped against the wall and smiled. This game was *incredible*. He touched his face. He still couldn't feel the visor. He couldn't believe that this level of immersion was possible. Now, he could relax and enjoy the rest of this insane virtual journey.

Or at least that was the plan, and it lasted right up until the lights came on. Then he saw it.

It was standing in the corner of a space that had no windows, no doors, and no identifiable source of light. And yet, there *was* light. It was as if the walls were sweating luminescence; just enough to allow Jack to make out the back of a strange figure. Every muscle in Jack's body fizzed with fight-or-flight energy.

And yet, he couldn't move an inch.

'Ekhrt tek rehrektern ...'

The sound was harsh. Guttural. Jack tried to open his mouth to speak, but he couldn't even part his lips.

'Svesticaross. Svesticarossur varociourest ...'

It was trying to communicate. Jack strained to hear

what it was saying but found he could not move, even just a little. He wrenched at his legs, tried to curl his fingers and blink his eyelids. Nothing. All he could do was watch as this mysterious thing uttered nonsense from across the gloom.

Then, with a final splutter, it turned around, revealing itself.

'In paralysis, there is no pain. Enjoy it. It will not last.'

The creature was over two metres tall. Broad shoulders framed a slender body that tapered into a single limb, with a bundle of thin, knotted tentacles – a hundred at least – splaying out from its base. Hanging down from the being's shoulders were an overlapping arrangement of translucent black wings, laced with purple veins: two shrouding the front of the body, two resting by its sides, and two hanging down its back. But it was the head that had Jack completely mesmerized.

The domed block was covered in a thin, translucent film of grey skin that made it possible to observe musculature and skeletal formations beneath the surface. There were indentations, curves and bulges where ears, a nose and a mouth might have once been – but the being had none of these. The only discernible facial feature it had were eyes – seven in all – mesmerizing and strange in equal measure. A single visor-like eye split the face in two, filled with a greenish-yellow liquid that sloshed around as it moved. At each end was a triangular cluster of three smaller eyes. The top pair were thin red slits, like knife wounds, and the orb was the colour of freshly spilled blood. The outermost pair were like cat's eyes, although they were purple, with flecks of silver. The lowest pair were the most disturbing, though – they looked *human*.

The being came closer, propelled across the floor on a writhing mass of tentacles. Jack remained motionless – although not by choice.

'I imagine you are wondering how I know your language,' it said. 'I imagine you are wondering how I am speaking at all ...'

As the creature approached, its front wings fell open slightly, and Jack caught a glimpse of multiple arms before one of them thrust its way through the gap. It held something in a three-fingered grasp: a small golden cuboid, with grooves cut down the length of each side.

'Mouths are a thing of the distant past for our species. The idea of consuming nutrients through an open orifice is repugnant. The idea of communicating through that same opening even more so. This device converts phrenolinguistics into what you would call "words". I don't enjoy demeaning myself by its use, but it is necessary in order to facilitate communication with ... lower lifeforms.'

Even though this creature had no mouth or nose, Jack could still perceive a sneer of revulsion hiding just beneath the surface of its skin. The remnants of a wrinkled nose, a downturned lip. Whatever this thing was, it *really* didn't like him.

'I imagine that you still think you are in that *insipid* game. It is hardly surprising you would deny the truth of your situation. You would rather believe that you, Jack Henry Delaney of Kingshold Road, student of Holmes Park High School and part-time car washer, are still sitting in your cramped terraced house on the edge of your bed in that tiny room of yours ... and that you could pull off your headset and quit whenever you want. By all means, try it.'

It took Jack a moment to realise that he was able to move his arms again; he'd been distracted by a sudden and severe sense of dread. How did this thing know so much about him? Where he lived, where he went to school ... *How did it know his name?*

Jack still couldn't speak, so he couldn't ask any of these questions. All he could do was feel for the visor again. He scratched and rubbed at his temples but only felt his skin. Then his arms fell limp. He was paralysed again.

'You have all reacted so differently,' the creature said. 'Cameron Yates and Ayomikun Osikoya-Arinola – their weakness ebbs from their every pore, doesn't it? When they were first paralysed, they didn't even try to lift their arms. Your friend Megan Joyce, however – she struggled even more than you. She was difficult. It took some convincing for her to accept her reality ...'

The mention of his friends' names made Jack's vision turn crimson, fear, loyalty and rage churning within him.

'If this were a *game*, do you think you would be able to feel … pain?' The corners of the creature's buried mouth turned upwards with the last word – an ancient smile breaking beneath its skin.

'I know those primitive interface devices can simulate impacts, minor discomforts – but what about *real* hurt? If this were a game, Jack Delaney, could it make you *bleed*?'

An electrical current suddenly surged up from the floor, funnelling right into Jack's spine. It tore into muscle fibres and shredded through nerves, lit up bone and spiked over every square inch of skin. His head was thrown backwards and his eyes rolled over white. His skin was on fire. His lungs were seared.

Jack was being burned alive.

'That was less than three of your seconds,' the creature announced, deactivating the current. 'Less than three seconds of *real* pain.'

Jack's body collapsed in a crumpled heap, his legs twitching, his throat heaving air into empty lungs until they filled enough for him to start coughing and retching. Eventually, he was able to pull his head off the floor. He tasted something warm and metallic. Jack reached up and touched his mouth in horror. He saw redness on his fingertips, fresh and wet.

Blood.

'Is this *real* enough for you, Jack Delaney?' said the creature, making its way back towards the corner of the room. Jack watched the creature tap at a panel of indentations on the wall. As the last command was entered, the creature turned to face Jack once more.

'Perhaps now you are ready to accept your reality ...'

Jack gripped the floor with stinging fingers as the nearest wall fell away completely, revealing the outside world.

Level 11: Evolution

The sky was alive.

Jack was on board a flying craft – just as he'd guessed – but he was flying through an *alien* atmosphere. He knew it wasn't Earth's, because Earth's sky wasn't thick with yellow clouds that belched forks of green lightning in a relentless onslaught of violent energy. Jack watched airborne currents rip from cloud to swollen cloud, filling them until they couldn't accommodate another molecule of light. The overloaded thunderclouds would explode, discharging their contents and illuminating the sky with emerald energy. This was happening everywhere, as far as Jack could see.

'Did you know that lightning strikes the surface of your planet a hundred times every second?'

Jack was so transfixed by the violent view that he hadn't realised that the creature had drawn up next to him.

'That's over eight-and-a-half *million* strikes, every day. The power from a single bolt is enough to power one of your electric bulbs for half an Earth year. And what do you do with all this energy? You funnel it into the ground and hope it doesn't hit you. You discard it like garbage,' the creature said, each translated word dripping with disgust. 'Your planet is wasted on you. It's no surprise you're so poorly developed as a species. Higher beings do not become such without developing better habits, especially when it comes to managing natural resources.'

The creature scuttled towards the control panel on the wall and started tapping in new commands. Jack uttered the first sound he had been able to make since the lights came on. It was a guttural, terrified scream – and it came as the floor beneath him fell away.

'Zarak! Zarak! Zarak!'

Jack only heard this strange noise when he'd stopped screaming, and he'd only stopped screaming because he hadn't hit the ground ... and he hadn't hit the ground because he hadn't actually fallen.

Although the outer layer of the ship had opened up below him, the internal floor of the cell – made of an almost imperceptible material – had remained in place. Jack was lying face down on the transparent surface. The new sound he could hear was coming from the creature's translator.

It was *laughing* at him.

Level 11: Evolution

'Do you think we would go to the effort of hauling you all the way across the galaxy just to dump you overboard? No, Jack Delaney – you have a far more important purpose to serve.'

The creature extended another hand through a gap in its wings and pointed the longest of its three fingers downwards. Jack followed it, and what he saw took away the breath that had only just settled back in his lungs.

It was a city; a massive metropolis that sprawled all the way to the horizon. From the smallest buildings to the huge towers that rose to surround a massive central hub, everything looked like it had grown up from the ground in its own unique and twisted way. And yet, Jack couldn't see any organic life anywhere – no fields, no tress, no greenery of any kind. But the buildings themselves looked alive. They swelled and surged with energy drawn up from the ground, energy that came from ...

'*Power vessels*. That's as close as I can get in your language.'

Jack saw them. Thick tubes full of crackling blue light formed an intricate network of energy conduits that ran like organic circuitry all over the city, pulsing down main highways and subdividing into grids, until every structure was met by its own power feed. Then the tubes looped back, rejoining a bigger vessel via a parallel pipe, all the way back to the centre core. From above, the whole thing reminded Jack of the human circulatory system. This city had grown out of the electrical lifeblood that rained, constantly, from the sky above.

'Each structure has the ability to absorb, store, and distribute the energy from the electrical storm,' the creature explained. Jack watched as emerald electricity tore through the sky, striking spires at the top of each building. Each hit made the structures swell, increasing their height fractionally, and any excess power was funnelled down into the power tubes.

'You see? Not an atom wasted. Which is crucial, especially now. Soon we will fly over a place where every spare spark is being put to use in our preparations for The Deletion.'

The creature's smooth skin buried a smirk, but not entirely.

'What is ... The ... Deletion?' Jack managed to reply, spluttering the first words he had spoken since his abduction. 'Why am ... I here? Who ... are ... you?'

'There is no word in your underdeveloped language for who we are. What would you call a technologically advanced interstellar colonial species with an empire spread over *fifteen* galaxies? As for The Deletion, this is our standard planetary occupation procedure. We have tried cohabitation in the past, but it's a messy business. We have found the easiest way is not to try to live in harmony with an indigenous species, but simply to wipe them out altogether. Extinction. Deletion. That is our intention for Earth.'

Level 11: Evolution

Jack's jaw fell open. He couldn't process what he was hearing – especially the idea of *him* having some "important purpose to serve" as part of humanity's extermination.

'Every planet we have taken possession of has been inhabited – some by lifeforms even lesser than you, if you can imagine such a thing, and some by races whose technological capabilities almost matched our own. All have fallen, in the end. We now control almost a hundred planets. However, there have been regrettable losses in the past, and we always learn from our ... mistakes.'

The creature spat the final word through its translation device as if it left a bad taste in its non-existent mouth.

'One lesson that we have mastered is the importance of *reconnaissance*.'

Jack knew what this meant. Ayo spoke about it all the time: scoping out your enemies and discovering their tactics and weaknesses before you attack.

'We have been watching your species for many of your solar cycles, looking for the best way to exterminate you,' the being continued. 'We noticed that infighting was a frequent occurrence on Earth, so we infiltrated your global military, feeding information and stoking the fires of war. In fact, we almost managed to have you wipe yourselves out a couple of times. Then, as your race made painfully slow strides in communication technology, we began spreading information to your whole population. We influenced your global politics, preyed on your prejudices, but we still couldn't quite get you across the threshold of all-out war. Then you made a leap – a leap that meant we had to accelerate our plans.'

The creature didn't give Jack the chance to guess at what that leap might have been; it was relishing the opportunity to explain humanity's demise too much to let the "lower lifeform" interrupt.

'You stopped putting people in machines,' it continued. 'You finally realised that, in war, no self-respecting civilisation puts soldiers on a battlefield. You engineer a violent, programmable attack organism. Or you put soldiers at the controls of war machines that can be piloted remotely. Earth's armies have started to do both. Attack drones. Chemical warfare. Remote-control warheads. Weaponised viruses. Robotic applications for the military. Self-driving army vehicles. Soon enough, all combat on Earth will be entirely remote-controlled. And who will be at the helm of these future machines of war?

It was then that Jack saw his place in this horrific nightmare.

'*You*, Jack. You, and people just like you. Your species calls them "gamers" now, but they will call them "soldiers" soon enough. It wasn't a difficult leap to predict, and we couldn't allow humankind to continue to advance to the point where they might actually put up a fight once we arrived …'

The creature moved closer to Jack. All of its eyes were fixed upon him, and the scowl under its skin creased its face as it continued.

'So we infiltrated your entertainment systems – where your most skilled future combatants lurk. *We* made that ridiculous game of yours. I'm sure the designers at the company would deny it. In fact, they probably didn't even realise it was happening – but we fed them every element of *Distant Dawn*, one way or another. We wanted to see what the future best of the best could do, especially when provided with weapons of war more advanced than anything your species has ever seen. We gave you information about our species – the so-called "Nograki" race – and we trialled our methods and tactics. We watched to see how you responded. Then we made ourselves better.'

The creature bent down, splaying its wings in an overt display of intimidation.

'We have now finished our analysis. Your planet's inhabitants remain sufficiently defenceless, and we are almost ready to begin The Deletion. In fact, if you look over there, you can see for yourself how *our* machines of war are progressing …'

In the distance, Jack could see a long valley that separated two areas of the electric city, fed by rows of thick power vessels. The collected energy bathed the valley in an ethereal glow. It was about half a kilometre wide, almost as deep, and stretched so far off that Jack couldn't see the end of it. But he *could* see what was inside it. Dropships. Not exactly like the Nograki vessels, but similar enough to be recognisable. They shared the same basic form as the modified Ex-Phase 8 craft: the heavy-duty nose cone, the pod ports in the midsection, the propulsion limbs dangling from the flanks. There were, however, two noticeable differences. The armour plating on the rear third of the ship was thicker, and the ship itself was *three times* bigger than any Nograki vessel Jack had ever seen ... and there was a whole fleet of them. The canyon was full of ships, processing along an assembly line, all in various stages of completion.

Jack could also see smaller machines hovering around each ship. He could see sparks where welds were being sealed. He could see huge panels and parts, chunks of armour and gun turrets drifting into position, carried up on plinths that glowed with the blue energy of the alien city. And, as he squinted, Jack made out the first living beings he'd seen on the planet besides his cruel captor. Tiny distant workers swarmed around the ships, fixing and moving and building. The only vessel not crawling with these creatures was the one nearest the end of the line. This ship was being fuelled; Jack watched energy from the power vessels gushing into it, surging through the hull and shocking the propulsion limbs into life. He saw it rise, escaping the bonds of its support structures. Finally, he watched the vast dropship fly through the storm, absorbing lightning strikes that increased its energy reserves as it drew up into the sky.

'You see what is possible when resources are used effectively?' the creature said. Even its lack of a mouth couldn't stop the smile of satisfaction protruding from beneath its skin.

'Killing whole civilisations?' Jack spat. His lethargy had turned to rage. Adrenaline was coursing through his tortured body. New-found fury fired up through his throat and exploded from his mouth. 'We definitely have a word for that – *genocide* – and only the worst people in our history have ever tried it.'

'You would call it natural selection!' the creature shouted through its translator, disgusted by the audacity of its captive. '*Your* species is undeserving of the treasures it has been gifted! Until now, you have existed without competition, so you take what you have for granted. But your time is over. We will take what is rightfully ours, by virtue of our strength, our power, and our intellect. We are better than you. You are finished.'

Jack scowled at the creature. He didn't fear it anymore – he hated it. He hated every word that came from its stupid little box, and he hated the expression that hid beneath its skin. Grimacing at the pain still tangible in every muscle, Jack forced himself off the floor and up onto one knee.

'If all this is true,' he began, glaring unflinchingly at his captor. 'If Earth is your target – why have you bothered dragging me all the way here?'

The creature assumed its full height, remembering its place as a superior species.

'You have been brought here to take part in a public demonstration – a spectacle for the citizens of our supreme society to enjoy. Nothing encourages loyalty and allegiance like witnessing the obliteration of a lesser species. You and your friends will fight our warriors. You will lose. We will celebrate the dawn of another arm of our cosmic empire while you lie in the dust, a testament to the ease with which your world will fall.'

Jack barely heard anything after the word "friends". The pain, the shock and the unbelievable sights had fogged his mind so much, he'd almost forgotten that the creature had spoken about the rest of the Mob. The anger that had been bubbling up in him suddenly subsided, usurped again by fear – the fear of losing his friends.

'Where are they?' he choked out.

'Your friends?' the alien replied calmly. 'They are already in the arena.'

Jack could see it now: a vast oval structure, right in the heart of the metropolis. Next to it, there was a second, equally formidable-looking structure, prison-like in its appearance. The two buildings were linked by a fortified tunnel. Jack could feel their energy throbbing from all the way across the city.

'We will soon arrive at the holding pen. You will have a short time to become acclimatised to your Wrakantrex.

Then you will join your friends and fight to the death – *your* death.'

Jack could barely hear the creature. His tears were pooling on the transparent floor, his fear growing as his mind brimmed with thoughts of his friends, trapped and tortured and terrified, just like he was.

The creature was already moving away – heading towards a vault that had opened in the wall – when Jack finally managed to call after it.

'What the hell is a *Wrakantrex*?'

'I believe,' the creature replied, 'that you call them "WarMechs".'

Level 12: Morituri Te Salutant

The outer walls of the ship closed. The electric city disappeared. Enveloped by the returning darkness, Jack was alone once more – alone and terrified.

Throwing out a trembling hand, Jack felt his way into the corner of the space, backed himself up against the wall, tucked his knees up under his chin, and hugged his shins. He clung to himself in desperation as he felt everything else slipping away: his friends, his family ... his life. He felt tears drip through the holes in the knees of his jeans. He was just a passenger now – not only aboard this alien vessel, but on this dire ride into the unknown. It was too much for Jack to take. He saw flashes of his friends, special moments and memories they had shared, firing through the haze and disappearing just as quickly. He saw his brother, Alexander, sleeping soundly in his cot.

Jack cried in the darkness. He began beating his hand against the cold floor, desperate to claw back some sense of control – even if only over himself. Eventually, Jack managed to pound out enough of the fear that had overwhelmed him and sit pensively in the dark. Even after his captor had tortured him and delivered such a dreadful message, a flicker of disbelief niggled in Jack's mind. Even the slightest sliver of rational thought made Jack question whether this was all really happening. But insane as it was, it *was* really happening. And why wouldn't it be? In a universe ninety-two billion light years wide, alien contact was inevitable. Why not here and now?

And yet, Jack was *still* searching for a way to convince himself that he was in a game. The creature was talking about WarMechs, for goodness' sake. He was going to wake up. He would get out of bed, go and check on Alexander, and everything would be okay. God, he hoped everything would be okay. He prayed he would see his brother again.

A body-jerking deceleration snapped Jack out of his anxiety trance. He could feel the craft manoeuvring. Then it halted. But he still couldn't see, which meant he didn't realise that the tentacles had returned – until they took hold of him. He wrestled against them with the little energy he could muster, but the serpentine limbs lifted him effortlessly off his feet. Then the floor beneath him fell away, transparent layer and all. A wild wind infiltrated the space. The air crackled with static electricity. Jack looked down and saw the prison-like structure at the centre of the city, about fifty metres below. There was an opening in its roof. It looked nowhere near big enough for him to fit through, but despite his protests, the tentacles suddenly slackened, and he was dropped from the craft. He plummeted like he was free-falling, even though the tentacles were still wrapped around him like bungee rope. Jack's cries trailed behind him like the ribbon on a kite as he plunged towards the tiny aperture. At the last desperate moment, he stopped screaming, shut his eyes, and braced for a horrific impact.

The impact never came. Instead, Jack felt a deceleration force so violent that he thought his internal organs might be pushed out through his nose.

Opening one cautious eye, he looked up past his feet to see the tentacles extending through the opening. He had made it through, and was swinging like a worm on a hook in the middle of another darkened space. The momentary relief of surviving the descent was short-lived as the tentacles released their grip and dropped him. He hit the ground. Hard. Jack held his ribs and his head in a daze, groaning and rolling over just in time to watch the cavity close up, plunging him into darkness once more.

This time, though, Jack had some idea of where he was. The structure linked to the arena where, if his alien captor was to be believed, he would fight against the race's toughest warriors ... in a WarMech. Jack wondered if they had their own virtual reality system here, to allow him to control the mech. But then he couldn't understand how controlling a robot in a fight with an alien could lead to his death ... unless it was a loser-gets-executed-type scenario. The thought sent a fearful shiver straight up into the base of Jack's skull as he imagined a grizzly myriad of methods of capital punishment – and those were just the ones his human brain could come up with. What might these sadistic alien creatures have in store for him?

Suddenly, a bright light filled the space, and with it came an answer to Jack's questions – of sorts. The view was fuzzy at first, but soon the image in front of him started to clear. And the clearer it got, the less sense it made.

Jack was looking at a foot. A huge metal foot.

Jack looked upwards. The foot connected to a leg, the leg to a torso, and from the torso sprouted the rest of a vast silver body. Jack couldn't believe what he was looking at. It was a WarMech – a *real* WarMech. Ten metres of armoured plates and weaponised limbs, standing there in the middle of a vast hangar. And, as if all of this wasn't enough for Jack to deal with, this wasn't just any WarMech. It was *his*. It was tHeScOuRgE, recreated in perfect detail, right down to the dints in the armour.

A set of ladders rested against the robot. They reached the chest cavity; the space where, in the game, the pilot would sit in their control pod. The hatch was open. Jack realised that he was meant to pilot the WarMech from *inside* the machine.

Jack didn't even think twice about whether or not he should climb the ladder. The moment he made it real, and reached out and touched *his* machine, caution and logic had been chucked out of the window. He gripped the ladder firmly and pulled himself up rung by rung, not looking down once. When he finally dragged himself over the precipice and saw the inside of the machine, it was all he could do not to fall back out again. It was exactly like it was in the game, down to the most intricate detail. But it was *real*.

Directly in front of him was the base of a chair, mounted on a multi-hinged arm, with a casing structure containing harnesses that would extend, wrap over Jack's shoulders and lock over his chest – just like in the game. He could see the outline of openings on the floor, and he knew that beneath them there would be a pair of mounts that would allow him to walk the mech with his own two feet. He scanned to the left and the right of the chair. Just as expected, there was a set of control grips, with a full complement of switch-triggers, sliders, tracker pads and slot selectors.

Jack didn't question how the alien race had managed to reproduce his WarMech, accurate to the smallest highly personalised detail. He was beginning to realise just how much they knew about *everything*: this robot was just one big hunk of proof of the creature's claims. They were inside humanity's technology. With Jack's world as connected as it was, he suspected that they could siphon information from any data source; it would be child's play for them to download specs for a player's robot from a game server that was already riddled with their coding. But instead of increasing Jack's fear, these revelations provided a glimmer of hope. There was something that his captors, in all their superiority, hadn't considered …

By creating such a faithful replica, the aliens had inadvertently given Jack a fighting chance. He'd used this very machine to kill thousands of Nograki enemies. He'd decimated monsters designed to reflect the warriors of this planet, and he was one of the best in the world at it. If his captor was to be believed, the Top Ten Nograki-killers were all somewhere on this hellhole of a planet. Jack knew the aliens were smart. They would have considered this, believing that to kill Earth's best combatants would be the ultimate proof of their superiority. But *Distant Dawn* was a game. *This* was real. They'd made it a fight for survival not style points, and in order to save their own lives, Earth's warriors would bring a war the likes of which their captors had never witnessed.

Jack turned around and began lowering himself into the pilot's seat. The torso restraints slid over his shoulders like metal serpents, their interlocking jaws snapping shut over his chest. He stretched out his hands and the control grips moved towards him. They felt familiar and welcoming – like the handles on his bike. Next, the panels on the floor opened up. For a moment, Jack's legs felt heavy again as they swung beneath him, then a pair of foot plates ascended, complete with cage-like boot structures that clamped around his lower legs. His feet were now the

WarMech's feet. His hands were the WarMech's hands. The transparent pod hatch swung shut. The displays on the inner surface burst into life. Jack settled into the seat like he was making himself comfortable on his bed at home. It all felt so familiar, so intuitive, and so overwhelmingly empowering. For the first time since he was snatched, Jack felt in control ... A feeling that lasted until the hangar doors in front of him opened, and he saw the inside of the alien arena.

Jack's mech staggered backwards, mimicking its pilot's horror. There were so many sickening sights within his single view that it was difficult to know exactly which one sent him reeling. It could have been the bunkers. The thick stone walls, intended to provide cover from enemy fire, had been melted like candlewax, dripping with smouldering toxins. Or it might have been all the bodies. They were strewn about the arena like discarded clothes. Some were biological extra-terrestrials, some were mechanical beings, some were a combination of the two, and some were made of much stranger things. All of them had one thing in common, though. They were dead.

But the most shocking spectacle was the crowd. A massive audience of alien creatures – more than a hundred thousand, maybe even double that – had packed out the six-tier-high arena. They were deathly silent. It was a menacing space, full and empty at the same time: full with beings bent on the destruction

of humanity, and empty of emotion and sound. Jack
realised that this was a power move; the arena and its
occupants were there to intimidate. And it was working.
Jack was frozen with fear. He might've stayed that way,
had it not been for a familiar sound.

'J-J-Jack? Is that y-y-y-you?'

The voice was coming through the comms system in
Jack's mech.

'Cameron? Cam, is that you? It's Jack – can you
hear me?'

'Jack! It's m-me! They t-t-took me! Did they h-hurt
you? Are you o–, are you o–, are you hurt?'

'I'm okay,' Jack replied, as convincingly as he could.
He could hear the fear in Cameron's voice, and even
though he was one more dead alien carcass away from a
breakdown himself, he tried to hold it together.

'I'm in my WarMech. They tried to hurt me, but I'm
okay. Where are you?'

'I'm in my m-m-mech t-too. They told me I have to
f-f-fight! They said they're going to m-m-mu–, to m-mu–,
they're going to kill everyone, starting with us!'

'I know. That's what they told me, too,' Jack said,
measuring his words as calmly as he could. 'But listen,
mate. They've made a mistake. They've put us in these
machines. *Our* machines.'

'We're on an alien p-p-planet, Jack! What are we
going to do?'

In that moment, Jack saw two sets of hangar

doors open up across the arena. Behind one he saw Cameron's WarMech, well and truly rooted to the spot. By contrast, the second set of doors had almost flown off their hinges. Standing behind them in all its graffitied glory was the Zuul mech. Then came a familiar voice.

'We rumble.'

'Megan!' Jack and Cameron shouted together. Zuul strode forwards into the arena; zero hesitation and no sign of fear. But then it faltered. It started to sway. It stumbled. It fell. The sound of the metal mech hitting the ground vibrated up through Jack's control pod. Before he knew it, he was bounding across the arena.

Jack leaped over the remains of slain creatures from all across the galaxy. He weaved around broken bunkers and stomped through pools of plasma. Jack's movements were fluid – the intuitive connection between him and his mech allowing it to become one big extension of his own body. Bursting through a cloud of purple dust, Jack's mech knelt down and gathered the Zuul mech into its arms.

'Megan! Are you okay? Meg!' Jack shook the painted robot. 'Zuul! Speak to me!'

Silence. Jack held the mech close enough that the control pods touched. He peered through the dusty glass, trying to catch a glimpse of his friend. After what felt like forever, a voice finally crackled through the comms.

'Dude ... I can't even think of a film quote ... messed up enough ... for my feelings right now.'

Jack cradled Megan's mech tighter, overwhelmed by the sound of her voice.

'What did they do to you?' he asked. Jack remembered what his captor had told him about how Megan had been treated. He felt the Zuul mech moving, trying to sit up, so he helped it on its way. It slumped forwards, resting its heavy arms on its knees. Then its head rose slowly.

'You know ... abduction, torture, electrocution. They made me listen to their plans to take over the world ... That was probably the worst part ...'

Megan shook her mech's head. 'But they did give me my very own Zuul to die in.'

Jack forced a fleeting smile through his apprehension. Megan returned the effort before she continued.

'Where are Cam and Ayo?' she asked. 'Are they all right?'

'I'm h-here! But I'm not all r-right!'

Jack turned to see the ForgeFire666 mech, standing over both of them.

'Are you o-o-okay, Meg?'

'Nothing a ShockSoda and a couple of paracetamol wouldn't fix, Cam. You didn't happen to bring any supplies to this alien craphole, did you?'

''Fraid n-not,' Cameron replied.

'Never mind. Help me up.'

The Zuul mech raised both arms. Cameron took hold of one and Jack the other, heaving the robot to its feet.

'Where's Ayo?' Megan said eventually.

The three robots scanned the arena. They could see multiple doorways built into the high walls that ring-fenced the fight zone. Some looked the same as the ones through which they had emerged, others looked much bigger, all of them were still closed. The arena remained silent, cold, and still. Until …

'Seek out. Take hold. Advance existence.'

The words caused the thousands of aliens in the crowd to move as one, each throwing out their four arms and pointing their clenched fists towards a single focal point in perfect unison. The WarMech pilots followed the target of this synchronised gesture and saw a figure standing on a hovering platform. The creature looked similar to Jack's captor, although even from a distance, Jack could tell that it was older and smaller. Its wings were shorter and its skin was greyer. And yet, this being commanded the attention of the entire crowd. A single movement of one of its hands was all it took to prompt thousands of beings to resume their stoic stillness. It surveyed the crowd as the platform beneath it rotated slowly. Then it repeated, 'Seek out. Take hold. Advance existence. This is our way. We toil to extend our empire. We reject inadequacy. We live to enrich the universe.'

As it spoke, Jack realised that the words were not for the crowd's benefit. The creature, like Jack's captor, had no mouth, and it was speaking through a translation device, the words beamed into the WarMechs. It was speaking to *them*.

'For the system to thrive, the motivation must be clear. Weakness – *your* weakness – will be exposed before all. The necessity of your extermination will be evident in your failure. Your death here will be proof of humanity's unworthiness to live on Earth.'

At this, doors began to open all around the arena, each revealing one of the mechs from the *Distant Dawn* Top Ten. Behind the last door was a dull-looking mech, the most unremarkable of the bunch, and yet it was the one that Jack had most hoped to see.

'Ayo!' he shouted. When Jack was met with nothing but silence, he realised that their comms must have been shut off. The hovering creature wasn't done talking.

'You will fight. You will perish. And your end will mark the beginning of our next mission.'

You don't know what's coming, Jack thought. *You're gonna regret bringing Earth's best fighters to this dive of a planet.*

As if in response to his thoughts, the creature on the platform spoke one last time.

'Our warriors have already had a taste of your kind ...'

The being extended one arm towards the far side of the arena, to a part of the stadium that remained unlit.

'... And it has made them hungry.'

Level 12: Morituri Te Salutant

A bright light shone on a slab of stone. Bent backwards over the top of it, lying broken and torn, were the remains of a WarMech.

It was _Carbon_Shift_.

Level 13: Freak Show

While he was normally calmer than a monk getting a massage, Ayo was now on the edge of a complete meltdown. Behind the blast shielding of his nondescript mech, he stared out at the madness surrounding him. It simply did not compute – just like the glitching weapons menu, which he frantically began to work his way through. And yet, there was no time to even attempt to process this horrifying reality, because the remaining doors around the arena's fight zone had started to open.

'W-w-what the hell is *that*?' Ayo heard Cameron yell over the reactivated comms. Ayo had absolutely no answer. From behind a dense set of doors, a creature emerged that looked nothing like any alien in the whole of *Distant Dawn*. It was at least ten metres tall. Its length was harder to estimate because more and more of its body kept emerging from the darkness. It had the body of a snake. A giant, armour-plated, copper-coloured snake, with twenty scuttling legs on each side: strong, dense, and tipped with menacing spikes. A pair of thick, triple-hinged lances jutted out halfway down its body, probing for something to stab at, and two huge, crab-like pincers snapped at the air up front. All the monster's facial features were shoved under a slab brow, with an enormous mouth that hung open below, filled with rows of barbed teeth. As the entirety of the beast emerged, the icing on the cake was revealed: a foot-long stinger on the end of its tail that couldn't have yelled "deadly" any louder if it had a skull and crossbones printed on it. As grotesque as the creature was, Ayo couldn't take his eyes off it – until his attention was snatched by Jack's mech, gesticulating frantically.

'There's another one!' Jack shouted, pointing towards a second snake-scorpion. 'And what is *that*?'

Ayo leaned forwards in his control pod, his nose almost touching the pod window. A different monster stood in the adjacent doorway, filling the frame. This one had two legs and two arms, but no hands. In their place, thick cylinders like beer barrels made from solid bone sprouted from its forearms. This thing had *hammers* for hands. Tufts of hair, pieces of metal, and even the odd claw and fang were deeply embedded in the bone: the remains of defeated races. The monster began banging these hammer-fists together like an ancient warrior beating battle drums. Then it lumbered out of its cell.

It had a domed skull crowned with spikes – perfect for headbutting, as well as knee and elbow spikes that pulsed with venom.

As he watched, Ayo realised that the drumming was getting both louder and more chaotic. He focused on the sound and detected three separate drum patterns. He looked across the arena. Two more hammer-fisted brutes were converging, their battle drums calling for the humans' oblivion.

By now, the WarMechs had all retreated towards the centre of the arena, forming a rough, disorganised, and mostly terrified circle. All except for Hephaestus. Just as he would have in a game of *Distant Dawn*, Ayo had already begun to make his way to the best and furthest vantage point he could find.

'¿Que diablos son esos?'

'Voglio mía madre!'

'Je vais être malade.'

The cries rang out over the comms like crossfire, as the circle of WarMechs drew closer together. Having failed to activate his mech's weapons system, Ayo abandoned his efforts and was now flipping through menus to find the translate function that would allow him to understand the other panicking players. Had they been back in *Distant Dawn*, this function would have been set to "on" by default. But here, it seemed that translation had been purposely deactivated for the global elite gamers turned galactic prisoners … as if their situation wasn't bad enough. Finally, Ayo found the right command. He instantly regretted activating it.

'I'M GONNA DIE! WE'RE ALL GONNA DIE!'

'GET ME OUT OF HERE!'

'NO! PLEASE GOD, NO!'

As the awful creatures closed in, the proclamations of dread became louder, more desperate, and increasingly difficult to listen to. Ayo's neurodivergence meant that he didn't relish being in noisy environments at the best of times, but here, in the midst of this madness, it was like someone was letting off firecrackers in his mind. He needed space to think. At least for a moment. Pulling up a further communications menu, he drew his fingertip across icons that represented each WarMech – highlighting all of them except the other members of the Mob. Then he tapped on another icon: a speaker with an "X" through it. The screaming stopped. The panic was muted, at least for now, and it allowed Ayo to refocus on the Mob, and on their emerging enemy.

So far, none of the alien creatures had attacked. They were still waiting on the *rest* of the monsters to join them, two of whom burst into the arena moments later – and made the snake-scorpions and the hammer trio look positively ordinary.

They were black from their start to their ends, both of which were tough to track as they didn't have fixed arms, legs or heads. The creatures shifted their shape constantly as they advanced. And yet, depending on the terrain, there was something recognisable in the way they moved. Over flat ground they stalked, low and sleek, taking on a catlike form. When they reached an obstacle they adopted a shape like an octopus – squeezing and sliding, moving over, around and through gaps in the rocks. When they reached a trench or a crater, they would spill out into a liquid-like form, trickling over the precipice and cresting over the other side like a breaking wave.

Ayo activated one of his mech's visual enhancements. He locked on and zoomed in, and the source of the alien's shape-shifting ability became clear. It wasn't one being. It was made up of thousands of slithering creatures, shifting and changing as one; six square metres of transmogrifying wormlike organisms, each capable of inflicting a venomous bite ...

... And somehow, the arena still wasn't finished churning out monsters.

'L-L-LOOK!' Cameron cried, the ForgeFire mech pointing a long metal finger upwards. Ayo had been so transfixed by the threats around him that he hadn't seen what was circling in the stormy skies above. It very quickly became his primary focus.

It was swimming through the air. Not flying, flapping or hovering – *swimming*. And while it swam, it ate. Like the filter-feeding sharks of Earth, which glide through water with their mouths hanging wide open, hoovering up plankton as they go, this thing was doing the same. Except that it wasn't consuming plankton.

It was eating lightning.

Even in the middle of this chaos, Ayo scolded himself for not noticing sooner that the arena hadn't been taking as much of an electrical battering as the rest of the city. Now he realised that this flying, scaly shark – all fifteen metres of it – had been absorbing the strikes that would otherwise have hit the arena, and *storing* the power. Its scaled skin was semi-transparent, which meant that Ayo could watch the light being channelled into some powerful organ in the centre of the body. Then he spotted them: openings that lined the creature's underbelly. As the lightning built up, these orifices began to glow. Ayo didn't need any further clues to work out the purpose of this sky-swimming, lightning-devouring beast. Soon enough, those orifices would open, and that stored-up lightning would turn into bombing ammunition.

But still, none of the assembled creatures attacked. Ayo heard Cameron stuttering over the comms.

'W-w-w-what should we d-do? Sh-shoot them?'

'I've been trying that for the last ten minutes. Your weapons aren't working either, I take it?' said Ayo, finally breaking his radio silence.

'AYO!' Cameron, Jack and Megan shouted together.

'Hi guys – I'd love to say it's good to see you all, but I'm up to my neck in faeces inside a robot that I created on my *computer in my bedroom*.'

'Well, it's good to hear your voice,' said Jack. 'Where are you, anyway? Where've you been?'

'As usual, Jack, I have taken up a position that offers maximum cover and minimum opportunity for direct engagement. Apart from that – and the whole being abducted, electrocuted, dumped in a cell and thrown into a gladiatorial arena thing – I've kept myself busy trying to fix my weapons. *Nothing* is working.'

'N-no w-weapons?' spluttered Cameron.

'What the hell are we supposed to do? Use harsh language - colonial marines-style?'

'The *Aliens* film, Megan? That's what you're thinking about now?' Ayo said in disbelief.

'I'm always thinking about it,' Megan retorted. 'So, what are our options?'

'I've been working through my mech's code,' Ayo continued. 'All the weapons systems are completely blocked ...'

Ayo spotted something that caused him to pause. After a moment, his dextrous digits continued to drag blocks of complex code around slowly, until a new and worrying display was revealed.

'... Are you just pausing for dramatic effect?' asked Jack.

'Shh!' hissed Ayo, tapping away at his mech's main control pad. 'I think – I think I've found something. A timer. It's ... it's counting down.'

'How l-l-long is l-l-left?' Cameron spluttered.

'Thirty seconds.'

No one needed to ask what happened after the timer hit zero. Ayo could already see the snake-scorpions snapping their pincers, the hammer-fisted bone-domes banging their hammer-hands together, and the morphing creatures shifting into a variety of menacing shapes. Above, the scaly sky-shark gorged itself on lightning.

'TEN SECONDS!' Ayo shouted, looking across the arena to see the Zuul mech drawing up to its full height.

'I'll beat these turd cubes with my bare metal fists if I have to!' Megan shouted, with all the bravado she could muster. 'I've got a brown belt in karate. Bring it on! Cobra Kai mother–'

A huge explosion tore Megan's threat in two.

Inside tHeScOuRgE, Jack's eyes were pinned open, his mouth agape as words of warning tried to escape … But it was no use. He'd spotted the threat too late. Now all he could do was watch as the lightning bomb sliced through the air: a sword blade charged with godly energy that cut – accurate and deadly – straight into Jeeroy-Lenkins, who was standing *right* in front of Jack. He watched in horror as the mech's armour glowed like a metal poker buried in the centre of a blistering furnace, and then, with a sickening inevitability, began to melt. The leg joints gave out first. They folded in on themselves, causing the WarMech to crumple to its knees in pitiful submission. It knelt there in the dust, convulsing violently, completely unable to break free from the smothering lightning. Eventually, the onslaught stopped … but the violence was far from over.

One of the snake-scorpions scuttled past at speed, lance extended, and decapitated the fallen mech. Its glowing head landed right at Jack's feet, the features melted into a grotesque death mask that stared up at him. Just when things looked like they couldn't possibly get any worse, Jack saw the limp, charred remains of a human body tumble from the unsealed control pod.

Jack didn't know what sickened him more: witnessing the real-life death of the player behind Jeeroy-Lenkins, or the fact that the second before the lightning had struck, he had seen a ring of red light appear at the foot of the knightly mech. A warning sign. A tell right before the lethal blow. He could have done something. He could have helped.

Jack drew his mech's arms up and balled the hands, ready to fight his enemy – with bare metal fists – just like Megan said. But then, through burning tears, Jack spotted something. A laser phasor had appeared from an opening on top of his right forearm. A nuke-fuelled grenade launcher had emerged from inside his mech's left arm. He glanced down at his control screens.

All his weapons systems were active.

Full fight mode.

Jack launched himself at the same crawling creature that had just decapitated Jeeroy-Lenkins, analysing the beast as he advanced. In no time he spotted a rhythm in the way it opened and closed its pincers, and a limit on the range of its lances. These were the kind of weaknesses Jack knew how to exploit. He waited until he'd reached the optimum distance, then planted his left foot heavily into the dirt, crouched and launched his mech into the air – sailing to the right just as the creature's pincer snapped to the left. He grabbed hold of the lance as it swung by him, *exactly* where Jack had anticipated it would, then his right foot came down hard on the centre of the serpentine body. Jack knew that this was its weakest point, and the heavy impact of the metal foot pinned the beast to the ground. Springing upwards with a second powerful leap, Jack tore the lancing limb clean off, and then, from the corner of his eye, he spotted the final threat – the stinging tail. It, too, was right where he wanted it. He drove his arm up to meet it, amputated spike in hand, and stabbed the monster through the base of its tail with its own weapon. As Jack's mech came back down to the ground, he drove the broken lance into the earth, skewering the monster. It writhed and struggled, spilling green plasma from its wounds. The more it thrashed, the more it risked ripping itself in two. Jack stared at the beast as he snapped two grenades into the chamber of the launcher on his arm. From that range, all it took was a flick of Jack's finger to reduce the snake-scorpion to a seaweed-coloured stain on the ground.

Game or no game, it was an epic kill ... and it was the spark that lit the fuse of violent pandemonium.

The silent arena erupted with sound. Metal feet shook the dirt; some charged forwards, others staggered backwards. An orchestra of gunfire echoed off the walls; strings replaced with laser shooters, woodwind with machine guns, brass for rocket-fuelled projectiles, percussion with bombs. The sound filled Jack's control pod as he scanned for his next kill, suddenly catching sight of the tail end of the second snake-scorpion. It was heading towards the east side of the arena – fast. If he'd killed one of those monsters, he could kill the other. Then he'd get started on the rest. He'd show his captors that they should never have let him inside a WarMech; that humans would *resist* with everything they had.

Backing up against a rocky structure about two-thirds of the way across the arena, Jack peered around the edge to witness a sight that boosted his confidence in the human resistance. SaiboTron had a barrel-fisted beast kneeling, defeated, at its feet. Its severed hammer-hands were rolling in the dirt. Raising its sword above its head, the silver WarMech prepared to deliver the final blow. However, what SaiboTron's pilot hadn't seen were the *other* two hammer-fisted creatures, charging out from cover on both sides.

It appeared that they'd let their fellow monster battle SaiboTron alone, using it as bait while they readied their ambush. They attacked, quickly and ferociously, and before SaiboTron even drew down its sword, the silver samurai was caught between two domed skulls. Jack winced at the sickening crunch. He saw the control pod crumple like a crushed ShockSoda can. No one inside could have survived the hit. And yet, even after the mech had fallen to the ground, the monsters pummelled the metal remains, reducing the mech to scrap with unmerciful savagery. Before Jack could gather his wits and make a move, the monsters disappeared into the maze of bunkers and barricades.

Jack gripped the edge of a wall so hard his mech's metal fingers broke a chunk off it. His chest burned and his stomach heaved at the sight before him. He couldn't bear to watch that happen to one more person – especially not one of his friends.

Mere moments later, Jack turned to see two shape-shifting creatures break from cover on the opposite side of the arena, and PrincessShatterSparkles and HudsonNotHicks run right into their path. Both WarMechs unleashed a full barrage of firepower at the writhing masses, switching through weapon after weapon. But the shells just sailed through gaps in the changing shapes, or took a clump out of the wormlike creatures only for the hole to be refilled just as quickly. Before Jack could close the distance to help, the shape-shifters had forced the two mechs into retreat, until they were back to back and confined to a small square of dirt. Once the creatures had the mechs where they wanted them, they spilled out across the arena like black lava to form a ring of fire – licking and spitting at the mechs, burning them with venomous bites and toxic saliva. But this was just a distraction. When the next lightning bomb rained down, it fell directly on the two WarMechs, melting them into one single mass. And when the black circle around them withdrew, all that Jack could see was a charred, contorted statue of the two machines of war, pink body parts and camouflaged limbs locked forever in a burnt embrace.

Level 14: Devastating News

When Cameron came across the burnt, twisted statue, it made him turn tail and run the opposite way.

Cameron was searching desperately for a level map to show him the layout of the area, and where he was. On certain *Distant Dawn* game modes, the map would also show the positions of teammates and enemies. But there was no map in Cameron's mech. There was no way of knowing where he or anyone else was, friend or foe. Cameron was alone. The longer this nightmare continued, the more intensely he felt it. Having stumbled further towards the centre of the arena, Cameron eventually spotted a deep scar in the earth – a bunker dug out by some poor, desperate lifeform before him. His mech clambered into the trench and sat on the ground. Drawing its legs up towards its chest and wrapping the armour-plated forearms around its knees, Cameron sobbed.

'... ameron? Cameron, are you there? Megan? Is anyone there?'

Cameron lifted his head.

'Can you hear me? Cameron? Megan? Ayo? Anyone!'

'I can hear you, J-Jack!' Cameron replied. He was so relieved to hear his friend's voice. Once the fighting had started, the noise and chaos had separated the Mob. He'd been alone since the first bullet flew.

'Cameron! Where are you?'

'I d-d-don't know,' Cameron said, peering above the brim of the trench. Everything looked the same: rocks and bodies and bullets.

'I got l-lost when the f-f-fighting started – all the n-noise – I c-couldn't hear anyone. I f-f-found Shatter-S-Sparkles and Hudson-n-n, Hudson-n-n, Hud–. Oh God, Jack, it w-was horrible. They were all b-burned and–'

'I know, buddy. Listen to me. We need to regroup. The Mob fights better together. I'm still where Sparkles and Hudson are. Can you find your way back?'

'I d-don't know,' said Cameron. 'I don't know where I am ...'

Silence.

'... Jack? Jack? Are you still there?'

'I'm here, mate,' Jack replied reassuringly, 'I'm just thinking ... Can you see the lighting shark?'

Cameron scanned the skies quickly. The bolt-spewing sky-shark wasn't hard to spot.

'Yeah.'

'Okay,' said Jack. 'Imagine this whole place is a clock face. If the shark is at twelve, I'm at four.'

'Got it,' Cameron said, shifting his mech up the side of the trench. 'I'm c-coming now.'

'Great – I'll try and contact Ayo and Meg. Be careful.'

'O-k-kay!' said Cameron. 'I'll see you soo–'

Cameron had barely dragged the ForgeFire666 mech from the trench when he found himself reeling backwards again – sent flying by a heavy hit. Just before his mech crashed back into the trench, he caught sight of the culprit behind the impact. BunnyQueen12 was running away from something, and had barged him into the trench in the process. Breathless, Cameron pulled his mech back onto its feet and grabbed hold of the rim of the bunker. As he dragged himself over the edge, he saw what BunnyQueen12 had been trying to evade. In the same moment, he realised exactly what the pilot of the big mech had done. BunnyQueen12 had knocked him down on purpose, leaving him stranded in the trench like an insect on its back; a nice hunk of bait. Now, the threat was standing over *him* instead ... in the form of two hammer-handed brutes.

'Jack! Help! The h-hammer monsters! Help!'

Cameron's mind was brimming with a panic that was bubbling over into his limbs. Fear melted his muscles and numbed his nerves. In the virtual world of *Distant Dawn*, Cameron had been a maestro, dealing destruction like a conductor leading an orchestra. He was a warrior who wielded life and death like surgical instruments. He was the global star of countless compilation videos that showcased his stratospheric Nograki kill count and super slaying style. He was *feared*. Now, he was just Cameron. Cameron the scared boy, looking up at the bullies of *this* world, powerless to stand up for himself. And here, his inability to fight back wouldn't cost him his lunch money – it was going to cost him his life.

Cameron raised an arm in a feeble attempt to fire his railgun, but the two monsters leaped into the trench and stomped down, one on each hand, pinning Cameron's mech to the ground. They lurched over him, leaning in closer until his control pod's window was filled by their awful faces. The creatures' hot breath fogged up the glass. Thick strings of red saliva dangled from their mouths, and Cameron could see chunks of meat of all different colours and textures stuck between their spiked teeth. Their beady little eyes gazed out from beneath heavy brows, looking him over hungrily. With a final, low growl, the monsters rose up and raised their barrelled fists high into the air. Cameron wrenched at his mech's controls, desperate to escape, but the muscular monsters had him at their mercy. He couldn't move. He couldn't fight back. All he could do was close his eyes.

Cameron heard two heavy thuds, and two wet splashes. Daring to peel one eye open, he found his pod window was soaked; a film of gooey purple liquid covered the curved surface, giving the tumultuous alien sky an almost calm lavender hue. He opened the other eye. He couldn't see the hammer-handed monsters, but there was another figure standing at the bunker's edge. As blurry as his view was, he recognised the form instantly. Cameron reached out and pressed a button on the side of his control pod. The pod window was wiped clean by an external mechanism, and it was confirmed: Th£D£V@ST@T0R was standing there, holding out its hand to him. Then it spoke.

'I saw what BunnyQueen12 did to you,' said a startlingly calm voice from inside the mech. 'Hardly in keeping with the spirit of cooperation – which is the only way we're going to beat these cretins. Wouldn't you agree, *Cameron*?'

Quad barrels on both the mech's forearms still smoked with plasma vapour, glowing with green heat. The WarMech had taken out both monsters. Cameron couldn't decide which to express first – his gratitude or his confusion. Th£D£V@ST@T0R's pilot knew his name. Maybe the Mob's *Distant Dawn* online chat hadn't been as secure as they'd thought. Maybe this pilot had been listening in. Compounding Cameron's confusion was another notion that kept pinging around his mind: *he knew this mech's voice*. During *Distant Dawn* games,

Th£D£V@ST@TOR

007

Cutting Edge Power Core with Enhanced Durability

Quad-barrelled Canons with Customisable Projectiles

Power-Transmitters for Object Weaponisation

Level-29 Experimental Armour Upgrade

Th£D£V@ST@TOR has almost every upgrade possible to purchase, from power-ups to special items, and even the capability to charge inanimate objects with plasma power – giving it the ability to use anything as a weapon.

Th£D£V@ST@T0R only ever used text chat. It was
notorious for it. It went to even more extreme lengths
to protect its anonymity than the Mob did. But now,
Cameron was finally hearing the player behind the
machine.

He took the outstretched metal hand and clambered
out of the bunker, standing pod to pod with his protector.

'M-M-M–, M-MMM–, MMM–'

The woman inside Th£D£V@ST@T0R gave a grim smile.

'"Miss Barrett", Cameron.'

Cameron was staring at his teacher. His teacher who
hated technology, confiscated phones, and refused to
take the register on anything but paper. *That* teacher
was the pilot of Th£D£V@ST@T0R.

And she had just saved Cameron's life.

It was *way* more than Cameron could cope with.
His mech began to sway as the blood rushed to his
dizzied head.

'Easy there, young man,' said Miss Barrett, steadying
Cameron's machine before it ended up at the bottom
of the trench for the third time. Dragging it clear,
she propped it against a bank of purple soil. When
Cameron's vision cleared, he saw the face of his teacher,
regarding him with something he'd never seen from her
before: genuine concern.

'Cameron, listen to me,' she said, grabbing his mech
by the shoulders. 'I'm not going to pretend I understand
what's going on here. One minute I was at home gaming

– oh, I game, by the way, and I'm very, *very* good at it – and the next I'm abducted, tortured, and dumped in a cell with a real-life version of my mech. Then, in the middle of a massive interplanetary battle, I rescue another anonymous player – only to look into their cockpit and discover that the gamer behind the legendary ForgeFire666 mech is a boy I know from the back row of my form room. It's all *way* too much to deal with, but right now we don't have much of a choice.'

Cameron looked at his teacher. The familiarity of her face in the midst of otherworldly madness provided a fleeting yet overwhelming moment of relief. His eyes brimmed with tears, and his bottom lip began to tremble.

'I want to g-go home!' he blurted.

'That's what we all want,' said Miss Barrett. 'Unfortunately, it seems like our ungracious hosts have other plans. We have to do something to change their minds – like prove to them that humanity is a force to be reckoned with.'

'You sound like J-Jack,' Cameron sniffed.

'Jack who?'

'Jack Delaney, Miss.'

'Jack *Delaney* is here? The boy who can't turn up to my class on time has managed to make it to an alien planet halfway across the universe?'

'Yes, M-Miss. He's the S-S-Scourge. Ayo and Megan are here t-too.'

Miss Barrett gave Cameron the same look of incredulity she would have if he'd told her that his non-existent dog had eaten his homework.

'Unbelievable! Four gamers in the global *Distant Dawn* Top Ten are in *my* class? Let me guess. Megan is Zuul – obvious from that obnoxious sticker-covered backpack of hers. And Ayo ... Ayo must be ...'

'H-Hephaestus, Miss!'

She nodded, calmly assimilating information that would – at any other time and in any other place – have bordered on brain-blending. An expression that Cameron had never seen from his teacher began spreading across Miss Barrett's face. She looked *impressed*.

'You guys are good. Elite fighters. But ForgeFire666 – you are *legendary*. I've seen you take out Nograkis in every way imaginable. I've studied your moves. You've made me a better fighter.'

'Only in the g-game, M-Mm-Miss. I can't fight like that in r-real life,' Cameron replied. As embarrassing as this admission was for him to make, he knew that it was true. His virtual self and his real-world self were on opposite ends of a spectrum that could have spanned from Earth all the way to this godforsaken planet. And he'd never felt that painful truth more than right then.

'I don't think you have much of a choice, young man,' Miss Barrett replied, teacher voice in full effect. 'In fact, I see only two options. You crawl back into that trench again and stay there, waiting for one of those intergalactic bullies to come and find you. Or, you come with me, find your friends, and we all fight together. You of all people know that I can't stand bullies, Cameron, and I'm certainly not hanging around here for that thing in the sky to dump lightning all over me. So I know what I'm going to do. And you need to decide, right now. Are you going to play this out like Cameron Yates? Or ForgeFire666 – the pain-dealing, send-'em-reeling, world-famous bringer of alien doom?'

Cameron stared at his mech's hand, lying limp in the purple dirt. What if the gap between Cameron Yates and ForgeFire666 wasn't quite as astronomical as he'd thought? What if his teacher had seen potential in him – even just a small, special something – that he'd never have credited himself with? What if the time had finally come to step out from behind his friends and his teacher and stand up to the bullies himself? A glimmer of hope reflected off his WarMech's armour. Cameron began to raise his mech's limb slowly, clenching the metal fist until warheads popped out of recesses in the knuckles, locked and ready to fire.

'*That's* more like it,' Miss Barrett said with a determined smile. 'Now, on your feet, ForgeFire,' she added, pulling him up out of the dirt. 'Let's go and find your fr–'

Miss Barrett's mouth hung open, the final word vanishing into silence. Her eyes popped wide for a heartbeat, then rolled back, the lids falling shut. Her body went limp. Her hands fell off the controls and her mech mirrored her, wilting like a flower. As desperate as he was to drag his eyes away, Cameron could not stop staring at the stinger that had penetrated his teacher's mech and punched right through her chest.

'MISS!'

Cameron screamed. He grabbed hold of the arm that was holding his, but before he could draw the mech closer it was wrenched away from him – flung like a ragdoll back into the trench – leaving only the torn-off robotic limb in his hand. There, standing in front of Cameron with its stinger tinged red, was the snake-scorpion.

Lightning cracked the sky open. Cameron stood, trembling. But it wasn't fear that shook his bones. It was fury. Pure hate-driven fury. The anger burned behind his red, tear-brimmed eyes as he stared at the savage serpent.

The creature hadn't attacked. It was still basking in the thrill of the execution. And this would be the last mistake it ever made.

Cameron planted one of his mech's legs into a mound of dirt and activated a single foot-booster that sent him soaring into a spinning leap. By the time the snake-scorpion had turned to aim a swipe of its lance at him, the robot had landed on its back, ripped off one of the spear-shaped appendages with one hand, and used the torn-off hand of Miss Barrett's mech to batter the slithering monster over the head. The creature – dazed and injured – was infuriated by the assault, rounding on Cameron as he jumped from its back, spilling plasma from the stub of its lance. Cameron met the creature's charge head-on, diving low at the last second and throwing a sonic punch into the ground, driving up a mound of purple earth that caused the snake-scorpion to rear up on its back legs, flinging its pincers out wide for balance. This was exactly what Cameron wanted. He arched a laser beam from left to right, lopping off both the monster's stretched-out pincers. With three of its five deadly limbs amputated, the injured snake-scorpion began to back away from Cameron's vengeful mech. But ForgeFire666 was far from finished. Turning the arm of his teacher's mech over in his hand, Cameron pulled the cover from a recess in the top, finding inside five nuke-fuelled grenades. As the creature hobbled backwards, tripping over alien remains. Cameron activated the grenades. He turned the robotic arm over and began manipulating the metal fingers. Then, unsheathing the chain spear from his forearm, he started towards the snake-scorpion, skewering Th£D£V@ST@T0R's arm to the tip of his spear.

'This is for M-m-mi–, M-m-mi–,' he started. Then he paused, took a deep breath and spoke again, as clearly as he'd ever uttered anything. 'This is for my teacher.'

Cameron threw his mech's arm out and sent the chain spear sailing through the air. The point of the blade sunk into the middle of the beast's body. It looked backwards at the object impaled in its midsection: a silver gauntlet full of live grenades, with a single digit sticking up. Th£D£V@ST@T0R's flipped middle finger was the last thing the serpent saw, before the explosion turned it into a vaporised cloud of green plasma.

Cameron slowly retracted the chain. Inside his splattered WarMech, he wasn't even *attempting* to calm down. He wasn't trying to breathe the burning fire out of his lungs, or lessen the tightness that tore at every muscle. Instead, he was bathing in the vengeance that had temporarily replaced all his crippling fears and anxieties. He had stood up to the bully. He hadn't run away. Within that brief moment of fury, Cameron had felt a spark of the fire of ForgeFire666. Deeply and intensely it burned in him, and it began to fuel a new determination. He would avenge his fallen protector. He would do for his friends what she had done for him.

He would not let the bullies triumph.

Level 15:
Duel of the
Fists

'Cameron! Ayo! Either of you out there?'

The voice snapped Cameron out of his rage-fuelled trance. He started back towards the trench, where the crumpled heap of metal that was Th£D£V@ST@T0R lay.

'Megan, I'm here,' Cameron replied. 'I'm with M-Mi–, I'm with Mm-Mm–'

'I'm with Jack!' Megan shouted back. Cameron could hear heavy gunfire over the comms. 'We're fighting the shifters! It's *not* going well. We could do with some help, buddy! We haven't seen Ayo for ages. I swear to the baby Jeebs, if he's been hiding this whole time I'm gonna find him and serve him up to these alien freaks mys– aaah!'

'M-Megan! Are you okay?' Cameron yelled.

Level 15: Duel of the Fists

'Tripped over a flippin' skeleton!' she yelled in annoyance.

'We need some help, Cam!' Jack shouted up. 'Our shots just pass through these things!'

'O-o-kay, I'm on my w-way,' Cameron stuttered. And yet, he didn't move. Instead, he craned his mech's head reluctantly over the edge of the trench. He didn't *want* to look inside the mech, but he wasn't going to leave Miss Barrett's remains out here in the middle of extra-terrestrial hell.

But there was a problem. There were no remains.

The mech was empty.

Across the arena, Megan and Jack were running low on weapons that worked and ammo to fire from them. The two had ripped through their inventory, with Megan complaining that the more imaginative weapons from the *Distant Dawn* game were missing – or in her words, that she couldn't 'Thanos-click these things into oblivion'. Instead, they were relying on old-fashioned bullets and fire, bombs and slugs, none of which were having much effect. And to make matters worse, the shape-shifters were getting closer – backing the mechs towards each other. It was only a matter of time until they'd form the ring of spitting black fire that would trap the WarMechs in one spot, and the sky-shark would arrive to finish the job. It was an inevitability that Megan, in her trademark wilful fashion, simply refused to accept.

'I've got a great idea!' she suddenly announced.

Usually, Megan's "great ideas" were described by the rest of the Mob as "dicey" at best, and at worst "insane in the membrane". And that's when they were playing a computer game, not fighting for their lives in an alien arena. However, their usual *kill it with fire and fury* approach wasn't working, and the shifters were closing in.

'Hit me!' Jack replied.

'We bring them in closer!' Megan shouted back.

'I'm not sure this is the right time for your *Top Gun* trick, Meg!'

'Trust me! We can't hurt them from distance – we might as well be firing at football netting. But if we engage hand-to-hand, or hand-to-whatever they've got, they'll have to solidify their bodies. *Then* we can hurt them ...'

There was a split second of silence. Then, 'Let's do it.'

Megan saw Jack retract all of his cannons and gun barrels, ball up his fists, raise his guard, and start towards the shifter. She did the same. The shape-changing mass in front of her seemed to shiver at the unexpected sight of a ten-metre machine of war striding straight towards it. It got stuck in flux, morphing between forms; odd shapes protruded, then receded again. Megan smirked as she hunched her shoulders and tightened her fists, causing foot-long metal spikes to pop out from her mech's knuckles. She had her enemy shook. The creature continued to spill random shapes as Megan approached, and only settled on its final form when the mech had closed the distance.

It was at that point that Megan hesitated. She stared at the shifter's chosen shape: a replica of her own WarMech.

'... Well, my mum's always saying that I'm my own worst enemy!' Megan shouted over the comms, as she shook off the surprise and continued forwards.

'I think it's time to channel those *Rocky* films you love so much,' Jack said. He cocked his fist and closed in on the creature opposite Megan's target, which had replicated *his* mech.

'Hell yeah! This is for Apollo!' Megan shouted. She launched herself at her foe. The impact of the spear tackle sent the shifter crashing to the ground; it spilled out into a pool beneath her mech. She rained down punches on the puddle of worms, flattening them into the dirt beneath her fists. But the creature was quick to react. It streamed through her legs and re-formed behind her. A heavy replica foot slammed into her back, winding her as her mech was sent crashing into the purple earth. The approaching steps of the shifter vibrated through her mech's fingertips as she caught her breath. She waited. She held out until she felt a heavy foot plant itself right next to her, indicating that the other was raised and ready to stomp. Rolling in the direction of the sound, Megan swept the standing leg of the creature and bounced her mech up onto its feet. But she didn't dive on top this time.

Megan glanced across to Jack, watching him swing a heavy fist square onto his target's replicated jaw, followed quickly by a left to the body that sent the monster reeling backwards. Jack seemed to be having better success with his prize-fighter approach, so Megan decided to follow suit. She waited until her foe was back on its feet, then unleashed a rocket-fuelled uppercut that almost took its head clean off.

This new plan of attack worked much better. In fact, it was soon going so well that Megan was *almost* enjoying it. She was quicker than the shifter, better able to control the mass of her machine, and it didn't hurt having elbow-mounted boosters to triple the power of each hit. It felt like working a punch bag – the shifter's swings were ill-timed and inaccurate. After a while, Megan started to wonder ... *are these things really trying?*

'MEGAN! MOVE!'

Megan didn't need telling twice. Instinctively, she tucked up and barrel-rolled to the right. A streaming shaft of lightning ripped into the earth next to her, burning the purple dirt. Megan shielded the view screen with her mech's forearm. The sky-shark was right overhead. The shifter had been absorbing the hits to keep her in one place.

'They're playing with us!' Jack shouted over the comms.

Megan clambered her mech up onto its feet. 'At least it's a fun game!' And she laid into the shifter once more.

'Not a game we can *win*! They aren't taking any damage – they're just trying to lure us into trouble!' replied Jack. 'We need to think. Think like we're still in *Distant Dawn*. These are the bosses, and there's always a way to beat the boss, right? They *must* have a weakness ...'

'Just keep yours busy!' shouted Megan, sinking another hard left into what was starting to feel like a Play-Doh foe. She slugged away; fists, elbows, knees and big metal feet rained down. But still, nothing stuck. The shifters would not yield. That was, until she activated a weapons system that had, mercifully, been included in her mech's build ...

'WOAH!' Megan heard Jack yell over the comms. She watched the head of his opponent explode into tiny pieces of slithering worm, spilling green blood for the first time ...

'SAY HELLO TO MY LITTLE FEATHERED FRIENDS!' Megan yelled. Hovering above Jack's mech, with its gun turrets ablaze, was one of Megan's drones. It spat bullets like hailstones over the shifter, and because the creature had solidified, the projectiles were actually doing some damage. Serious damage. At Megan's order, Jack continued to bombard the creature's body with heavy blows, and each hit was rewarded by wet slaps of writhing alien flesh hitting the ground – blown off by the unrelenting fire from the drone. Behind, Megan was doing the same – pummelling the shifter relentlessly while her other drone blew pieces off it.

We're gonna do it, she thought. *We're gonna beat them. We're gonna wi–*

Megan's ambitions were dashed by a missed punch, the momentum of which almost spun her completely. Her enemy was no longer there; it had collapsed into a pool on the ground and was flowing away at speed. It covered the distance between itself and her gunner drone's position in no time. Once it was directly underneath, the shifter shot upwards in the form of a towering spike. Megan watched in horror as the drone was impaled on the tip. Spitting sparks and smoke, the drone's lights blinked, then went dark.

'Aw crap,' Megan muttered. She turned to see an identical shaft in front of Jack's mech, with a metal bird skewered on the tip. Megan started to back her mech up, and Jack did the same. As the two came together, the shifters reassumed their catlike stalking states.

'I don't know what else we can do!' Megan yelled. Jack was silent for a moment.

'You trust me, right?' he said.

'I mean, I'd trust you to, like, borrow my limited-edition copy of *Flight of the Navigator*, or–'

'Meg! You trust me, *right*?'

'Course I do,' she replied.

'Then stand your ground. Don't move, whatever happens. And, when I say, you jump and you split your mech. Send your parts as far out as you can.'

'If *I* had suggested that plan, you'd call it insane ...' Megan said, already planting her feet. She watched the two shifters closing the gap, stalking their prey, waiting for the perfect moment to attack.

'Wait ...' said Jack. Megan's mech twitched nervously. A snout emerged from the monster in front and split in half, exposing two rows of black teeth. Each one was formed from the spitting head of an alien worm, dripping with violet, metal-melting venom ...

'Wait!' Jack shouted. Every fibre of Megan's being told her to run – her unshakable Raid Mob bond stretched to breaking point as the shape-shifters advanced, growing in size with each step. But Megan held her shredded nerve.

'WAIT!' Jack yelled again. And then, just as the creatures were about to leap, it appeared: a red circle of light glowing beneath their feet.

'NOW!' he screamed.

Inside her control pod, Megan pulled a booster trigger. It felt like a bomb had gone off beneath her seat. Her mech erupted into the air, then four more explosions sounded as her robot's limbs flew off in different directions. Watching from her heightening vantage point, she saw Jack pull his mech downwards and roll right. His shape-shifting enemy, already committed to its attack, soared straight past his machine. In one fluid motion, Jack popped up from his roll and drew his arm upwards – the fire fist function fuelled and ready. The torso of Megan's mech was now hanging in the air. On either side of what remained of her machine, two leaping shifters were about to engulf her completely. And, to make matters worse, all three combatants were bathed in that deep crimson glow that signalled the coming of the sky-fire.

At the last possible second, Megan spotted a metal fist sailing right towards the remains of her mech on a trail of blue flame. Its impact pushed the torso clear of the path of the converging creatures. Unable to stop themselves, the shape-shifters clashed together in a mid-air collision of worms and teeth and blackness, and at the very same moment, the lightning bomb came down.

The light was so intense it burned, even as Megan scrunched her eyes closed. It filled her hovering pod, and the warmth tingled hot over her skin. Then as quickly as it had erupted, the electricity dissipated and the light dulled. The lightning had done to the shifters what it had done to PrincessShatterSparkles and HudsonNotHicks, although the remaining statue was even more grotesque. The black creatures had burned grey; ashen like the embers of a dying fire. Aberrant forms stuck out of the heap of charred alien flesh: a clawed hand here, a scaled tail there; half a face that looked more human than was comfortable.

But no matter how ghastly the remains were, they were remains nonetheless.

The shifters were dead.

Megan had already managed to recall her limbs and recombine her mech. Landing heavily, she strode around the statue and whistled as she looked it up and down.

'Gutsy move, man ... But don't ever hit me again.'

'Thanks for trusting me,' Jack said, drawing up his arm as his fire-powered fist flew back and locked into place. 'I think – I *think* we've almost won.'

'The place is definitely a lot quieter than it was. And a lot squelchier,' Megan added, lifting her mech's foot from a deep puddle of alien blood.

A peel of thunder drew her attention from the ground to the skies above, where she spotted the sky-shark, still gobbling down lightning, preparing for its next shelling.

'How the hell do we take *that* thing out?' she said.

Suddenly, a familiar voice came from behind them. 'G-g-guys!'

The ForgeFire666 mech bounded towards them.

'G-guys – you won't believe who's h-h-here! I almost got killed, but I was saved by M-M-Mi–, M-M-Mi–'

'MAY I INTERRUPT?' came another instantly recognisable voice.

'AYO! Where the *hell* are you?' Megan shouted, looking around. 'And where have you been?'

'Look up!' Ayo shouted back.

Megan, Jack and Cameron scanned the stormy skies.

Megan locked on to the shark. The image on her view screen magnified until it showed something that, even on this insane alien world, she simply could not believe.

The Hephaestus mech was riding the lightning shark.

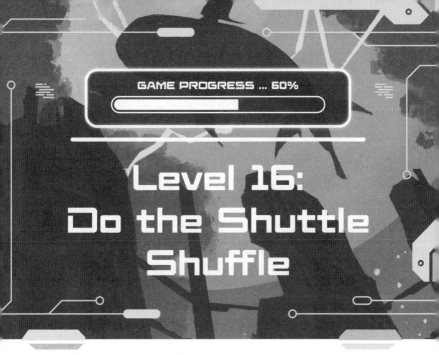

Level 16:
Do the Shuttle Shuffle

'... Can everyone else see Ayo riding the sky-shark?'

Megan's question hung, unanswered, as the three mech pilots stared upwards. A lot of unbelievable things had happened to them in the last few hours, but for Jack, this was about as nuts as he could handle.

'Yup,' he managed eventually.

'Cool. Cool cool cool,' Megan replied. 'Just checking – thought for a second I might've been having a FREAKIN' PSYCHEDELIC EPISODE! AYO! WHAT IN GOD'S NAME ARE YOU DOING UP THERE?'

'Well,' Ayo began, his speech broken by thunderous explosions, 'while you were all wast*FIZZ* time with those creepy-crawlies down th*CRAAACK* – and probably assuming that I was camping – I was worki*RAZZ* on a way to take out our biggest threat!'

'BY RIDING IT?' Jack shouted up.

'How else wer*FIZZ* we going to hurt it?' Ayo replied. 'I'm not sure if you've not*KRA-KOOM*ced, but the underside of this thing isn't exactly its weak spot*TIZZ*...'

'H-h-how did you g-g-get up there?' asked Cameron.

'I highjacked the hovering platfor*SNAP*. I extracted the translation unit from *CRACK* the comms system. It was pretty eas*SIZZLE* to find the appropriate subdirectories after that. Would you like *BOOM* to know more, or am I okay to focus on KILLING THE GIANT LIGHTNING MONSTER?'

The view from Jack's monitor was surreal. Ayo's robot had planted its feet into the sky-shark's back, an improvised lasso of metal fibre extending from one arm, attached to the creature via a grappling hook. The ride looked rough. The beast knew there was a stowaway on board. It had begun swinging its mass from side to side in an effort to shake the mech off. This proved problematic, and not just for Ayo.

'TAKE COVER!' Jack shouted. Lightning bombs were dropping thick and fast, with no red glow to signal where they might land. The mechs scattered. Jack skidded his mech behind a mound of rubble before drawing up his monitor view again.

'What are you going to do?' he shouted up.

'There's a blowhole ... WOAH! ... on its back,' replied Ayo, his words bumping over the turbulence. 'It opens after every ... few strikes. I'm going to attempt to drop ... a bomb ins-side.'

'You're going to *blow up* the thing that you're *standing on top of*?' exclaimed Megan in utter disbelief. 'Aren't you supposed to be the smart one?'

'Is there an-n-nother way?' Cameron asked.

'Not unless ... I can get this thing ... to roll over ... for a tummy rub,' replied Ayo. 'Then you could gun it down ... AH! ... at your leisure. As is, I'll have to hope the delay on the bomb ... will give me enough time to bail.'

'Can we do anything to help?' Jack shouted.

'Yes. Whether I make it or not ... don't ever call me a camper ... again,' replied Ayo.

Jack spotted a glowing green warhead appear inside a cavity on the Hephaestus mech's forearm. He recognised it as a Level 5 Reaper Shell – a *serious* piece of explosive power in the world of *Distant Dawn*. He watched Ayo prime the device then drop it.

'Jump!' Jack shouted. But there was a problem. The grappling hook would not detach. Jack watched as Ayo released his robot's foot grips, sending it tumbling along the creature's back and off its tail, until the lasso pulled taut. Now, Ayo was being dragged through the sky like a fish on the end of a line – and the bomb was ticking. The last thing Jack saw before the explosion was the arm of Ayo's mech, morphing and rising into the air. After that, there was nothing except a ball of green light, an ear-shattering eruption, and a cloud of detonation dust ...

Level 5 Reaper Shell

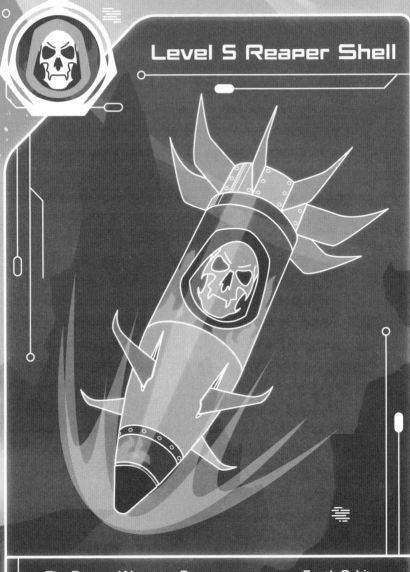

The Reaper Weapons Programme was an Earth Orbit Defence initiative, headed up by Colonel J. Hardcastle with the express intention of giving the Nograki invaders "a dose of their own doo-doo". Salvaged alien power cores were used to fuel experimental missiles – the most powerful designated the "Level 5 Reaper Shell".

Level 16: Do the Shuttle Shuffle

The rapid expulsion of destructive energy from the Reaper Shell combined with the concentrated lightning from the sky-shark was enough to shake the entire arena. It blew the doors off the holding cells and put cracks in the walls that ran all the way from the ground to the front row of the stands, threatening to spill stunned alien audience members onto the battlefield. What it didn't manage to do, however, was fell the Raid Mob. Jack was the first to emerge from the dust cloud, scanning the skies desperately.

'AYO? AYO! SOUND OFF, MAN!' Megan shouted, climbing out from a nearby bunker, with Cameron following behind.

'Is he – is he d-d-dea–'

'*Don't* say it!' Megan snapped.

Jack couldn't speak. He wanted to offer some reassurance to his friends, but he couldn't get past the awfulness of what had just happened. The truth was, *no one* could've survived that blast. Ayo was not okay. He'd sacrificed himself to save them. This realisation weighed so heavily on Jack that it had him pinned at the centre of his chest. He could taste survivor's guilt in every breath.

'L-L-LOOK!'

Jack blinked away hot tears and snapped his head upwards. An object had pierced the cloud: a dull, grey mass, with limp limbs hanging from a motionless torso.

'AYO!' Jack cried. 'AYO! ARE YOU OKAY?' No response. Jack zoomed in on the robot and saw that Ayo was flying deadstick – he wasn't in control. Whether that was down to damage from the explosion or because Ayo was unconscious, Jack didn't know. What he *did* know was that if Ayo's mech hit the ground from that height, whatever state he was in would get a whole lot worse.

'We need to slow him down!' Jack shouted.

'Anyone hiding any emergency crash mats, projectile parachutes or Christmas miracles they might not have told the group about?' cried Megan, struggling to hide her desperation.

'W-What about ... w-what about the sh-shuttle sh-shuffle?'

The two mechs turned to face Cameron's.

'That took us *fifty* tries!' Megan exclaimed, her WarMech's arms flapping to punctuate her exasperation.

'And it was in the middle of a *game*, Cam,' added Jack. 'There are no extra lives or continues here. What if we get it wrong?'

'You got a b-better idea?'

Jack remembered the shuttle shuffle. It had been the Mob's name for an audacious move they'd pulled off in *Distant Dawn*, during a mission where a transport shuttle full of colonists had malfunctioned. *Forty-nine times*, that ship had hit the ground, killing everyone on board. They'd tried everything to stop it crashing, including fashioning safety nets out of metal grappling cords and melting the ground to soften the landing. The only thing that had worked was the shuttle shuffle.

Jack shook his head at the sheer madness of the idea – but Cameron was right. He didn't have a single better suggestion.

'Same order as last time, then?' Jack pulled up a screen that tracked the Hephaestus mech's path, speed, distance and position.

'Let's do it!' Megan shouted back. 'Give me a boost!' She backed up her mech and aimed it towards her falling friend. Cameron sprinted off in the opposite direction, and Jack crouched where he was.

'GO!' Jack shouted. Megan roared as she took off, pummelling the ground, building speed. The thrusters on her mech's back ignited. She closed in on Jack. The quadpistons in his mech's legs were primed and ready to fire. Planting her robot's foot in the purple dirt, Megan leaped into the air, landing squarely on tHeScOuRgE's shoulders. Jack dipped his WarMech under the weight, then fired the quadpistons, sending his robot springing up and using the momentum to launch Zuul off his back. The combined thrust sent the Zuul mech soaring upwards. Megan powered into the red sky, heading straight for Ayo's flight path. The WarMechs couldn't technically fly, so this was as close as they could get.

'I see him!' Megan yelled as she rocketed higher, tracking Ayo. 'Get ready, Cam!'

Inside his WarMech, Jack was willing them on. He knew that if Megan could intersect with Ayo's flight, she could push him off his course and take a big chunk out of his descent speed. Then Cameron would do the same. It would be up to Jack to take the final hit, slowing Ayo's mech enough to bring it down safely. It was like trying to hit a falling penny with a dart. Three times in a row.

'Five ... four ... three ...' Megan started counting, adjusting her WarMech's boosters as she closed in. Ayo's mech was falling fast, and she was still roaring towards it. 'Two ... ONE!'

The mechs collided in a mid-air shower of sparks. Jack watched the Zuul mech grab hold of Ayo's machine, directing it towards a horizontal flight path. This was Cameron's signal. Now, Megan would have to pass the robot off to Cameron mid-flight, like a relay baton. A ten-metre long, robotic relay baton, filled with explosives and bullets.

'Let's go, Cam!'

Jack was already crouched in the dirt, quadpistons recharged and primed. He watched as Cameron moved without hesitation – the sleek mech cutting a fierce shape across the arena. In a blur of mechanical movement and thruster fire, Cameron was in the air.

'C-c-coming in hot!' he shouted as he flew towards the mechs.

'I see you!' Megan replied. 'Watch the proximity warning. I'll release him at twenty metres.'

'G-got it!'

'Ready ... ready ... NOW!'

Megan released her grip and sent her mech into a

spinning barrel roll that pulled it off the flight path. For a moment, Ayo's mech became a sinking stone once more ...

'YES, CAM!' Jack yelled excitedly. Cameron had managed to boost his mech onto the perfect flight path. He gripped hold of Ayo's falling mech and pushed it onto an opposite course, taking another chunk out of its descent speed. Jack checked Cameron's trajectory and took up his position.

Numbers crashed around his brain. His max jump height. His take-off speed and boost velocity. His fuel levels and burn time. The speed and angle of Cameron's descent, and the time window between his release and Jack's grab. *This is the kind of maths they should be teaching at school*, Jack thought as he punched a metal toe into the ground and pushed off into a heavy sprint. *I've never needed Roman numerals to save my friend's life ...*

'I'm l-letting go!' Cameron shouted as he released the heavy mech and spun out sideways, leaving Ayo's machine falling through the air again. Thick dust from the Reaper Shell explosion trailed behind Ayo's robot, leaving a zigzag trace that led all the way back to the huge cloud above. Jack powered up to intersect the mech's path, igniting the quadpistons once more and exploding into the air. In moments, he was half a heartbeat away from collision.

'I'm coming for you, mate – just hang on ...'

Jack smashed into Ayo's mech, managing to grab hold of it. The dramatic shift in direction meant that their descent speed was now no faster than if they were coming off a regular boosted jump. Landing a boosted jump on your own was easy. Landing a boosted jump with another WarMech on your shoulders was not.

'YOU'VE GOT THIS, JACK!'

'YOU CAN D-D-DO IT!'

Jack wrangled and wrestled with the Hephaestus mech, manoeuvring as best he could, until the limp robot was draped across his shoulders. A proximity alert rang in his ears. His entire control pod flashed red – a warning that, in *Distant Dawn*, would have signalled low health, and likely imminent death. Jack diverted all power to his leg thrusters, then waited for the optimal moment to slam on the brakes as the purple ground raced up to meet him.

'JACK! AYO!'

'S-S-SPEAK TO US!'

The voices sounded like they were coming from the edge of a dream. Jack stirred where he lay; he felt thickness in his aching head.

'Come on, big guy. Let's get you out of here.'

Jack felt himself moving. He forced his eyes open. Between crimson blinks, he saw the purple dirt of the arena. He began to understand that he was lying, half-buried, in a very large crater of his own making. He lifted his lolling head, and through his pod window he could see his robot's long, scarred metal arms stretched out in front of him. One was in the grip of the Zuul mech, the other in the hands of ForgeFire666.

'Where – where is Ay-Ay-o?' Jack spluttered, tasting fresh blood in his mouth. He groaned as his machine was heaved over the brim of the crater and lowered onto the ground. The other two mechs collapsed in tired heaps on either side of him. The Zuul mech stretched out its graffitied arm, indicating to the side.

'AYO!'

The Hephaestus mech was sitting up in the dirt a few yards away, having also been dragged from its crater. It was peppered with burn marks and impacted plates, but it was in one piece. Through strained eyes, Jack could just about make out Ayo in the control pod. Blood stained the side of his face, and the left lens of his glasses was cracked. But Jack could also see a wide, grateful smile.

'Thanks, guys.'

Jack collapsed back into his seat, equal parts relieved and happy. He even considered sending his rocket-powered fist around the group to collect some congratulatory bumps, but he doubted they had the energy left.

'You'd have done it for us, Ayo,' Megan huffed, still catching her breath.

'Plus, you k-killed the sky-shark,' Cameron added.

'Yeah – you're right. We're even.'

Jack continued to grin inside his mech. For a moment, he forgot where they were. For a moment, it felt like a normal night playing *Distant Dawn*, with the infamous Raid Mob bathing in the exhausted glory of completing another elite mission. But this fleeting relief was obliterated by a single word.

'VERMIN!'

The Mob looked up – their attention drawn to a voice that seemed to come from the walls. They'd all been so busy fighting for their lives, they hadn't noticed that, all around them, the once still and stoic crowd were more than a little riled. Wings were flapping in agitation, and three-fingered hands began to rise up, curled into angry fists. Their leader's wizened, almost featureless face appeared as a giant hologram, projected above the slab of stone where the remains of _Carbon_Shift_ lay. The vestigial muscles beneath the surface of its wrinkled, grey skin twisted and knotted as it addressed the Mob.

'Your purpose was to perish! That is *all* you were brought here to do!'

Jack was stuck halfway between rage and disbelief. The creature was scolding them for *not dying*.

'Since you have proved ineffective in demonstrating humankind's combat weaknesses, you will be used to exhibit your race's *moral* flaws instead. Your dysfunctional, disloyal, selfish natures will be laid bare. And *then* you will die. All of you.'

If this was a game of *Distant Dawn*, Jack knew that it would be Megan's job as the mouthiest member of the Mob to respond to such talk. He could almost imagine her now: *'Come and have a go yourself, you wrinkly sack of crap – I've flushed bigger turds than you.'* But before any of them could speak, the four mechs collapsed. Inside, the pilots could not move; they had been paralysed again. All they could do was stare up at the stormy sky, until several flying machines hovered into view. Each heavy-duty alien drone lowered cables from its belly that hooked onto the WarMechs and dragged them towards a set of doors. The four robots, who minutes ago had been flying and battling and shooting and *winning*, bumped and thudded along as they were hauled unceremoniously across the ground.

From the corner of his eye, Jack saw the remains of the other elite fighters' machines, lying beside vanquished aliens from across the galaxy. So much death. And, as he was pulled into the darkness, Jack couldn't help but contemplate how much life the Mob could possibly have left to live.

Level 17: Group Therapy

'In paralysis, there is no pain. Enjoy it. It will not last.'

Ayo remembered his captor's first translated words. He wondered if the other members of the Mob had been fed the same lie. There *was* pain in forced numbness. The pain of helplessness. As such, when a dull ache began to throb on the side of his head, where his temple was still encrusted with dried blood, Ayo felt a sense of relief. The pain made him feel alive and in control again – things he no longer took for granted.

As the feeling seeped back into his aching limbs, Ayo started to shift his weight, orientating himself as best he could in the dark. He was lying on his back. His feet were still latched into his mech's leg controls. He felt like he might have twisted his left knee, and the fuzziness of a concussion lingered across his forehead, but he was alive. And, while he was alive, there was still a fight to be fought.

Level 17: Group Therapy

'Your dysfunctional, disloyal, selfish natures ...'

Ayo tried desperately to understand what the creature had said to them. The Raid Mob *was* built on dysfunction: Cameron's anxiety and his comfort eating; Megan's abrasive temperament – the shield she threw up around other girls to avoid the pain of developing unrequited feelings; Jack – the kid from the broken home, on the broken street, in the middle of the broken estate; and him, with a list of traits that would light up a test sheet for almost any social developmental disorder, if his parents ever let him take one. But *disloyal*? No way. The Raid Mob practically lived for each other. They were a family, where all those struggles were accepted and valued just as much as the skills that made them the greatest gaming team on the planet. If these things wanted to demonstrate disloyalty, they'd made a significant mistake in picking them.

Fumbling in the dark, Ayo found the edge of a control screen and tapped at it. Nothing. He flicked ignition switches and weapon selectors. No response. His mech had been completely disabled. Ayo sank down into his rig. He removed his glasses and wiped them on his shirt, then replaced them, straightening them meticulously even though he still couldn't see a thing through them in the pitch-black space. Then, taking a long, deep breath, he closed his eyes and focused on the images just *behind* his eyelids. He began scrolling through information in his mind, like a living computer. Mech schematics. Game programming. Console manuals. Patches and updates. Cheat codes. Everything Ayo knew about the dynamics of *Distant Dawn* flicked through his mind, until ...

The redundancy backup subsystems.

Ayo's eyes snapped open. Reaching forwards, he began feeling around beneath the main display panel. He was searching for a concealed panel, behind which lay a fuse board, and behind that ...

It didn't take Ayo more than five minutes to implement his solution, but by his standards, it was still too long, 'Is this on? Is it working now? I swear on Sun Tzu and the whole Han Dynasty, this alien tech can just fu–'

'AYO! AYO I CAN HEAR YOU!' Jack's excited voice came through loud and clear in the dark.

'Finally! You know, for an advanced race, their coding is so needlessly cumbersome,' said Ayo, still working away inside his mech, his face now lit up by the green glow of an active comms system. 'Give me a minute. I'm bringing everyone's comms online.'

Ayo continued to tap instructions into a keypad. One by one, he saw green orbs shine out in the darkness – the Mob's control pods bathed in an emerald hue that signalled their successful reconnection.

'Is everyone okay?' Ayo asked as he looked around the group. The mechs had been strewn haphazardly around a large, empty holding cell.

'I think we left "okay" behind when we got abducted, dude.' It was Megan. Ayo managed a smile at the sound of her voice.

'You remember the "game over" scene in *Aliens*?' she continued. 'The bit where Bill Paxton loses it and tries to put a six-year-old in charge of a marine rescue mission?'

'How could we forget?' replied Ayo. 'You've only made us watch it thirty-eight times. I've kept count.'

'Well, *that's* about where I am right now. Full *game over* mode. I mean, we beat their elite warriors. Doesn't that mean we win? Doesn't that mean we get to go home?'

'In films maybe,' Jack said. 'I keep thinking this must all be a dream. Like I'm gonna wake up and it'll all be done, and then I'll find you guys online and tell you about it.'

'I don't think we're gonna get the dream ending here, Jack,' Megan snorted. 'How you doing, Cam? You're being characteristically quiet. You holding up okay?'

There was no reply. Jack spoke up.

'Cameron? You all right, man? We're all scared – but we're here for each other.'

A low static crackle hissed over the comms channel, but no words followed.

Ayo struggled to supress his impatience. He needed to know that Cameron was okay. 'Just cough or something.'

Then came two very unexpected words.

'Miss Barrett.'

The quiet returned, but this time it was a stunned silence. The words were so deliberate, so clear and determinedly spoken, as if they had been rehearsed a hundred times.

'Miss Barrett?' Ayo repeated. 'What about her, Cam?'

'She s-s-saved me. Out there. She s-saved my l-l-life.'

Ayo didn't know what to say. There was no more room in his maxed-out mind to compute such an illogical response, and there were certainly no words in his stock empathy phrase bank that would do for this situation. Fortunately for him, Jack entered the chat.

'Miss Barrett is our *teacher*, Cam,' Jack offered, as gently as he could. 'She's not here. *We're* here for you though, aren't we?'

'Course we are, man! Raid Mobbin' forever!' Megan said, the worry evident beneath her forced enthusiasm.

'Miss B-B-B,' Cameron began, faltering at the name this time. Across the comms, Ayo heard him take a deep breath before he continued. 'Miss Barrett was The Devastator.'

The rest of the Mob was stunned back into silence again. Miss Barrett. *Miss Barrett*, their technophobic teacher, was Th£D£V@ST@T0R. Miss Barrett, the woman who once tried to set up a calligraphy club in school to, quote, "avoid the tragic death of penmanship" was Th£D£V@ST@T0R – a world-renowned, elite gamer. The probability that half of the global *Distant Dawn* Top Ten sat in the same school room every day and didn't realise it was so unlikely, the rest of the Mob simply couldn't believe it.

'Cameron,' Ayo began. 'Miss Barrett? Are you sur–'

'SHE SAVED ME!' Cameron shouted, fiery emotion flooding the comms channel. 'She s-saved me – just like she always d-d-did. It was h-h-her. She s-saved me and she s-spoke to m-me, and those m-monsters k-k-killed her. If she h-hadn't been h-helping me, she'd s-still be alive.'

Ayo didn't know what to say, and it seemed as though Jack and Megan didn't either. What he did know, however, was that as implausible as Cameron's revelations seemed, they must somehow be true. Ayo knew Cameron through and through, and he wasn't a liar. And if that was the case, then Cameron's distress was not being caused by the surprise presence of his teacher, but by her loss – and the guilt that came with it if losing her life had saved his.

'Six people have died, Cam,' Jack began. 'Seven, if we assume Carbon Shift went the same way. And not one of those deaths – not a *single* one – was the fault of a human. We're all fighting for our lives here. We could have lost Ayo today. But we didn't. Whatever these scumbags have in store for us, we will war against it, like we always do. And when we beat them you can carve Miss Barrett's name into their gravestones ...'

A series of sniffles sounded across the comms.

'Thanks, J-J-Jack,' Cameron managed eventually.

'Miss Barrett, eh?' Megan chimed in, clearly doing

her best to lighten the mood slightly. 'Now that's a commitment to anonymity that puts even you to shame, Ayo.'

'Hugely impressive,' remarked Ayo – and he meant it. He was genuinely amazed. It took a lot to shift him from his customary neutral disposition, but the Barrett revelation had managed it. 'She led a complete double life. With that level of dedication, it's actually not that surprising that she was Top Ten material. And I must say, I *did* find it suspicious when she was absent on the same day that the RealFeel sets were released.'

'Ahh give over! You never had the faintest idea!' said Megan. 'All I know is, that woman just went from hellspawn to hero in my book. The Devastator was *legit*.'

'The w-w-weirdest thing was, I s-saw her die,' said Cameron. 'But w-when I went back to h-her mech, she w-w-wasn't there.'

Just as Ayo was beginning to get a handle on the situation, this extra revelation sent the Mob back into a state of stunned silence.

'Do you think she escaped?' asked Ayo finally.

'No. Not p-p-possible. Her injury was too – too – t-too–'

'Let's not focus on that right now,' Jack cut in before Cameron could get too upset. 'We can't undo what happened, but we can make sure no one else suffers the same fate. Could *we* escape? You've got the comms working again, Ayo – could you activate the escape handles?'

'Erm, why would we want to get *out* of our armoured machines, Jack?' asked Megan. 'Until we know what's coming, I'm kind of okay with being surrounded by metal.'

'Metal that *they* control,' Jack shot back. 'Metal that they can use to paralyse us whenever they please. It'd be different if we were in charge, but surely it's better to be on the outside of what is basically a prison cell on legs?'

'I'm working on that,' Ayo said, in his way-calmer-than-he-should-be-for-the-situation tone. 'I'm trying to find the control subroutines for the mechs, but there's so little order to their programming. One minute I'm in the directory for the comms system, the next I'm in the programs they use to control refuse drones. I could have a few rubbish-bots bring us some recycling if you'd like?'

'Keep digging, man,' said Megan.

'Grounds maintenance? Would that be useful? Because that's actually where I am right now.' Ayo frowned, the confused code reflecting off his broken glasses. 'This system is just atrocious. Wait ... now I'm on their military sub-server.'

'Anything juicy?' asked Megan.

'Weapons inventories. Ship schematics. Looks like they're producing two classes of vessel – those big dropships and some smaller, scouting crafts. They're getting close to their construction target.'

'How close?' asked Jack.

'96% complete.'

'Ayo?' said Jack.

'Yeah?'

'Find us a way to get control of our goddamn mechs, will you?'

Ayo didn't respond – he was too busy tearing through the alien subsystems. He'd already assimilated their code structure, and now he was bearing down on the needle in the extra-terrestrial haystack that would unlock all the pointy parts of their mechs.

'We need to turn this abduction into an all-out assault,' Jack mused. 'The people on Earth have no idea what's coming. We need to stop those ships from leaving this planet. If we get control of our mechs, we can do to this place what we did to the Nograki stronghold on Arkelios-7. You guys remember that?'

'Yeah,' Megan replied flatly, 'and once we've finished, we can pick up a slingshot and some pebbles and go to hell to beat up the devil! Come on, man – I'm always down for a ruck, but we're not in a computer game anymore. We're on *their* planet. *Survival* is the aim, plain and simple.'

'Survival for what?' said Jack. 'If we continue to play the game by their rules, then–'

'WE AREN'T PLAYING! THIS ISN'T A GAME, JACK!' Megan shouted, her voice suddenly cracking. 'I know you struggle to see the difference, but this is *real*. People are dying. People that we know. *We* could die.'

Ayo's frantic tapping slowed to a stop at the sound of this outburst. He didn't need to see Megan's face to know that she was genuinely upset – something she rarely, if ever, allowed herself to be in front of anyone. Even them.

'I'm sorry, Meg,' said Jack eventually. 'It's just – I just hate these things. I want to go home. I miss my brother, and I can't bear to think about what'll happen to him if they get to Earth.'

Megan sighed over the comms. It sounded like she was trying to breathe out the anguish before she spoke.

'I get it, man,' she said. 'As annoying as my parents are, I can't stop thinking about them. I want to get home too. I want to protect my family. But we can't do anything if we're dead, which we will be if we go all Arkelios-7 on these freaks. We need to bide our time – give Hackerman over there a chance to work his magic. And, if worse comes to worst, I'll be right by your side, blasting until the barrels are empty. You know that.'

'Mm-mmm-me too,' said Cameron.

'Thank-you,' said Jack.

'Well,' Ayo said, firing a few final commands into a keypad, 'if you've all quite finished your group therapy session, I think I might have found something ... It's a *total* mess in here, but I think I've located the right directories that will allow me t–'

Ayo's speech was cut off by the grating creak of the doors opening again. Several beams of light shone through the entrance, searching the space. They quickly settled on Ayo's machine.

'Ayo! Ayo, what's going on?' Jack shouted.

'I – err – I don't know.' Ayo began tapping furiously at the control pad as four drones hovered into view. Each released a cable that clinked as it attached to his mech. With a synchronised pull, the drones lifted Hephaestus off the ground. Purple dust and detonation ash tumbled from the mech's limbs as it was carried out like an injured athlete ... only Ayo's machine was being *returned* to the field of play.

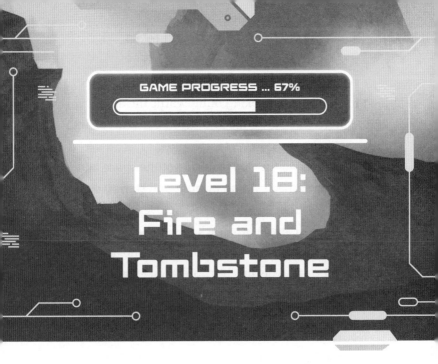

Level 18: Fire and Tombstone

Moments after Ayo and Hephaestus were taken, the remaining mechs' systems started to come back online. Jack looked all around his control pod as screens blinked into life. He grabbed hold of the control grips and twisted his body, testing the movement of his machine, rocking it up onto its side. Once there, he saw the Zuul and ForgeFire666 mechs moving too. Ignoring the pain in his ribs and head, Jack pushed his mech up onto its arms, dragged its feet underneath its body, and heaved himself upwards until tHeScOuRgE was back on its own two feet.

'Are you all right?' he said to Megan as his robot took hold of hers, grabbing it by its outstretched arm and helping it up.

'Ask me again when we get out *there*,' she replied. Megan was already looking out towards the arena, where there was now a mech-shaped path carved into the purple dirt.

Jack glanced to the opposite side of the space and saw Cameron's mech sitting upright and staring out in the same direction. Sliding his thumb over the weapon selector on the control grip, Jack pulled up his favourite railgun from his inventory and pushed it into an empty slot. Then he lifted his mech's right arm, expecting the weapon to appear from the recess on the top. It did not.

'Anybody's weapons systems working?' he asked.

'Nothing,' said Megan.

'N-nope,' said Cameron.

'Another fair fight then,' said Jack, returning his mech's arm to its side.

'W-W-Whatever is out th-there, we face it together,' said Cameron, taking a firm step forwards.

'Together,' said Megan.

'Together,' repeated Jack.

They followed a path out of the cell and into the arena, where they were met by the hostile alien crowd. The fevered hum of their beating wings vibrated through Jack's mech and crawled over his skin. The path led towards the far wall of the arena, ending at the stone upon which the remains of _Carbon_Shift_ still lay. Behind that stood an elevated platform that looked like a stage.

Level 18: Fire and Tombstone

Jack scanned the arena. No sign of any waiting enemies. No sign of the remains of the other mechs, either, aside from the mangled mess of _Carbon_Shift_. And, most gut-wrenchingly, no sign of Ayo.

'W-W-What are they g-going to do to us?' Cameron stuttered.

'I don't know,' Jack said slowly. 'Keep your head up. Don't show them fear – that's what they want.'

Jack knew that these things had dragged them across the stars to make a spectacle of the weakness of humans. If they didn't show any, then regardless of their fate, they'd have beaten their captors.

'Well, they won't be getting a drop of fear from me,' said Megan defiantly. She took the lead, suddenly storming up the path towards a ramp that led to the platform. As the trio made their way past the remains of _Carbon_Shift_, Jack remembered how the player behind the mech had disappeared mid-game the night when they'd all been booted off *Distant Dawn*. He remembered how the footage from the stream, which hinted at some kind of abduction or kidnapping, had been dismissed the next day as a prank or a publicity stunt done for clicks and views. He baulked at the idea that this player, this human, had actually been *here* – facing a gruesome fate all by himself. In the midst of his own awful situation, for a brief moment Jack felt lucky. He was lucky to be there with his friends, walking united up that ramp, all determined to face their foe head on – to survive and to reunite with their missing teammate. As unthinkable as it might have seemed before Jack had laid eyes on the crumpled remains of the _Carbon_Shift_ WarMech, he realised that his situation could actually have been a whole lot worse.

Then his situation got a whole lot worse.

As the mechs stood on the platform, facing outwards towards the crowd, Jack found his machine immobilised. Only the comms system remained active. On the other side of the arena, a second platform began rising slowly from beneath the ground – and atop this platform was the Hephaestus mech.

Its entire lower half had been encased in what looked like a concrete cage, trapping the mech in one spot, but leaving its top half free to move. And that top half was armed. Hephaestus was carrying a weapon that Jack recognised from a specialist mode on *Distant Dawn* called "CanniBallistic Combat". This mode enabled players to engage in mech-on-mech death matches, where if you destroyed another WarMech you gained all its upgrades, skins and points. They were risky, and usually played by only the most desperate or the most reckless players. Ayo's mech had been fitted with a long-barrelled, hyper-fuelled, top-of-the-line weapon from the CanniBallistic Combat catalogue. Its official designation was the "X-13 Anti-Mech Railgun", but the *Distant Dawn* community affectionately called it "The Tombstone".

X-13 Anti-Mech Railgun

Scope with Enhanced
Microelectronic Sensor

10-Stack Plasma Core

R.I.P

Reinforced Conducting
Rails with Sub-Shock Guards

WarMech-Piercing Rounds

This pumped-up bringer of doom comes
exclusively from *Distant Dawn*'s CanniBallistic
Combat catalogue. It can only be used for
mech-on-mech warfare, and its reputation for
putting even the biggest WarMechs on the ground
has led to it being known as "The Tombstone".

It was a gun specifically designed to destroy even the toughest WarMech.

'Ayo! Are you okay?' Jack shouted up. There was no response.

'AYO!' Megan yelled. 'Are you in there? Give us a wave – preferably not with your Tombstone arm.'

Still nothing. Jack couldn't tell if Ayo was inside his machine; he tried to draw up a magnifying screen, but all his displays had been disabled. Then, before he could speak again, another voice cut him off. It came from beside Ayo's mech. The hologram of the alien leader had returned.

'You were brought here to die,' it began, buried musculature pulling its blank face into a wrinkled mask of barely hidden revulsion. 'You failed. Now you will be exterminated by the hand of one of your own.'

It was at that moment Jack knew Ayo *was* inside his machine, because the Hephaestus mech jolted at this shock announcement. It looked more able to move than the other mechs, if only fractionally, and it was warring against its forced limitations.

The creature continued. 'The history of your pitiable planet is steeped in blood, spilled by your own kind. As a species, you barely need an excuse to kill each other. Hate, fear, jealousy, greed, territorialism: you kill for anything. Your bonds are so easily broken, and your spirits along with them. That is why, within the next five of your Earth minutes, this human, "Ayomikun", is going to execute each and every one of you.'

Jack turned inside his control pod, looking at Megan and Cameron.

'No way! There's no way! Ayo's not gonna kill *us*! No way!' spluttered Megan.

'He c-c-cou–, he c-c-cou–, he won't!'

'Of course he won't,' Jack replied. 'Nothing could make him do that to u–'

Jack was interrupted by the appearance of another hologram on the opposite side of Ayo's machine where it struggled to free itself. What it showed stunned all three of them into silence. It was an image of Ayo's parents.

The two of them were sitting in the living room of Ayo's house. His dad was on the couch, and his mum was sitting in a tall armchair, both of them with computers on their laps. Jack watched Ayo's dad take occasional sips of tea from a grey china cup, while Ayo's mum never so much as glanced up from her screen as she worked. It wasn't an uncommon scene in the ever-industrious Osikoya-Arinola household, but it was one that the Mob hadn't expected to see from across space. As Jack watched, he realised where the image was coming from. He knew that in that living room, standing in front of the couch and the armchair, there was a TV: a TV with a built-in camera for motion capture and webcam chat. The aliens had activated that camera and hacked the feed.

Before this realisation had time to sink in, the

holographic image shifted. It split in two, displaying a close-up of Ayo's parents, one on either side. These were the feeds from the laptop cameras. They both tapped away, oblivious. Ayo's dad's teacup hovered into view every now and then. His mum's face crumpled as she read something she didn't like.

'You can stop what is about to happen at any time, Ayomikun. You know what you have to do.'

Suddenly, both of Ayo's parents' faces contorted in shock, expelling shrieks of panic. They disappeared as the holographic images span and tumbled, coming to a violent halt and showing only floor, furniture legs, and frantic feet. Jack recognised that they had both simultaneously dropped, or maybe even thrown down, their computers. As the holographic feed switched back to the TV camera view, he could see why. Both laptops had caught fire.

The Mob watched as Ayo's dad batted at his laptop with a sofa cushion, while his mum ran to fetch a pair of oven gloves to pat out the flames. Mr and Mrs Osikoya-Arinola's baffled and increasingly panicked exclamations rattled around the arena and into the Mob's ears. As they fought to extinguish the flames, Jack saw a smart speaker on the back wall catch fire.

The realisation of what was happening felt like a punch to the gut. Just like the laptops, the smart speaker was under alien control. Somehow, they'd created a power surge that blew the batteries. As smoke began to creep across the room, the pair finally made a run for it out into the hall and towards the front door.

They're going to be okay, thought Jack. Ayo's parents would get out of the house, they would be safe, and Ayo certainly wouldn't off his best friends over a fire-damaged living room. Jack was almost on the verge of laughing at the aliens' second failed scheme, until he saw Ayo's parents returning to the living room.

'What the hell are you doing!' yelled Megan. 'Get out!'

'The doors are locked,' said Jack, emptily. 'So are the windows.' The words tumbled from his mouth as though they had life of their own. The locks on the doors and windows were electronic. The Osikoya-Arinolas had them installed, along with security cameras and window shutters, so they could check on the safety of their house when they were away on business. The Mob used to joke that Ayo lived in a prison when his parents were away. Now it was Ayo's parents who were trapped.

'There are eighteen more devices under our control,' said the alien leader. Its wrinkled face now twisted into a half-veiled expression of pleasure. 'We will ignite one more every thirty seconds. We will unlock the front door when you do what you have been brought here to do, Ayomikun.'

The Hephaestus mech had stopped struggling against its restraints. Beside it, the holographic display, which was now fogged with smoke, showed Ayo's dad reaching for a dining chair and dragging it towards the front

window. He lifted the chair, but before he could throw
it, the shutters slammed down. They were heavy-duty:
designed to keep thieves out. They were so impenetrable
they even blocked sunlight. The space was lit only by fire
now; the back of the room was wallpapered with flames,
fuelled further by an electronic picture frame that had
caught fire and was now spitting sparks into the blaze.

The Mob watched Ayo watching his parents, who
were crouching down and holding each other as the
thick, choking smoke that had slowly filled the room
began to descend on them. They watched Ayo watching
his parents, who were slowly dying in front of his eyes.
And then they watched Ayo raise his robot's arm and
point the Tombstone weapon straight at them.

'Ayo ... Ayo don't do this.' The bone-chilling fear
of staring down the barrels of a gun engulfed Jack's
concern for the panicked screams and choked coughs
that echoed around the arena. As the volume from the
feed increased, Jack saw the barrel of the Tombstone
weapon shaking in response. The Hephaestus mech
turned its head, as if it couldn't watch the actions of its
own pilot.

'Ayo – please,' Jack started – but a final, desperate cry
from Ayo's mum was all it took. The Tombstone erupted.
A burning projectile screamed across the arena. Jack
closed his eyes. The explosion was massive. The world
inside his head went black, and a cacophonous ringing
trilled through his skull. But, after a long moment had

passed, he opened his eyes. He was okay. He looked across at Hephaestus; the Tombstone hung loose by its side. The barrels glowed green, smoke rising into the air. But Jack was still standing.

'MMMM-MM-MEGAN!'

Jack looked down. The Zuul mech lay motionless on the ground beside him. The torso had been engulfed by green fire. Jack couldn't see the control pod for the flames. He tried to move, tried to help his friend, but his machine wouldn't respond. By the time he looked back across the arena through eyes brimming with tears, the Hephaestus mech had raised its arm again, and had taken aim at Cameron's mech.

'DON'T DO IT, AYO!' Jack screamed.

Beside Ayo's machine, the hologram showed his mum cradling his dad, covering her face against the thickening smoke. Ayo's dad wasn't moving.

'PLEA–'

Jack's appeal was shattered by the sound of the Tombstone discharging for a second time. Jack caught a glimpse of Cameron's terrified face before the ForgeFire666 mech was hit by a near-deafening emerald explosion.

'NOOO!' Jack screamed, clawing at his control pod window. He pressed his face to the edge of the glass and saw Cameron's mech ablaze in green flames, limbs twisted and scorched. He reached up and started tugging at the escape hatch release – not knowing what he would do if he managed to get out. When the handle did nothing, he returned to the window and banged on the glass, bitter tears tumbling down his cheeks.

The hologram showed Ayo's mum and dad lying in a crumpled heap on the floor of their burning living room. His mum was still moving – barely. The fire had spread across the walls. Both the couch and the armchair were aflame. Their time was almost up ... which meant Jack's was done.

'Ayo – please. We can find a way ...' Jack started, pressing his hands against the glass and imploring his friend to stop. Then he heard it – the sound he'd assumed had been cut off from him and the rest of the Mob.

He heard Ayo's voice.

'Sorry, Jack. There's no other way.'

The Hephaestus mech raised its arm. Jack stared straight down the barrels of the Tombstone. There was an explosion. The world went green – then black.

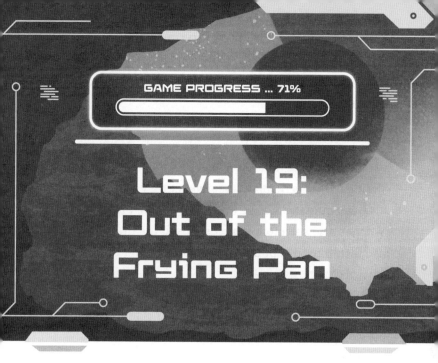

Level 19:
Out of the
Frying Pan

The sound of water bubbling came from somewhere in the hazy distance. Even to ears that still rang with explosions, the gurgling sound was very clearly not the froth of some peaceful stream. The pops and splutters sounded as if they came from a spitting volcano. It was hot, too. And the weight didn't help either; the dense pressure from above inducing the fear of being buried.

A lake of fire. The feeling of being entombed. If this was the afterlife, it didn't feel like the *Good Place*.

But was Hell supposed to be *green*?

When he finally opened his eyes, that's all Jack could see. His vision was so blurred that the world was just a wash of fuzzy green shapes. However, as he lay there – wherever *there* was – he realised one very important thing.

He was alive.

As his surroundings became clearer, Jack saw that he was still inside his WarMech. The green light was coming from his display screens; not only was Jack alive, his mech was alive too. All the dials, displays, switches and selectors that comprised the interior of his mech's control pod were on, uninhibited by alien constraints.

Jack's pod window was coated in a thick layer of green sludge. Jack activated the wiping blade, spraying it with a power decontaminant at the same time. It was a decision he instantly came to regret.

A decapitated alien head was staring right at him, looking through the only one of five eyeballs that remained in its socket. Two had been gauged out, and the other two were dangling by long, stringy red veins, smushed into ovals against Jack's pod window. The alien still wore the expression that had been etched into its face at the moment of its death. Its mouth hung open, revealing a row of irregular yellow teeth shoved haphazardly into rotting green gums, and its nose, with its three separate nostrils, was pushed up against the glass. The rest of Jack's view screen was completely covered with body parts: torn off legs and arms, chunks of skin and fragments of broken bones, plus a whole host of other parts that he didn't recognise. Jack now knew the reason he felt like he'd been buried. He had been. He was in a mass grave.

Jack took hold of both the control grips, jammed his feet into the leg holsters and began to move his mech. He dragged the arms across the front of his machine, trying to clear his view and create a path. The problem was that each swipe only caused a fresh and equally disgusting batch of alien body parts to tumble down over his mech. Instead, Jack tried stretching the arms out ahead of him and sweeping from the middle outwards, while kicking the legs against the biological mulch that lay underneath him. Jack swam his machine up through the death pile, thrashing and kicking past bones, flesh and blood until, with a final heave, he broke the surface.

He wasn't in Hell, but where he was didn't seem all that much better.

Jack found himself in what looked like a giant hangar, sitting on top of a pile of alien remains that formed the bank of a boiling river filled with liquid metal. This silver stream flowed down the centre of the space, popping and fizzing, each bursting bubble producing a shower of sparks. Looking closer, Jack saw that the edges of the stream were electrified – the liquid metal was being charged with the same energy that flowed throughout the alien city. Jack followed the direction of the stream and saw that it disappeared around a dark meander about a hundred metres away. Then, glancing back, Jack saw the source of the stream – a source that explained the immense heat as well as the grim purpose of the death pile.

A vast furnace was burning at the far end of the hangar. It was lined with portholes that glowed white-hot, and exhaust ports that spat thick plumes of red gas. On either side of the furnace there were two vast funnels. The one on the left attached at the top and was being fed a constant stream of scrap metal by the same drone-like machines that had dragged the mechs from the arena. What was happening in the funnel on the right-hand side of the furnace was a rather grizzlier affair. It was fitted lower down the structure, its contents feeding the fire at the base of the furnace. Instead of scrap metal, this funnel was being filled with leftover body parts. As if the humiliation of defeat wasn't enough, the remains of these poor vanquished lifeforms were being burned to fuel the aliens' metal factory. Jack was trying to process this level of diabolical when, from the corner of his eye, he saw movement on the opposite body-filled bank of the river. Something else had survived. Something *inhuman*.

Jack struggled for grip as he pushed back against loose skulls and squelchy flesh, drawing his robot's right arm up so that a grenade-launcher popped out like a nuke-fuelled jack-in-the-box. He aimed at the shifting body parts with his finger hovering over the trigger. He watched as a giant head rose up from the death pile. A pair of beady eyes shone red in the darkness, set deep beneath a heavy brow. A brim of brilliant yellow spikes encircled the creature's head like a grotesque crown.

'It smells worse than the inside of a tauntaun in here!'

For a split second, the *Star Wars* reference caught Jack completely off guard. Then –

'MEGAN! Meg, is that you?'

'Jack? Jack! Where are you?'

The alien head turned quizzically. Jack realised that Megan's mech was buried beneath it.

'Keep pushing up!'

'I'm trying!' Megan's voice sounded. 'I can't see a thing!'

Jack saw the Zuul mech's arms, plastered with graffiti, gaming logos, and the blood of a hundred different aliens, emerging slowly from the sludge. With what looked like considerable effort, Megan finally managed to shove off the decapitated alien head. Jack beamed as his friend's robot rose from the death pile.

'WHAT IN THE NAME OF LUKE SKYWALKER'S LOST HAND IS GOING ON?' Megan yelled. 'I thought we were dead! What *is* this place? What is *that* thing!' she spat, pointing her mech's arm at the furnace. 'And *that*!' she added, pointing towards the molten metal river. 'How are we *alive*? And WHY THE HELL AM I SITTING IN A POOL OF DEAD ALIENS?'

'I thought we were dead too,' Jack replied. 'Ayo was supposed to kill us – maybe he thinks he did. I don't think we'd be down here unless they thought we were dead.'

'Where's "down here"?' Megan asked, struggling to free the bottom half of her mech from the sludge. 'And where's Cameron? He up to his wig in alien guts somewhere around here too?'

'I don't know,' said Jack. 'I haven't spotted any other movement yet. We can search for him once you get yourself out. As for this place, it's a factory, a recycling plant, and a crematorium,' he added, indicating the furnace. 'Scrap material goes in the top, dead alien parts get burned at the bottom, and the molten metal that comes out is electrically charged,' he said, pointing down the length of the river. 'I reckon it's the metal that they're using to make their ships.'

'Wow. You seem to know a lot about our current, insane predicament,' huffed Megan, finally freeing her robot.

'I've been awake a bit longer than you. Plus, I paid attention during the tour. I've seen the dropship assembly line. I think it's close by.'

'Oh yeah? I was a bit too busy getting tortured, almost to death, to take in the sights,' said Megan. 'So, what d'you think they've got planned for us now?'

'The top funnel for our mechs and the bottom one for us,' said Jack. 'There is some good news, though.'

'Well, we are overdue,' Megan replied with a chuckle of minor relief. 'Lay it on me, bro.'

'Activate your display screens.'

After a long pause, weapons began popping out all

over Megan's mech. Cavities in the arms, shoulders and torso opened, revealing a plethora of offensive tech.

'Are you thinking what I'm thinking?' said Megan, her words already dripping with vengeance.

'I'm thinking that I know what you're thinking, and I'm thinking that too, but not yet. First of all, we need to find the rest of the Mob.'

'There's only *one* other member as far as I'm concerned,' Megan replied, staring vindictively at the cannons on her mech's forearms. 'If I see that scrawny, disloyal, backstabbing turdmudgeon – he's toast.'

'I don't think Ayo tried to kill us,' said Jack. 'If he had – if he'd *really* tried, we'd be talking to each other at the pearly gates right now. I think there's something else going on.'

'I'm literally sat on top of a pile of death.'

'You're alive, aren't you?' Jack replied.

'Maybe Ayo missed his shots,' huffed Megan dismissively.

'Come on, Meg,' Jack replied. 'How many times have you seen the camper miss? He was supposed to execute us, yet here we are. I saw you and Cam both covered in flames – the hit from the Tombstone should have ended you. But look at your mech! Look at mine!'

The Zuul mech tilted as Megan leaned forwards, her face appearing at the control pod window, inspecting her WarMech.

'There's no damage,' she said.

'I know,' replied Jack. 'There's just this weird green residue.'

'But we were completely KO'd, and our mechs were bricked,' said Megan, scraping up the green goop and inspecting it. 'Who, or what, brought us back online?'

Jack didn't know. He replayed the last moments in the arena. Flashes of Ayo's parents. The Tombstone pointing at him. Ayo's last words.

There's no other way ...

Before this train of thought could reach the station, it was derailed by the arrival of five drones hovering down through gaps in the ceiling. Cables shot out and pulled taut, struggling to heave a hefty object from the death pile. It was covered in alien entrails and slime – but even so, Jack and Megan recognised the drones' cargo immediately.

'CAMERON!' they shouted in unison, scrambling against the ever-shifting pile of remains in an attempt to get closer to their friend's WarMech. It was hard to get a foot or handhold, but the two mechs managed to drag themselves slowly upstream.

'We're coming, buddy! Just hang on!'

Jack didn't know what state Cameron or his mech were in. He assumed unconscious for the former – otherwise Cameron would have shouted for help already – but he didn't know whether the ForgeFire666 mech was dead as DVD, or combat ready. He saw Megan's mech making good progress, moving faster than he was. But Cameron's mech was on *Jack's* side of the molten metal river. He felt a tug of war coming on, and he'd need Megan to help stack the odds in his favour.

'Meg! Pull up and start shooting! I'll grab Cam!'

Megan didn't need telling twice. Projectiles tore through two drones before they'd even realised they were being attacked. The remaining three took evasive action while heaving their load towards the furnace. The machines had already managed to unearth Cameron's mech, which was now lying on its front. The metal limbs were limp; the whole body was deadweight.

'I've got you, mate!' Jack lunged forwards and grabbed the ForgeFire666 mech's left arm and leg. But the more Jack pulled against the straining drones, the deeper he sank back into the pile. And the drones were canny – they shifted quickly, using Jack's mech as cover while pulling in the opposite direction.

'Move, will you! I can't shoot *around* you!' shouted Megan, having been forced into ceasefire.

'I'm a bit – stuck – right – now!' Jack strained. The drones had managed to get Cameron's mech on its side, and Jack could see through the pod window that the robot was still offline. It was just Cameron inside, lying limp and unresponsive.

'I'm gonna get you out of there!' Jack shouted. But as the last word left his mouth, Jack lost his grip on the slime-covered mech. tHeScOuRgE fell backwards, sending a foul wave of rotten flesh into the air as it splashed down into the death pile. The drones pulled hard, staying low. They used the uncovered mass of Cameron's mech for cover, once again forcing Megan to stop shooting. Jack could hear ForgeFire666 being hauled closer to the blazing furnace.

Then, one by one, the flying machines exploded.

Jack watched as the last grappling lines were severed, and Cameron's mech fell back into the decomposing mulch. He saw lights illuminate the interior of the control pod, he heard joints creak into motion, and finally, he watched the robot's arm rise up from the bed of remains – until, with an outstretched finger, it managed to draw Jack's attention towards the roof of the hangar. There, suspended from the grappling lines of two more drones, was an astonishing figure: the Hephaestus mech.

Megan raised her weapons. Jack wasn't sure if she was planning to shoot the drones or the mech, but before she did either a voice called out.

'Please don't. It's hard enough to control two of these drones *and* shoot three others *and* reprogram Cam's mech all at the same time ...'

Emerging from the slime, the ForgeFire666 mech rolled over onto its elbow. Cameron was alive and awake – and yet, he said nothing. He merely joined the other two Mob members in gobsmacked silence as they watched Ayo's machine descend. None of them said a word, not even when the grey WarMech touched down and the drones carrying it simultaneously dropped out of the air, instantly deactivated.

'Ewww.'

The Hephaestus mech raised a foot. Strings of biological waste clung to the base like melted cheese on a slice of pizza.

'Well, that's gross. How are we all? As well as can be expected?'

Jack was dumbfounded. There were too many concepts to deal with all at once. He, Megan and Cameron were alive. Their mechs worked. Ayo hadn't killed them. Ayo was alive. Ayo seemed to be in control of both their robots *and* the enemy drones. Clearly, Ayo knew more than they did. He managed to blurt out, 'What the hell is going on, Ayo?'

'Well, I'm sure you've worked out at least a few things,' Ayo replied in his usual abnormally calm way, all while struggling to keep his footing. 'Most importantly, you aren't dead.'

'But you sh-sh-shot us!' Cameron managed, finding his voice.

'I did – sorry about that. However, if I'd used the ammo they wanted me to, you'd have plenty more to complain about than a coating of incendiary residue. Except you wouldn't. Because you'd be dead.'

'You swapped out the ammo?' Jack echoed. 'But we were all knocked out?'

'You would not believe the extra functions they've built into our mechs,' Ayo continued matter-of-factly. 'Well, maybe you would, because they are horrible aliens bent on the destruction of humanity. These suits can electrify us, poison us, *and* render us unconscious. It's grossly unpleasant when they do it, but it came in quite handy when I needed it.'

'But you sh-shot us!' Cameron repeated, still clearly scarred.

'With what amounts to a *firework*,' Ayo replied sharply, his patience clearly wearing thin. 'Then I put you to sleep, intent on reviving you when I'd managed to escape. I can only apologise for your current surroundings. I assumed they'd leave us in the arena and we'd make our escape after they left ...'

'Escape?' said Megan, lowering her weapons – her mistrust seemingly giving way to confusion.

'Of course. That's still the plan, isn't it? Going back to our families and such?'

There was another silence. This time it wasn't one of bewilderment or disbelief, but of sadness. Jack watched as Ayo tramped around obliviously in the death pile. Eventually, Jack managed to push out four very difficult words.

'What about ... your parents?'

Ayo wiggled an alien's scaly arm off the top of his mech's foot.

'Huh? My parents?'

Jack hesitated ... but Megan wasn't so tactful.

'They're dead, Ayo.'

Without even pausing, Ayo simply replied, 'No they aren't.'

Jack could feel the desperation rising in his throat.

'We saw them, Ayo. They died at your house. Those things, they caused a fire and–'

'You saw what they *wanted* you to see, Jack,' said Ayo. 'You didn't see what *I* saw. What *they* missed. My parents are not dead.'

'How do you know that?' asked Megan, sounding frustrated at her lack of grip on a situation that Ayo seemed to understand so clearly.

'Three reasons,' he announced. 'One, the picture frame that caught fire. Mum broke it last week. Smashed it to pieces. Two, my dad's bowtie. He wears a bowtie once a week, when he lectures to the undergraduates. He thinks it makes him look trendy. He lectures on a Friday. Today is Tuesday. Three, the oven gloves. There are no oven gloves in our house. We don't live in Victorian times. We have a single rubber heat-proof mitt. Not much use as a fire extinguisher. But then, the aliens wouldn't have known that because there are *no cameras in the kitchen.*'

'So where did that footage come from, then?' said Megan, still almost as confused as she was angry.

'They *made* it,' huffed Ayo, frustrated that the rest of the Mob hadn't caught up yet. 'They stitched it together from images captured around our home – a few days ago, by the looks of things. And where they were missing information – like the oven gloves – they improvised and assumed we wouldn't notice.'

'You really th-think they could d-do that?'

Ayo snorted. 'They are an advanced race who have perfected interstellar flight. They have built real versions of our mechs. They have, according to their leader, infiltrated Earth's computer systems at the highest levels. Do I think they could map stolen images over wireframe computer models and throw together some grainy footage for a five-minute hologram clip? I think they could have shown us an alien spaceship blowing up the White House with E.T. flying off in the pilot seat if they'd wanted. I think they found the task *so* easy, in fact, that they forgot to check the details, or assumed we wouldn't spot the inconsistencies because we'd all be distracted and unfocused.'

Jack almost laughed at the idea of Ayo being unfocused. The aliens had picked the wrong audience for a sloppy production.

'I still can't believe you noticed those tiny details in the middle of all that madness,' he said.

'My ability to fixate on things that others barely notice came in handy at just the right moment,' Ayo shrugged.

'Sounds like a superpower to me,' Jack smiled.

'I'd rather have adamantium claws,' Ayo replied flatly. 'The point is, it was fake. And as soon as I knew it was fake, I concentrated on the task I'd started in the holding cell: getting control of our mechs, starting with my own.'

'So that's how you were able to swap out the ammo and activate the tranquilisers,' said Jack. The ForgeFire666 WarMech's head shook in disbelief, mimicking its pilot, and an impressed chuckle sounded from the direction of Megan's now much more relaxed mech.

'Well done, Watson, you got there eventually. Now, considering that you were all consigned to this revolting scrap pile, plus the fact that they dumped me here too – alive but immobilised, quite unsporting really – I think it's safe to assume that they think we're dead. Which means we are finally free to get on with it,' said Ayo. As he spoke he began to move, traipsing his mech through the rot and heading determinedly towards the meander in the river of metal.

'G-get on with w-w-hat?' asked Cameron, scrambling in the muck to bring his mech to its feet.

'Getting the hell out of here,' said Megan.

Level 20: In the Midst of Chaos

Cameron followed his teammates, lumbering unsteadily through the death pile, still trying to shake off the grogginess of the tranquilizer. His mech's legs felt heavier than ever as he dragged them up out of the rotting mulch and planted them down again. It was like walking through a bog in metal wellies. The sweat of exertion and heat dripped onto the control pod window as Cameron looked down at his WarMech's legs, heaving them towards a place where the liquid metal disappeared over a precipice like a mercury waterfall. When he finally reached the edge of the opening – a rounded cavity dug out of a cliff face – the relief and horror struck him in equal measures. The sudden coolness pushing a shiver up his already chilled spine.

'I saw this,' said Jack, as the Mob dared to look down into the valley below. 'I saw this from the dropship. All these ships. They're heading for Earth.'

Craning his mech carefully over the edge of the precipice, Cameron watched the shimmering liquid spill into a vast receptacle. It crackled with energy as it was funnelled down one of the seemingly endless power vessels that lined the valley, all carrying the fuel from their own furnaces down into the gulf in order to power a vast assembly line. There, in varied states of completion, were the triple-sized, super-armoured cousins of the Ex-Phase 8 dropships. They moved down a procession line that buzzed and sparked with activity. The aliens were certainly working hard to prepare for the end of humankind.

There was another enterprise occurring in the glowing valley that Cameron was the first to spot. Spread out below the procession of dropships, there was a second, separate assembly line.

'Are those the s-s-scout sh-ships you talked about, Ayo?'

Cameron was pointing at a line of starfighters. They were smaller than the dropships, but what they lacked in size they made up for in stealth. With their dynamic, angular design and flat matte armour panels, they looked like they could cut through any atmosphere and leave nothing more behind them than a gentle gust of wind.

Nograki Fleet

Powered by the same perpetual lightning energy that pulses through their capital city, the alien fleet is an intergalactic force responsible for the demise of no less than fifteen galaxies. The armada includes vast dropships, rapid scout ships, and heavily weaponised assault crafts – enough to crush any planetary resistance.

'So we find a way down, boost one of those speedy ships, and we're back to Earth before you can say "put the kettle on",' said Megan.

'How will we fly one of those th-things?' asked Cameron. Prior to his vengeful battle with the snake-scorpion – and before that, his pep talk from his teacher – an enquiry like this would have betrayed equal parts panic and hopeless resignation. Now, however, it sounded far more like a determined search for a solution.

'From what I've managed to dig up, flying them won't be a problem,' said Ayo. 'Mainly because they're all going to the same place. All the crafts have remote flight capabilities. They've been pre-programmed with the navigation parameters for Earth.'

'You're right – *that's* not the problem,' said Jack, staring pensively into the gulf.

'*You're* right,' said Ayo. 'So what *is* the problem?'

Cameron could tell that, as usual, Ayo was a few steps ahead – and waiting for someone else to catch up.

'The problem is, if we run ... they'll follow us. Nothing will change.'

'Soooooo ...?' Ayo asked.

'So we need to make sure they *can't* follow us. We need to destroy the rest of them.'

'You really are coming on nicely, Jack,' said Ayo. 'Now, for ten bonus points, can you tell me how we might accomplish such a feat?'

'Oooh, oooh! I want ten points!' said Megan, hopping

about on the ledge so much that stones began to loosen and tumble down the cliff.

'Yes, Megan?' said Ayo quickly, fearful of a rockslide.

'So we find a way down, boost one of those *big* ships, use the payload on board to bomb the crap out of the central power station and *then* haul ass ... and we're back to Earth before you can say "get the biscuits out".'

'Missing a little finesse, and a few minor details, but worthy of eight points at least,' said Ayo. Megan smiled proudly inside her mech, and gave him a metal thumbs-up.

'That one,' said Cameron, indicating the ship at the front of the assembly line that was being fuelled for launch. The prospect of escaping this awful place had him more fired up than ever before. 'That looks ripe for the t-taking.'

'Agreed,' said Ayo. 'These scumbags fake-killed my parents. Let's teach them a lesson.'

'Punch it!' Megan shouted.

The journey down into the valley had been fraught. Trying to descend the hillside in four giant WarMechs was hard enough; smuggling them aboard an alien spacecraft was even harder. Thankfully, the stealthiest camper in the history of *Distant Dawn* had been there to lead the way. Thanks to Ayo, the alien race didn't have a clue what was happening. That is, until the dropship's surprise departure sent the entire assembly line into chaos. Propulsion components and warheads fell from hovering platforms, tumbling to the ground and shaking the valley with explosive impacts. The fuel line snapped free, spitting liquid energy in all directions, while power vessels surged and overloaded, showering the canyon with lightning-powered shards of rock.

But the *real* destruction started when the dropship's immense exhausts fired, blowing with enough force to push the second dropship in the assembly line off its mountings. It went reeling backwards, crushing the scout ships below. The domino effect was catastrophic. Explosion after explosion erupted around the felled ships, and torrents of spilt energy fed a fire that engulfed the entire valley in blue flame.

'That's a damned good start!' said Jack, leaning on Ayo's shoulders as Ayo steered the ship. 'Now let's really let 'em have it!'

Ayo glanced back at the assembly line, which lay in total ruin. The carcasses of dropships spat and fizzed, melting in the searing fire, while the air was punctuated by explosions as more spilt warheads ignited, feeding the inferno. Flames danced on the surface of his glasses, and a satisfied grin spread across his face. The aliens had made him watch as they burned his house down – it was fitting that he returned the favour. Only this was no high-tech simulation. Leaving genuine devastation in his wake, Ayo pushed the craft upwards, soaring high above the blasts. The runaway dropship was now flying at speed towards its new target: the central hub. The heart of the city.

'Errr ... guys? W-W-What's that?' said Cameron.

'That,' Megan replied, 'is the wrong kind of attention.'

A third type of flying craft was approaching: one Ayo had never seen before. They had the sleekness of the scout ships, but were also heavily weaponised. These were military vessels - a hundred of them - flying in formation in ten rows of ten. Purple propulsion fumes trailed out behind, leaving a square prism of violet smoke as they tore through the sky. Ayo was as impressed as he was intimidated by the precision and coordination.

'LOOK OUT!' Jack shouted.

A hundred ignition flashes lit up the sky. A hundred rockets tipped with explosive payloads punctured the air. A hundred well-aimed explosions enveloped the dropship in a ball of purple fire. The dropship's shields and armour plating were strong, but the sheer power of the barrage was still more than enough to knock the vast vessel off course. Smoke started streaming from impacted sections, and at least two of the propulsion tentacles were blown off altogether.

'Get us back on track!' shouted Megan, appearing at Ayo's other shoulder.

'Indispensable advice,' said Ayo, struggling to get the ship straightened up.

Level 20: In the Midst of Chaos

'They're c-co-com–, they're co-c-com–, they're going to attack again!' Cameron yelled in alarm. Ayo watched as the armada swung around in perfect unison for another gunning run. The dropship swooped, dropping altitude fast. This was risky; the lightning-rod spires that stretched up from the buildings quickly became obstacles in the ship's flightpath: but the manoeuvre was dramatic enough to force the attack ships to abort their run. None of them, it seemed, wanted to risk slamming an errant rocket into the power grid, especially as the assembly canyon chaos was already causing blackouts across the city. But as the dropship moved through a less built-up area, it was tagged by a streak of lightning. While the vessel was built to absorb that kind of charge, the damage it had already suffered meant that this surge blew out three more propulsion tentacles. This wouldn't be a problem if the Mob wanted to keep the ship on its low trajectory, but Ayo knew that the dropship's most effective weapons were the ones in the firing ports on its belly. For those weapons to work, it had to be *above* its target.

Ayo now had two problems. The damaged ship didn't have enough propulsion power to reach the altitude needed for a bombing run. And, even if it did, the armada of assault crafts were waiting there to shoot it to smithereens. He scrambled for a solution that wouldn't come as the central hub loomed in the distance. Then Megan said: 'Hey – what about that Sun Who guy?'

'Sun who?'

'Sun Who! Your virtual assistant – that military strategy guy.'

'Sun *Tzu*,' Ayo replied.

'Yeah – him! What would he suggest in a situation like this?'

Ayo thought for a second.

'He would probably say that *invincibility lies in the defence; the possibility of victory in the attack.*'

Jack squeezed Ayo's shoulder.

'We aren't invincible, man. But if we attack with everything we've got, then it'll be humanity's victory.'

There was silence, and then ...

'Yeah! Who wants to live forever?'

'Did you just name drop the Queen song from *Highlander*, Megan?' said Ayo.

Megan beamed. 'You got the reference! I'm so proud!'

Ayo felt three hands unite on his shoulders as he accelerated the ship, low and fast, straight at the central hub.

The armada above must've realised what he was doing, because a hail of rocket fire rained down on the dropship. Collateral damage was now acceptable, it seemed, as long as it took the explosive-laden dropship off its collision course. But the assault came too late. The sudden jump in speed had given the dropship the edge, and most of the armada's rockets were falling short. A handful found their way through, and the rear of the dropship was peppered with explosions, but it wasn't enough to stay its progress. With smoke spewing from its lacerated flanks, and propulsion tentacles throbbing on the brink of overload, the ship closed in on the energy source.

'TEN SECONDS!' Ayo shouted. The hands gripped his shoulders tighter. He pushed the engines for all they were worth, and as the hub loomed, he armed every heavy-impact warhead on board. All *forty* of them.

The outcome was an explosion that tore the entire sprawling metropolis to pieces.

When the dropship collided with the central hub, the force of the warheads ignited the energy of the heavens. The explosion bordered on stellar – like the death of a star. There was a rapid implosion and a moment of absolute silence before the materials at the centre began to burn with unbridled power, erupting in a sphere of white light. This incandescent fireball enveloped the city within seconds. It razed every structure. The armada, the arena, the entire energy grid – everything burned until there was nothing left of the civilisation but fire and ash ...

... And one alien scout ship.

With four human occupants.

'Sun Tzu would also say that *all warfare is based on deception,*' said Ayo, smugly.

He and the Mob watched the wreckage of the dropship safely from the bridge of a scout ship that hovered high above the burning city, shrouded in thick cloud cover. In Ayo's hand was a small tablet. He had detached it from the inside of his mech's control pod and used it to override the dropship's remote systems sending it to it's fiery fate unmanned.

'Could Sun Who give you any piloting tips?' scoffed Megan. 'Because that whole sitch went from Plan A for Aerial Assault to Plan K for Kamikaze *real* quick.'

'Well, *you* try controlling a giant dropship with a remote control.'

"IMPACT WARNING", "TOTAL SYSTEM FAILURE", and "REMOTE PILOT LINK LOST" now blinked on the tablet screen, obscuring a set of touch-sensitive flight controls.

'You should've let *me* fly it,' Megan continued, 'then we'd be taking a dropship home instead of this dinky thing.'

'I thought it more important that our most skilled pilots be at the helm of the ship that we were actually *in*,' Ayo replied, removing his glasses and wiping them on his shirt before repositioning them on his face. 'The dropship was a decoy and a weapon. Its fate was inconsequential.'

Jack, who was standing next to Ayo in the ship's bridge, jumped in.

'You guys are unreal – you all did great! The plan worked! They took the dropship bait, the grid was destroyed, we escaped, and this place – well, look at it. There's no threat here anymore. I think … I think we might have just saved humanity.'

Jack scanned the cityscape and spotted the remains of the arena: the place where so many innocent souls from across the galaxies had lost their lives, just to feed the greed of this cruel civilization. He thought about the humans included in this. Fellow gamers. Even his own teacher, Miss Barrett. None of them had fought in vain. The Mob would take their legacy home, along with this ship and what they had stored in its cargo hold. They would tell their story. They would expose the threat that had secretly infiltrated humanity; the threat *they* had destroyed. They would make sure the names of Earth's heroes were known to everyone ...

'I can't believe I have to sit on your knee to fly this thing.'

Megan's interruption shattered the silence. She'd left her seat as soon as they'd brought the craft to its covered position, and now she was looking back towards it, and its occupant, with unabashed reluctance.

'It's n-n-not that comfortable f-f-for me either, you know!' Cameron replied. He was sitting in the pilot's chair – a single seat in the centre of the bridge, surrounded by controls that were not built for a human.

'It *is* pretty impressive that the two of you managed to steer a ship with controls intended for a four-armed alien,' said Jack. 'Even if you looked like a loved-up pair of –'

'Utter another word and I'll sling you out the cargo hold,' said Megan, scowling as Jack stifled a chuckle. Then she turned to Ayo. 'Are we going to have to fly home like that?'

'Yes – unless you grow an extra pair of arms.'

'What about a remote pilot program like the one you used?'

'Not for this type of craft,' Ayo replied. 'But you'll only have to pilot us along the atmospheric exit path. The autopilot and warptronic systems should do the rest.'

'Warptronic?' Megan repeated. 'You just making up sci-fi words now?

'Well, that's the translation. It's propulsion tech that bends space. It's like their version of a hyperdrive, I'd imagine,' said Ayo, clearly doing his best to speak Megan's language.

'Like the Millennium Falcon?'

'Yes, exactly like that. Except this is real, and it works.'

'It might well do,' she replied, 'but you never saw Han Solo sitting on Chewie's knee ...'

'Does that mm-m-make me Chewie?' said Cameron, offended.

'Guys! It's only temporary!' said Jack. 'Soon we'll be off this godforsaken rock and – what was it you said, Meg? Back home in time for–'

'A brew and a biscuit!'

'Right,' Jack grinned. 'Let's go home.'

Megan nodded, striding towards the pilot's chair, giving Cameron a fist bump before taking up her position and pulling harness straps over the two of them. Cameron grabbed hold of the lower set of grips, while Megan held on to the upper controls. They began to push the craft gently upwards. The ride was shaky at first, but the pair synced their movements quickly. Soon they were soaring through the dense yellow clouds, towards the planet's upper atmosphere.

'Wait a minute, something weird's going on. You feel that?' asked Megan.

'Y-Y-Yeah, the controls have gone all l-l-light.'

'IS THIS NORMAL?' Megan shouted over her shoulder. Ayo's voice cannoned back from the rear of the bridge.

'I THINK WE'VE REACHED THE END OF THE ATMOSPHERIC EXIT PATH.'

'SO NOW WHAT?'

'NOW WE WAIT FOR THE WARPTRONIC SYSTEM TO KICK IN AND TAKE US HO–'

Before Ayo could even complete the word, the ship warped. It vanished in an instant – leaving behind nothing more than the faintest trail of space dust.

Level 21: Playground Bully

The Mob's scout ship ripped through re-entry with such
speed that Megan and Cameron, who were now back
in control, had almost no time to orientate themselves.
Suddenly, Cameron hauled the craft over to the left.

'WOAH! WHAT ARE YOU DOING!'

'LOOK!' shouted Cameron. 'THE R-RIVER!'

'WHICH RIVER?' Megan shouted back.

'THE ONE NEXT T-TO THE MM-MM-MMMM–'

'THE MOTORWAY! THAT MEANS WE'RE ALMOST THERE!'

The landing was coming up fast. Cameron pushed the
craft towards the target while Megan increased the rate
of descent. It was going to be a rough landing.

'HOLD ON TO YOUR BUTTS!' Megan yelled, gripping
the controls tightly as Cameron course-corrected. They

held their nerve, and held the line, all the way in.

The first impact sent the ship ricocheting straight back into the air, riding a tidal wave of dirt. After three more heavy bounces, the craft finally dug in. Its nose cut through the earth and left a scar half a mile long before it eventually scraped to a stop.

'You okay?' Megan managed. Her chest hurt where the harness had pulled tight; she could only imagine what Cameron felt like underneath her.

'I'm o-okay. Are y-y-you guys okay?'

Simultaneous groans rang from the rear of the bridge.

Megan unbuckled the harness and stood, steadying herself against the pilot's seat. Her ears were ringing from the pressure of the rapid descent, but she could have sworn she heard *voices*. She hobbled towards the exit hatch.

'Ready for one last bit of teamwork?' she said, looking back at Cameron. Stepping forwards, Cameron grabbed two of the four door handles, while Megan grabbed the others. The door flew open. A ramp extended downwards. Megan stuck her head out and looked around.

'Hi, everyone! It's, err, great to be back!'

Megan was addressing a crowd of over a hundred stunned, familiar faces. They had landed the scout ship on their school's playing field.

No one replied to Megan's greeting. She almost felt disappointed. For a moment, she'd expected a hero's welcome – which was ridiculous, really, as no one knew what the Mob had done. All they knew was that Megan Joyce from Miss Barrett's form had just crashed a spaceship into the school's football pitch.

So, naturally, they got their phones out and started taking pictures.

Megan took a few steps down the ramp. Cameron's head poked out after her, sending a fresh wave of murmurs through the crowd. As quickly as Cameron had emerged, he retreated.

Megan turned back and grabbed Cameron's arm, squeezing it encouragingly. 'It's okay. We'll go at the same time.' But the look on Cameron's face told her everything she needed to know. 'Hey – you're ForgeFire666. You just defeated an alien race bent on exterminating mankind. Maybe now's the time to start letting your inner badass out ...'

Megan smiled as she watched Cameron's expression shift. A look of resolve set in, and they began to descend the ramp together.

'STAND BACK, EVERYONE! EVERYONE, STAND BACK!'

The sudden, panicked voice belonged to Mr Woods, the school's headteacher: a tall, skittish man with an odd habit of repeating himself, only backwards.

'Megan! Cameron! What on Earth is this? What is *this*?'

'If you think *this* is mad, you'd better sit down, Sir.'

To Megan's surprise, Mr Woods *did* sit down. Or rather, he *fell* down, then scrambled backwards, just like everyone else in the crowd. It was an understandable response to the sudden presence of two ten-metre tall, heavily-armoured robots. Ayo and Jack had returned to their mechs, which had been stashed in the ship's cargo bay along with Megan's and Cameron's. They were now sitting in their control pods, staring down at the shocked crowd.

'Greetings, all,' said Ayo, sounding more like an alien invader than was perhaps advisable.

'Hi, everyone! Err – sorry about the pitch!' Jack added.

'We've got quite a story to tell,' said Megan as Hephaestus and tHeScOuRgE drew up next to her. 'Could I please borrow someone's phone?'

The crowd remained at a distance, phones aloft. Megan soon realised that what they were seeing wasn't actually all that alien. These kids had seen these robots *plenty*. On streams and Let's Plays, all over social media – not to mention in the game of *Distant Dawn* itself, which pretty much every one of them played. She could even hear the words 'Hephaestus' and 'Scourge' bouncing around the crowd.

'A *phone*, someone?' she said again. 'If you could just give the Insta stories a rest for two seconds so we can call the authorities?'

A Year Seven boy with a freckled face and a phone bigger than his head broke from the crowd. He offered the phone to Megan, never taking his gaze from Jack's mech.

'That's tHeScOuRgE, isn't it?' he squeaked.

'Yeah, yeah, don't wet yourself. My mech's in the

back, too,' said Megan as she typed "99–" into the phone. Two things stopped her hitting the last nine. The first was the boy's sudden, hasty retreat. The second was all the other pupils doing the same. Megan looked behind her. It was all she could do not to turn and run away herself.

Another scout ship sat at the far end of the field. It wasn't lying in a crater, which meant it had been landed by a pilot who knew what they were doing. One who was now standing beside the craft, looking straight at the Raid Mob.

It was the alien leader. It had followed them.

'*Back inside!*' Megan hissed, pulling Cameron up the ramp while Jack and Ayo turned to face the invader, weapons erupting all over their mechs.

'YOU!'

The alien's single word cannoned across the playing field, louder than it had been in the arena.

'You have desecrated the seat of the most eminent power in the Universe! You have impeded *progress*! You ... will ... all ... DIE!'

'Not today,' said Megan as she emerged from the rear of the ship, drawing the Zuul mech to its full height. The ForgeFire666 robot followed close behind. Both WarMechs had every weapon primed and ready to shoot.

The sound of shredded metal clawed the air, causing the panicked crowd to scramble for cover as something began tearing its way out of the enemy's cargo hold. In an instant, the hull of the ship was cleaved clean in two by a machine that made the Mob shrink back.

It was a WarMech – but unlike any the Mob had ever seen. It was twice as big as their's, with limbs as thick as buses. Its movements shook the ground. The alien leader spread its decrepit wings and flapped up to the height of the giant's chest, disappearing into an open control pod.

'*We* engineered these machines of war, remember?' it taunted. '*We* are the game makers. *We* make the rules. And now, for you, it's GAME OVER.'

Megan watched as two missile tubes opened on the giant mech's torso, and a pair of warheads screamed across the playing field towards them. The explosion sent white-hot shards of metal flying from the Mob's scout ship in all directions.

'Anyone got any suggestions!' Jack shouted, rolling his mech over onto its side after leaping for cover.

'Get it a date with the *COUGH* Statue of Liberty?' spluttered Megan.

Cameron shouted from behind the wreckage of the ship. 'Ayo? What w-w-would Sun Who ss-ss-say?'

'I don't know. But here's what *I'll* say – and it's not my usual take: we need to get closer.'

'I agree. Toe-to-toe, cancel out the long-range fire,' said Jack. 'It's big, but we're fast – let's take advantage.'

'On it!' shouted Megan, already launching Zuul into a sprint. The four WarMechs streaked across the field, darting, ducking and dodging a barrage of

Wrakantrex

While humans know them as "WarMechs", the alien invaders call them "Wrakantrex"– this is the biggest they have ever built. Twice the size of the Raid Mob's mechs, and filled to bursting with powerful projectiles, it makes four-on-one look like good odds.

explosives. Four moving targets proved too difficult to hit, and by the time the smoke cleared, the Mob had closed the distance. Ayo fired a grappling hook into the Wrakantrex's shoulder armour and pulled his mech up onto its back. The weight of the Hephaestus mech tipped the giant backwards, while tHeScOuRgE and ForgeFire666 threw themselves at a leg each, causing it to stumble. But it did not fall. Even when Megan threw a double-fisted punch right into its metal solar plexus, the Wrakantrex remained standing.

'KEEP PUSHIIIII– AAAARGH!'

The giant managed to shrug Ayo's machine from its back and grab hold of it, lifting it high above its head. Then the giant threw the grey mech down right on top of Zuul. The pair crashed to the ground in a tangle of metal limbs. Megan's pod window crashed into Ayo's. They exchanged pained glances before the giant raised its arms again, warheads ready to fire at them.

'NO!' shouted Cameron. He fired his chain spear around the giant's arms and pulled. The missiles missed their target, obliterating a storage shed instead. The Zuul and Hephaestus mechs scrambled to avoid a second attack, but it never came – because the giant's arms were still aimed at the smouldering remains of the shed. A shed that had been used for cover by a group of terrified kids.

Megan recognised a face amongst the group. Franky McGrath. FrankenDeath14. The bully who'd tormented Cameron almost every day was standing there, trembling and crying. Then she watched Cameron move without the slightest hesitation. He rocketed towards the group, planted his mech's foot and leaped into the giant's line of fire, just as it let loose a hail of projectiles.

Megan's eyes widened as Cameron's mech was peppered with explosives. It took the full impact of the Wrakantrex's assault, protecting the cowering kids – including that trouser-stain Frank McGrath – until the enemy mech's blaster ran dry, and Cameron's WarMech was left smouldering on the grass.

Enraged, Megan fired from every port and hatch on her mech. tHeScOuRgE and Hephaestus followed suit, lighting up the back of the giant robot. The onslaught drew its attention, but it wasn't enough to cause any substantial damage. They weren't going to beat this thing in a firefight.

'You two pull him away from Cam and the school!' Jack shouted. 'I've got an idea!'

The Mob members didn't question the order. They kept up the barrage, even when the giant mech began returning fire. The football pitch became a lethal fireworks display. Tracer rounds streamed through the air, warheads skimmed targets and sparks flew as mechs ducked and rolled, popping up and firing at their impossible enemy again and again.

'Whatever you're planning, Jack, hurry it up!' Megan shouted.

'I second that,' added Ayo.

'Guys – you aren't going to like this, but the next time that thing reloads, I need you to stop firing.'

'Can you repeat that into my good ear? Either one will do,' said Megan, her face creased with confusion as she continued to pump round after round from every available weapon.

'I need you to just stand there – both of you. Please. You trust me, right?'

'God, I hate when he does this!' screamed Megan. 'Yes, I trust you!'

'Against every logical and statistical impulse – I also trust you,' said Ayo.

'Thank you. Just wait for that reload.'

The Zuul and Hephaestus mechs continued their barrage until the giant's weapons went quiet. Their simultaneous ceasefire seemed to take the huge mech by surprise. It stood still for a moment ... then two missile tubes opened up on its torso.

'Err ... Jack?'

'You are pushing the trust of the group, Jack.'

The missile tubes glowed red. Nothing would stop the ignition now.

'JACK!'

Megan and Ayo screamed in unison, but neither of them twitched a single metal fibre. The only moving mech on the field was Jack's, executing a quadpiston-powered leap onto the giant Wrakantrex's back.

'The bigger they are, the more explosives they carry,'

came his voice, as he stuffed both his mech's metal fists into the missile tubes, blocking them completely. In a fluid, perfectly timed movement, Jack detached the fists and engaged the powerful pistons in his WarMech's legs, backflipping free and clear of the interstellar interloper. Megan and Ayo watched in awe as explosions engulfed the enemy mech in a vast, violent ball of flame. Cannon fire erupted inside its body as the stored ammunition ignited, sending projectiles bursting outwards through its armour. It was self-destruction on an epic scale. Finally, the Wrakantrex buckled at the knees before falling flat on its front, completely enveloped by a searing inferno.

'G-g-guys?'

The stuttering voice was quiet and distant. It took a moment for Megan to hear it, and a moment longer for her to realise that it wasn't coming through the comms.

'Cameron? Cam! Are you okay?'

Cameron had escaped his mech, which lay, bullet-ridden and smouldering, on the edge of the field. Megan knelt her mech down and popped open the control pod, with Ayo doing the same beside her. Clambering to the ground, Megan sprinted towards Cameron and hugged him tightly. Ayo stumbled towards the group, breathless and bruised, and Megan drew him in.

'W-W-Where's Jack? Is h-h-he okay?'

The Mob scanned the battlefield, but all they could see was fire and smoke and smouldering metal. That

was, until a creaking, battered, scarred – and now handless – mech emerged from the burning haze.

'... Man, that landing was *rough*.' tHeScOuRgE walked towards the Mob. 'Thanks for trusting me, guys. That was *way* closer than I planned.'

Megan looked up towards the dented WarMech's control pod, nodding with respect. Metal rasped and groaned as Jack's WarMech took a knee. The control pod popped open and Jack came down off his rig. Taking a seat on the edge of the pod, with his legs dangling over the lip, he smiled at the rest of the Raid Mob.

'Well,' he started, 'thanks to the shuttle shuffle, I've had plenty of practice timing quadpiston jumps. One jump to plant the fists,' he pointed to his mech's handless arms, 'and another one to get clear of the blast!'

Sliding down his mech's metal shin, Jack joined the rest of the Mob, where they fell into a group hug. It was an embrace filled with joy and relief. The nightmare was finally over. They had defeated their enemy, both as alien prisoners and home-turf defenders. And they'd done it all together – the notorious Raid Mob proving just as formidable in the real world as they were online.

Above the spits and pops of the crackling fire behind them, the Mob heard the sound of sirens blaring.

'Looks like someone finally called the authorities,' said Megan. 'Good thing, too – I think we could all do with some medical attention.'

'Unfortunately, I can't stick around.'

Jack let the group go and clambered back up his mech's leg. Hauling himself into the control pod, he climbed back into the rig and drew his back up to its full height. It turned and broke into a lumbering sprint, running past the side of the school.

None of the Mob said anything. They knew exactly where Jack was going – or, more precisely, *who* he was going to.

Rounding the corner of his street, breathless and aching, Jack saw his house. He saw the hole in the roof through which he'd been abducted. It was now the quickest way to get to where he needed to be. Approaching the front wall, Jack carefully positioned his mech's feet as close to it as he could, then leaned the robot over so that the control pod was level with the hole in the roof. He pushed open the hatch and clambered down, landing heavily on top of a pile of broken roof tiles and ceiling plaster. He was back in his tiny bedroom.

Jack opened the door and bounded across the landing. Jack pushed open the door opposite his own and went inside. As quietly as he could manage, he peered over the edge of the cot.

Lying there, grinning and burbling, was Alexander. Jack's chest burned with love, shoving a lump up into his throat, and pushing the widest smile he may ever have smiled across his face. He reached down into the cot, cradling his baby brother in his arms. A tiny hand reached upwards, resting over Jack's heart.

Now everything was okay.

But then, something strange – something terrible – began to happen. The bundle in Jack's arms started to disintegrate. The smiling infant transformed to black sand and slipped through his fingers, no matter how tightly he tried to grasp it. Panic surging through him, Jack looked around; the same thing was happening everywhere. Everything in the room was falling away, disintegrating and disappearing – and not just that. Jack drew his empty hands to his face and watched in horror as the tips of his fingers began to fall away to nothingness. He tried to scream, but even his voice had vanished. Jack's entire world crumbled, piece by piece, until there was nothing but absolute blackness.

Absolute blackness and two short words blinking in the middle of the void.

GAME

OVER

Level 22: Only the Beginning

'JACK!'

A voice penetrated the abyss, which had swallowed up everything except those two stark words.

'JACK! WILL YOU GET OFF THAT BLOODY THING AND ANSWER THE DOOR!'

This time, Jack recognised the voice. He tried to move towards the sound, vague sensations spreading across his invisible form. He became able to distinguish hands from arms, fingers from hands. He felt the weight of his body through the soles of his feet. Soon enough, Jack could feel every part of himself, but he still could not see any of it.

Jack tried rubbing his eyes – but he couldn't. There was something in the way. Jack grasped at it and pulled.

Level 22: Only the Beginning

Suddenly, the hovering words and darkness evaporated, replaced by a wash of brilliant white light. Instinctively, Jack scrunched his eyes closed and covered his face. After a few moments, he managed to open his eyes.

Jack was in his bedroom.

He was in his bedroom, sitting on his bed, holding something in his hand – a hand covered by a glowing white glove.

He was holding the Hailstorm Games Fullmmersion Visor.

Bright daylight was pouring in through the window. Disorientated, Jack looked to the ceiling. He expected to see the gaping hole through which he'd been abducted, but there weren't even the *remnants* of a hole. The same dingy yellow paint and mould patches that Jack had always known stared back at him, untouched.

Then Jack spotted something blinking on his TV screen.

GAME OVER

As he stared at them, the letters began to shift ...

GNSER TH DVER

And change ...

GNSWER TH DVOR

Until finally ...

ANSWER THE DOOR

Jack recoiled in shock. He struggled to stand, throwing out his gloved hands to steady himself. Every muscle in his body ached.

Staggering into the hall, Jack pushed open the door opposite. He found Alexander standing in his cot, gurgling away. When he saw Jack he burst into a huge smile, instantly mirrored on Jack's weary, pallid face. Jack approached the cot, knelt down, and took hold of his brother's tiny outstretched hand.

'Alex!' said Jack, smiling through overwhelmed tears. 'I don't know what's been going on, but I know I've missed you, little man.'

'JACK! THERE'S SOMEONE AT THE DOOR!'

Jack's face scrunched up at the sound of his mum's voice. He vaguely remembered her leaving before he'd entered the *Distant Dawn* Elite Mission the night before. He also remembered taking precautions to make sure he didn't stay in the game too long. He pulled his phone out of his pocket. *Twelve* missed alarms.

Have I really only been gone one night? Jack thought, his mind hazy. *Did I even go anywhere at all?*

Jack heard the sound of knocking, followed by his

mum huffing her way to the front door, unlocking it, and greeting whoever was there with an impolite 'What do you want?' Then a second voice rang up the stairs. 'Mr Delaney? We are representatives from Hailstorm Games. The company would like to speak to you about your prize.'

'Prize?' Jack repeated, barely taking in the words.

'What prize? What's he won?' Jack heard his mum say, suddenly interested in the visitors. Then she screeched, 'JACK! WHY ARE THE POLICE HERE?'

Stunned, Jack looked at his brother again.

'I've got to go and sort a few things out, okay? I'll be back to check on you before bedtime.'

Jack squeezed his brother's hand gently and felt tiny fingers close around his.

Gripping the handrail, Jack edged downstairs. When he reached the bottom, he saw two large men standing on the pavement outside his open front door. Both were dressed in smart grey suits, with cabled ear pieces and dark sunglasses. Jack steadied himself against the hallway wall as he slowly approached the front door – the combination of the stark sunlight and the surprising guests causing him to squint. Jack leaned his head slowly out into the street. What he saw, coupled with the sound that instantly erupted, almost caused him to faint on the spot.

The street was blocked off by police cars at both ends. Officers were posted at the door of each house, and only one car remained on the street: an imposing black 4X4, with windows tinted so dark it would be impossible to catch a glimpse of anyone inside. And yet, none of this drew Jack's attention. It was what was *behind* the police barricades that sent his jaw to the pavement.

A massive crowd of people, mostly kids and teenagers, had filled both ends of Jack's street. At the sight of him, they all erupted, breaking into a deafening chant.

'SCOURGE! SCOURGE! SCOURGE!'

'We have a vehicle waiting to take you to the Hailstorm Games Campus, Mr Delaney,' began one of the suited men. 'We also have your favourite refreshments prepared. We understand that you might be fatigued after your adventure.'

Jack could barely hear the man over the growing sound of the crowd. The multiplying madness was *way* too much. Jack felt his legs start to wobble. One of the suited men dived into the doorway to catch him, and before his shell-shocked mum could object, the man bundled Jack into the car. A cold hit of air conditioning was just enough to keep him conscious as the vehicle sped Jack out of the estate.

'ShockSoda, Sir?'

The suited man who'd spoken to Jack at his house opened a partition between their seats. Inside was a mini fridge, stocked with the Mob's drink of choice in every flavour. Through his daze, the sight of the

ShockSoda stash was enough to remind Jack that he hadn't actually drunk anything for hours. He reached for a can of Tropical Storm.

'Sir, if you don't mind ...'

The man pulled the compartment out further to reveal a pair of chilled crystal champagne glasses – nothing like the plastic tumblers and stolen pint glasses Jack was used to. The man emptied half the can of ShockSoda into the glass before handing it to Jack.

'You must also get your sugars up,' he added, tapping a touch screen mounted on the armrest. In response, a fold-down table lowered from the seat in front of Jack, with four shelves behind it, each stocked with all his favourite snacks.

Jack didn't need telling twice. Before long, he'd polished off two ShockSodas, three packets of crisps, three chocolate bars, and two packs of sweets. With his belly full and his head clearing, the need for answers grew stronger. First and foremost, he needed to know if the Mob was okay. He didn't even know if this whole thing involved them, or if it had only happened to him.

He reached for his phone, but the suited man stopped him.

'Sir, we advise you not to use your phone until we reach the campus.'

'Why not?' Jack asked.

'It may ... come as a shock, Sir.'

'I'll just check my notifications,' said Jack. He took out his phone and unlocked the screen. His face turned white. His shaking hand dropping the phone onto the floor.

The suited man gave Jack a look that said something slightly more polite than "I told you so". Jack picked his phone up and looked at it again, just to be sure he'd seen what he thought he saw.

Across three social media accounts, Jack had 2.7 million friend and follower requests.

'Perhaps it's best just to leave that for now, Sir,' the suited man said. 'We are almost at the campus, and I imagine it's Megan, Ayomikun and Cameron who you'd like to speak to most.'

Jack shot a look at the suited man. His ShockSoda-filled stomach turned at the mention of the Mob – they must have been involved in this madness too – and this guy knew something about it.

'How do you know who ... What has happened to ... How do you know about ...'

'I'm sure these questions have endings, Mr Delaney, and I'm equally sure that they will be answered soon. We're nearing the campus, and I've just received word that your friends are awaiting your arrival. As is the head of the company.'

The vehicle began to slow, and Jack looked out of the window at a sight that he had only dreamed about seeing: the headquarters of Hailstorm Games. The

campus's central building was huge; too tall to see the
top from inside the car. Its design was based on a double
helix, with two towers twisted together, mirroring the
shape of DNA: the genetic instructions for all living things.

The vehicle came to a halt in front of a grandiose
glass entrance. Jack reached for the door handle, but the
suited man spoke up again.

'Sir, if you don't mind ...'

Jack paused. The driver opened the door for him. Jack
slid out awkwardly and the car sped away, leaving him
alone at the entrance to Hailstorm Games HQ.

A long glass tunnel led Jack into the building. The
walls were lined with virtual figures: 3D, life-sized
renderings of soldiers in the exosuit uniforms of the
Earth Orbit Defence – the military fighting force from
Distant Dawn. As Jack passed by, each one stood to
attention, saluting him before speaking in turn.

'Thank you, Sir.'

'Great job, Sir.'

'Semper fi, Sir.'

By the time Jack neared the doorway at the end of
the tunnel, he was returning his "comrades'" salutes.
He almost didn't notice that a large and imposing virtual
figure had materialised out of thin air, right in front
of him.

'Woah!' Jack exclaimed. 'Colonel Hardcastle?'

He was exactly as Jack had imagined, right down to
the perfectly starched uniform draped in medals and the

caterpillar moustache that hung over two rows of yellow teeth, with a soggy cigar clamped between them.

'Private Jack Delaney!' the Colonel announced. 'You've made me prouder than my prize bull, and he's won the county fair Bull Monty Award three years a-runnin'.'

'Err ... thanks?' said Jack.

'It's "thanks, *Sir*", Mr Delaney. You and your goon squad might be our universal saviours and all, but dammit son, respect the chain of command!'

Jack couldn't help but smile. He drew his feet together, cocked his elbow and raised a hand to his brow. The Colonel returned his salute, and the door behind him slid open.

Rapturous applause greeted Jack as he stepped into a vast atrium filled with rows of what Jack assumed must be Hailstorm Games employees. The hairs on his neck stood up as straight as the soldiers he'd just finished saluting. He walked slowly down the centre aisle, trying not to trip over his own feet. It was all very confusing – but it was a *really good* kind of confusing.

'JACK!'

The shout drew Jack's attention towards the front, where he could see four high-back chairs, each one glowing blue at the edges like thrones from the future. Seated on three of them were the other members of the Raid Mob. Jack broke into a run and the Mob all got up from their seats. Megan threw her arms around him and squeezed far too hard before Cameron added to the crush. Ayo wrapped his gangly arms around the whole bunch. The three of them had massive smiles on their faces; they seemed to know something Jack didn't.

'Guys! What the actual hell is going on?'

'We won!' squeaked Megan excitedly.

'We w-w-won, Jack!

'Yes, Jack. Apparently we are the winners.'

Jack was as excited as he was confused. 'What have we won?'

'WE DON'T KNOW!' Megan looked like she was about to explode. 'But now that you're here we can finally find out!'

'PLEASE TAKE YOUR SEATS!' came an unseen voice over a loudspeaker. 'AND PREPARE FOR A SPECIAL PRESENTATION FROM OUR FOUNDER AND CEO, MR MILES MORGAN.'

The gathered crowd sat down, and there was a moment of anticipatory silence.

'Good morning, everybody! And a great morning to you four, our competition winners!'

The head of Hailstorm Games burst through a nearby doorway, looking *way* younger than the founder of the biggest computer software company in the world should, and dressed to match. He looked like the type to hang out at Megan's dad's coffee place, except for a few small, but very telling, details. He wore Gold & Wood TITAN glasses, which Jack knew cost thousands of pounds. A vintage "FLYNN LIVES" t-shirt sat beneath a Brioni blazer that cost the same as a Mercedes, and he had a Richard Mille 68-01 Kongo watch strapped around his wrist – worth a cool three-quarters of a million.

'Look at his shoes!' Megan whispered excitedly.

They were pretty hard to miss, coming halfway up his shins and being lit up along each side. They were Nike MAGs: Marty McFly's self-lacing trainers from *Back to the Future II*. Thirty grand. This guy was *loaded* – with enthusiasm as well as money. He seemed even more excited for the Mob to be there than they did.

'Before we get to all the awesomeness we have in store, some housekeeping,' he said. 'I know what you've experienced has been extreme, and may have left you confused. In fact, it's likely and completely understandable that you've been questioning reality itself. That was our absolute intent. However, there are some reassurances that I'd like to offer.'

Miles Morgan took a deep breath, then spoke like he was reading out small print for a TV ad.

'You were *not* abducted – you were *not* taken to space – you have *not* visited an alien planet – you were *not* tortured – you certainly were *not* nearly killed – *no one* around you was killed or harmed in any way – your families' identities are safe – *your* identities *have* been revealed to the world and you are now the four most famous gamers in history ... Any questions?'

All four of the Mob raised their hands.

Jack noticed a look flicker across Miles's face, similar to that of a child who'd been told they couldn't go out to play until they'd finished their dinner. 'Okay. I get it. You've all been through something big. Fire away,' he said. He pointed at Cameron.

'W-W-When did all this s-start?'

'Good question, great question. We gave you the outpost mission to help you get used to the VR controls, but the actual experience began when you joined the mission to Maximalum. After you started that game, everything you went through was part of the competition, right up until you removed your headsets this morning. Next?'

Jack was amazed at how flippantly Miles answered. It was as if having to explain the most mind-bending experience of their lives was an everyday occurrence.

'How is it possible that there were people we *knew* in the game?' asked Jack.

'Well, that depends,' said Miles. 'In terms of your school friends, that was an easy one. Ten minutes after the stream went live, we released an app offering people the chance to appear in the game. They uploaded a selfie and, if selected, they got rendered in. Some even add scripted vocals. Almost every kid in your school entered, so it was easy to throw in faces you knew. Even your teachers were up for it after they found out who The Devastator really was!'

'What about our families?'

'Ahh, yes. Your brother, for example, was rendered based on photos from your Cloud account. Ayo's parents appeared via images captured from home devices. Although, we were very disappointed to have missed that picture frame and those oven gloves, Mr Osikoya-Arinola – that was a *great* spot.'

'Wait a minute. You mean that what the aliens said *they* did – hacking devices and stealing information – those are the things that *you* actually did?' blurted Megan.

'Yes, indeed!' replied Miles.

Jack was stunned into silence by the reply. He folded his arms tightly across his chest as if to protect himself against any further invasions of his privacy. He felt like someone had been spying on him. Miles Morgan, apparently oblivious to the turn of mood in the room, continued on.

'Rest assured, your families only appeared as themselves to *you* in the game. To all the people watching the streams, they were rendered completely differently.'

'*All* the p-p-people? H-H-How many people s-saw us?'

Miles looked off to the side. One of his employees, who was holding a tablet, raised five fingers.

'Five million, Ken? Five million concurrent viewers? Oh, five–zero? Fifty million viewers globally! That's spread across YouTube, Twitch, and our own streaming channels and app, but still, it's a record-breaker no matter how you square it!'

The announcement sent Cameron into a coughing fit. Megan began slapping him on the back, and Ayo took over the questioning.

'The Raid Mob have always worked hard to maintain our anonymity. You have spied on us, taken information from our private devices, and shared our identities on a global platform. What made you think that this would be tolerated?'

Miles looked at Ayo with utter confusion.

'You did.'

The Mob returned Miles's mystified gaze.

'When you gave us *permission* to do those things,' he continued.

The Mob's frowns deepened.

'When you signed a form that expressly gave us consent to – what was the wording again? Ken?'

The tablet-wielding employee reappeared, handing the device to Miles. Adjusting his expensive glasses, Miles began to read in his fine-print voice.

'Section 7, Subsection C, Point 6: I, the user, hereby agree that my likeness may be used within all of *Distant Dawn*'s Fullmmersion gameplay environments, including residential and educational settings, even those deemed "private property". Point 7: I agree that visual information may be collected from any of my online accounts for the purpose of in-game renders ...'

'I never agreed to that!' Ayo began, but Miles wasn't finished.

'Section 8, Subsection B, Point 4: I, the user, hereby give permission that any and all data collected may be used as part of a global broadcast, and linked to both my *Distant Dawn* gamer tag and my legal identity. I surrender all rights to anonymity as a condition of my entry into the competition ...'

The Mob sat in stunned silence.

'See, it's that last bit that really sums it up,' Miles continued. 'You wouldn't even have been allowed into the competition unless you were okay with going public. But you guys knew that. You all signed. You agreed to every single one of those conditions.'

'We didn't sign anything!' Megan finally managed, giving words to Jack's thoughts. 'And we certainly never read anything that said any of–'

She paused, and as she did, a memory flashed through Jack's mind. He glanced at his teammates. If their expressions were anything to go by, it appeared they'd all had the same realisation.

'The terms and conditions ...' they all groaned in eerie unison.

'Of course!' exclaimed Miles, seemingly happy that they were all back on the same page. 'We'd never do anything without the express consent of our users!'

'Yeah ... see, the thing is, we don't usually read that stuff,' said Megan. 'I mean, we kind of do. We let Ayo take care of it. He reads everything. Twice.'

'Well then, I assume he understood the risks and obligations on all of your behalf,' said Miles. 'Although, really, in the digital age, you should all be taking responsibility for your own data protec–'

'I didn't read it either,' Ayo announced.

'So you all agreed to a life-changing, globally-broadcast surrender of almost all your privacy … without reading the contract?' said Miles, his enthusiasm ebbing slightly.

The Mob nodded their collective heads.

'Well, I suppose it's a good job you won then! If there's one thing I can guarantee, it's that what you've gained from winning is far better than what you gave up to play. We can't turn back time – not *yet* anyway – but the quicker we move on, the better you will feel about all this. Now, were there any more questions?'

Megan put her hand up.

'Yes, Zuul?' Miles said, forcing a smile to mask his impatience.

'Yeah, so, I've used VR before, and if what you've said is true – that I never left my gaming chair – how did you manage to make it feel like I've been piloting a giant robot, flown through space, and got beaten up more times than I can count? I am *aching*, man!'

Miles's smile widened.

'Finally!' he said. 'The fun part. Let me show you how we made you believe you were abducted, taken across the stars, and left to fight for your lives on an alien planet. And then, let me show you how this is only the beginning.'

Level 23: Making Sense of It All

The Raid Mob found themselves rushed into a transparent lift by Miles Morgan, who was soon pacing the width of the space in excited agitation. He placed his hand on a scanner. A robotic voice rang out.

'Hello, Mr. Morgan. Thanks for coming back early.'

'No problem, Master C,' Miles replied, smiling knowingly at the Mob. 'Take us to the BioMovements lab, please.'

There was a pause. The lift doors slid shut. The robotic voice spoke once more.

'End of line.'

'Your lift operator is the Master Control Program from *Tron*!' said Megan excitedly. *Tron* was one of the Mob's collective favourite films. Funnily enough, it was about a gamer who got trapped inside a computer simulation.

'I'm so glad it's not wasted on you!' Miles replied contently. 'So many of the corporate suits I have in here don't even recognise half the voices I give this thing. Ah! Here we are!'

The lift doors opened. The Mob gawped. The left side of the space was occupied by a medical research lab, with artificial human bodies covered in electrodes, scanners mapping muscle activity, and rows of synthetic brains lining the far wall. At least Jack hoped they were synthetic. The right side of the space was partitioned into glass cubicles. Inside each one were two people; one tapping notes into a tablet, the other sitting in a chair wearing the Fullmmersion kit. A large screen showed what the test subjects were experiencing in VR: kayaking down white-water rapids; riding an elephant through a rainforest; skydiving over a city full of neon skyscrapers at night. And these were just the "realistic" simulations.

Further down the row, one test subject was piloting a Spitfire in a simulation of the Battle of Dunkirk, while their neighbour flew a starfighter in the Battle of Coruscant. The further the Mob looked, the crazier the simulations got. One worker was driving a race car on a track shaped like a rollercoaster suspended high above the clouds, while another played chess – against a robot – on the moon.

'What's the biggest problem with Virtual Reality?'

Miles asked – but he didn't wait for a reply. '*Actual* reality. The real world gets right in the way of full immersion. You used to strap on a headset, grab a pair of hand controllers, and that was that. You *saw* the reality. You *heard* the reality. But what about something so simple as movement? If you wanted to walk in those old simulations, you pushed a joystick with your thumb. Your *thumb!*' Miles repeated incredulously. 'Those systems discovered their limits very quickly.'

As he spoke, Miles led the group to the biological research area. They were standing in front of an odd-looking model. It had a brain, eyeballs, nose, mouth, and ears, but the remainder of the body was comprised solely of a spine, and sprouting from between the vertebrae was a maze of stringy, sprawling vessels.

'At Hailstorm Games we realised that, if the virtual reality experience relied on physical spaces, it was always going to be limited. At first we looked at solving this problem with augmented reality – combining VR with the real world. But ultimately, we still had to impose boundaries. Users will always find physical limits in the real world. So we started thinking about reality itself. What makes your reality real? What makes you *believe*?'

Jack suddenly realised why Miles had brought them to this model in particular.

'Your senses?' he offered.

'Exactly!' said Miles excitedly. 'You believe your *senses*

– the tools we have to help us understand the world. And, as magnificent and complex and impressive as the senses are, they are all susceptible to manipulation. For example, I hand you an ice-cold ShockSoda. You recognise its shape, its design. You take hold of it and feel the cold, wet metal. The fruity smell drifts through your nostrils before the can touches your lips. Finally, the taste hits your tongue. If you experience all those things, then the drink was real, right?'

'... Right?' Jack repeated, still not quite sure where Miles was going.

'Right,' said Miles, 'but what did you *really* experience? Your sense of sight recorded an image that your brain recognised. Your memory loaded up a ton of sensory expectations, and your senses confirmed them. Your brain thinks you held and drank a ShockSoda because your senses told it so. So why can't we start talking to those senses directly – get some control over the messages being sent to your brain? If we give your sense of touch, hearing, smell, and taste the inputs that match whatever you're seeing, then no matter how crazy what you're seeing is, you will be so much more likely to believe it. *That* is what we did with the Fullmmersion experience,' said Miles.

He drew a VR visor from a nearby display.

'This visor not only feeds you visual information, but it has been fitted with an olfactory simulator capable of producing over a thousand distinct odours and odour combinations. The earpieces can replicate the entire audible range of humans, but can also target vibrations towards the vestibular system – the part of your ear canal essential to your sense of balance. With the right frequency, this thing can make you believe you are upside down, soaring through the air, falling, swimming, running – anything! Pair that with these beauties,' said Miles, picking up a tube of the circular stick-on discs, 'and we can stimulate your muscles and your nervous systems with sensations of movement, gravity, temperature, impacts – anything we'd need to convince you that you were in a completely different world, free to move in any way you wanted, all without leaving your seat ...'

Miles placed the items down and looked back at the Mob.

'That's why everything you experienced felt so real. Because, as far as both your bodies and your brains were concerned, it *was* real. And as crazy as you might have thought that experience was, you have only just begun to explore the system's capabilities. I want to show you something else we've been working on ...'

Miles led the group back towards the lift. After giving the robotic operator its instructions and smiling at the *Tron* voice response, Miles turned to them.

'It's funny what you can get from a person's browser history. I think I'd be able to take a good crack at *your* favourite films.'

The Mob said nothing, but Megan cracked a half

smile. Thanks to her, they were all *proper* film nerds: their favourite films weren't exactly modern, or mainstream, or even age-appropriate. There was no way Miles would guess them all correctly.

'*Big Trouble in Little China*!' he blurted. 'That's yours, Jack – right? You watch it at Megan's, mostly, but you have downloaded several copies on your own computer from a torrent site. Searching for the best resolution, I'd guess?'

'Y-Yeah – that's right!' said Jack.

'And you,' said Miles, looking at Cameron. 'You tell your friends that your favourite film is ... *Flight of the Navigator*.'

Jack, Megan and Ayo all nodded, but Cameron began to flush red.

'But it *isn't* your favourite film, is it? You don't even like it that much. The Puckmaren freaks you out. No, your *actual* favourite film ...'

The rest of the Mob leaned in. There was very little that they didn't know about each other, so this was like gold dust.

'... Is a secret!' Miles concluded. 'And it's a secret that stays between you, me, and your internet service provider. Now, Ayo, your favourite film is a *Monty Python* one, and I wholeheartedly approve. But as for which film – *The Meaning of Life*? Really?'

'Absolutely,' replied Ayo. 'And I've written an essay on the subject that proves it.'

'I've read it!' Miles replied. 'Megan. I think your

favourite film was my safest guess. So much so that, for this demonstration, I have integrated it into the simulation. I want to show you how we plan to revolutionise the way the world consumes video media.'

The lift door slid open. Miles went to lead the group out, then stopped. He hesitated. He turned to Megan.

'... It's *Aliens*, right?'

Considering all the mind-melting Hailstorm tech, Jack felt a pang of disappointment when Miles led them into a small cinema room with regular seats, pointed at a medium-sized screen.

There wasn't even any popcorn.

The lights went dark and the film started. The Mob knew *Aliens* line by line, thanks to Megan. They also knew *everything* about her hero, Private Jenette Vasquez, the tough-talking, hard-as-coffin-nails space marine. As Vasquez's first scene approached, Jack wondered where Megan had gone – she'd been led away by one of Miles's technicians. She was going to miss her favourite character in her favourite film.

Except she wouldn't. Because Megan *was* her favourite character. She was *in* her favourite film.

Megan was on the screen. She was in full costume, right in amongst the other characters, ripping pull-ups and admiring her own biceps. And that's how it continued. Whenever Vasquez appeared, it was Megan. She explored the abandoned power station, survived a spaceship crash, battled tons of aliens, shouted a lot, and when the moment came, she died one of the most heroic deaths of the franchise.

Two minutes later, Megan burst through a door at the side of the screening room, alive and well – and more excited than Jack had ever seen her.

'I WAS VASQUEZ! I WAS IN THE FILM! IT WAS SO REAL! I SAW RIPLEY! I KILLED SO MANY ALIENS! I SWORE SO MUCH!'

Miles began applauding as the film faded to black.

'That is just one of the ways we anticipate our users will consume media in the very near future,' he said proudly. 'A Fullmmersion experience of film. Imagine it. Jack, you could be Jack Burton! Ayo could be one of the Crimson Permanent Assurance pirates! Cameron could be Simba! Oh – oh I'm so sorry, Cameron!'

'SIMBA! From *The Lion King*!' Megan guffawed as Cameron turned red again.

'The point is, you can be anyone in any film. Our programmers have developed software that will digitise *any* visual media and turn it into an inhabitable virtual space. You'll be able to visit *Jurassic Park*, *Gotham City*, the *Fury Road*, the *Matrix* – anywhere! TV shows, too, and music videos. All of it will feel as real as the simulations you've already experienced.'

The Mob were buzzing – and Miles still wasn't finished.

'Now, we have one more place to go. And when I say "go", it should come as no surprise by now that we don't actually have to move to get there.'

Miles opened a container at the side of the room, revealing another set of VR visors.

'We are headed towards the last stop on our tour. We will travel a great distance to get there. When we arrive, you will find your prize.'

The Mob grabbed the visors and strapped them to their heads. Jack sat back in his seat, and the world went dark.

Level 24: The Prize

The Raid Mob found themselves standing on a barren, rocky surface. The ground was chalky and pock-marked, and grey as far as the eye could see – from deep craters to jagged rises, and everything in between. The sky above was black, apart from two orbs that shone out from the darkness. One was the Sun. The other was Earth.

'Looks pretty fragile out there all alone, doesn't it?' said Miles, kicking up moon dust with his expensive trainers. 'When we're there it seems so big, and so divided. For thousands of years we have sought to split it up; giving names to the bits we've grabbed for ourselves and saying "go away – this part is ours". And this behaviour isn't just a human habit. It never was. Territoriality is as old as life itself.'

Miles was staring sombrely at the Earth, while his words were dripping with sadness.

'And yet, although humankind has been around for only 200,000 years, we have accomplished feats that no other living creature has even come close to. Over five billion species have existed over the course of our planet's history. Only *one* of them ever invented a computer. Only *one* of them ever managed to send members of its own kind into space. Only *one* of them knows that *anything* existed before them, or beyond them. *Us*. And how did we manage all those things? Territoriality? Greed?'

Miles's expression shifted. A more hopeful look took hold.

'Through connection, communication and cooperation. So, my question is this: what could a more connected world achieve? What is humankind's *real* capability?'

Jack suddenly felt himself go light, as if the mass of his body had ebbed away. He was floating. He looked at the rest of the Mob; their feet hovered a few inches off the ground, and their hands rose up involuntarily. They all looked at Miles, and Miles looked back at them.

'Hold on tight,' he said with a smile.

The Raid Mob were launched from the surface of the moon. They shot into space at an incredible speed, cutting through the cosmic fabric. Mars flashed beneath them as they headed towards the vast asteroid belt that separated the inner planets from the gas giants. Instinctively, Jack crossed his arms over his face as he was threaded like a human needle through the dense field of rocks. But even when they swung around the striped orb of Jupiter and skidded along the rings of Saturn, they met no resistance. By the time they'd passed Neptune, even Cameron had managed to relax a little. The edge of the solar system loomed, and looking back, the Mob spotted Earth – now a tiny speck in the blackness.

Gradually, the stars began to converge around them, grouping together as they flew further into wild, open space. A moment later, this view was obscured as they were enveloped by a thick cosmic cloud. Sparks of green and blue and red danced inside the galactic fog – a blanket of nebulas that seemed to stretch on and on. Jack couldn't help himself: he reached out his hand. He wanted to touch this mystical material, this dense collection of the remnants of supernova explosions and the shed skin of dead stars. It danced between his fingers like shifting sand. Finally, Jack broke free of the clinging cosmic fog and looked back on what he had left behind: a vast spiral in space. The Milky Way galaxy. Home to Earth, and *a hundred billion* other planets.

Then the journey through space continued.

It wasn't long before Jack was looking at a sea of lights. It was not dissimilar to the view from his bedroom window on a cold, clear night. Each cluster, with billions of stars and planets, formed a building block of an unimaginably vast universe. The majesty of all creation was unveiled for Jack and his friends.

The Mob came to a stop on the edge of the known universe, where they were joined by Miles.

'This is my favourite place,' he said. 'And this is the first time I've ever brought anyone else here. I couldn't think of a better place for your prize-giving.'

The light of the entire universe danced in the Mob's bright eyes.

'Your prize is all of *this*. Everything I have shown you today, and much, much more. It is all yours. You each now own shares in Hailstorm Games. You will also own part of the Hailstorm Campus – namely the individual properties that will be built especially for you, for domestic, academic, and eventually professional purposes. Your educational futures will be fully funded by Hailstorm Games, and you may study anywhere in the world. When you complete your qualifications, you will all have jobs waiting for you at the company. You will each have a prize money deposit that will become accessible at the age of 21. It will be worth five million pounds.'

The Mob were speechless. Jack's eyes were so wide they reflected the whole of the known universe. Then, Miles continued.

'My competition was never about kills or style points. It was never about views and likes. If it was, Carbon Shift would have won; he was the first to be taken into the abduction simulation. But we soon found out that he'd been cheating with aimbots and wallhacks – hence his WarMech's fate. After that, I made sure that no *one* person would be able to complete the challenge. It would take a collective effort; the effort of a group of people who weren't just out for themselves – out to conquer and keep – but to connect and share, and feel belonging and attachment. You, the Raid Mob, have proved that you have the qualities that are key to making real progress as part of a connected race. You cooperate, you communicate, you are loyal, and you put each other before yourselves. When you believed someone else was in danger, you stood up for them. You have demonstrated what is needed to take my company in a direction that will benefit humanity. I believe that technology is the key to unlocking our potential and creating a world where real cooperation takes us to places beyond our wildest imaginings. I want you four to help me get to those places ...'

Miles turned, looking out beyond the edge of the universe and into the unknown.

'... And then, I want you to take it further.'

Miles looked back at the group.

'Sound good?' he said.

Jack found himself staring out into the same abyss. What he might once have seen as a bleak and empty space now seemed to be bursting with opportunity and excitement. Turning back towards his friends, he saw his own beaming smile mirrored on all their faces.

This was going to be fun.

'*Five million pounds!* That's a whoooole lot of red bandanas!' Megan bounced down the corridor with the others in tow. 'And we get our own digs too! Custom made! I'm going to have a cinema room with reclining seats that look like hypersleep chambers! And I'm going to have a life-sized xenomorph replica in every room – even the toilets!'

'My home will be a fortress of facts and information,' said Ayo. 'Every wall will be covered in bookshelves, and I'm going to oversee the construction of an underground computer lab that'll make Bill Gates quake in his chinos.'

'You g-guys have seen *Richie R-R-Rich*, right?' Cameron said. 'Well I'm gonna d-d-d-do what he did ...'

'Build a McDonalds in your house?' Megan guessed.

'Yup!' Cameron responded, licking his lips in eager anticipation. 'Only, they'll h-have ShockSoda on tap in every f-f-flavour, and a milkshake bar, and a massiv–'

Cameron's excited voice faded as Jack fell further behind his friends. He hadn't said anything since leaving the simulation. He was in shock. It was all so utterly life-changing, especially to him, and it had him in a daze. He followed the sound of his friends' eager voices, until something pulled him from his trance.

'Jack!' a voice whispered. 'Jack! Wait a second!'

Jack stopped and turned. Miles Morgan had paused in the middle of the corridor.

'Come here a moment.'

Jack's arm drifted upwards, pointing after his friends.

'Ken will take care of them,' said Miles. 'I want to show you something.'

Jack walked back to Miles, a sudden curiosity rousing him from his stupor as he was led towards a heavy-looking door. Miles placed his palm on a security scanner. A narrow hatch opened, and a small metal sphere hovered out on a robotic arm. Miles removed his glasses and looked directly at it. There was a beep and an amber light.

'Enter voice code passphrase now.'

Miles spoke slowly and deliberately.

'You can close your eyes to reality, but not to memories.'

The light turned green and the heavy door swung open. Jack saw that it led to a walkway, which in turn led to the opposite side of the Hailstorm Games building – into the right-hand helix tower.

'Follow me.'

Jack continued in his dazed state. On the other side of the walkway there were more security checks, scanners, and even an enhanced X-ray gate to pass through before gaining access to a long white corridor. There were doors at regular intervals. Each door was fitted with heavy-duty digital locks. It looked like a hi-tech prison.

Miles stopped outside the first door. His face was set in stone, and he looked at Jack as if he was trying to peer into his mind.

'Behind this door is the future of my company, Jack,' he said. 'What waits for you inside this room makes the technology you've seen so far look like the abacus. You will be the only non-employee to see it.'

'But … why?' Jack suddenly felt hot and dizzy, blood rushing to his head.

'Why you?' said Miles. 'Because I have a feeling, Jack. And I need a way to find out if I can trust that feeling. Inside this room are two things: a chair and a helmet. The helmet is a little cumbersome – I'm working on scaling it down – but all you need to do is sit down and put it on. The device will take care of the rest.'

Without waiting for a response, Miles reached into his pocket and pulled out a transparent key card inlaid with complex chips that glowed blue. He held it against the doorframe. The digital locks popped. The door hissed as hydraulic hinges pulled it open. Jack saw four white walls, a white ceiling, a white floor, a chair, and a helmet.

The starkness of the surroundings started to make Jack feel trapped – like he'd seen too much, and now there was no turning back. 'Do I have a choice?'

'Jack, I understand that you feel like you haven't had a choice over a lot of things in your life,' said Miles softly. 'I can assure you – that isn't the case here. The choice is absolutely yours.'

Jack felt forces pulling him back and pushing him forwards all at once. Questions bounced around his mind. *Why are the rest of the Raid Mob not here? What is the "feeling" that Miles talked about? What is with all the extra secrecy and security? What could I be letting myself in for this time?* Jack teetered in the doorway, on the brink of two different paths; paths that could take him to very different places.

Then he stepped towards the chair.

Miles spoke clearly. 'Think of a time, a memory – something that you did, or that someone did to you – that you would *change*, if you could.'

Jack picked up the helmet from the chair. He turned it over in his hands. The design was like the Fullmmersion kit – sleek and smooth, delicate yet powerful. Jack sat down in the chair, and the door behind him closed. He placed the helmet on his head. A pair of circular disks, mounted on small probes, extended down from the brim on each side.

The moment they pressed gently onto Jack's temples, the white room disappeared, and everything went black.

It took Jack a moment to recognise the place where he found himself. He was in the kitchen of the house he used to live in, before he moved to the estate. Everything was there, correct down to the smallest detail. But Jack wasn't concentrating on the furniture, or the wall tiles, or the photographs on the fridge door. He was transfixed by two things: the glow coming from the middle of the room, and the figure behind it.

Twelve candles burned on a colourful cake in the centre of the dining table, the light flickering across the face of the only other person there. Jack's mum was sitting at the table. She had one hand on her distended tummy, and the other held to the side of her face. In the dim light, Jack could see that she was crying. He knew that she wasn't able to see him; he was only there to watch.

He knew what was going to happen next. He remembered it clearly. He would run in, so excited for his birthday cake and his presents that he wouldn't even notice his mum was upset. He'd ask where his dad was. His mum would tell him that his dad wasn't going to be there for his birthday. Jack would ask questions; the answers would make him mad. He'd ask why, over and over. His questions would turn into demands, then into blame. Jack would tell his mum that she was always yelling at dad and it was no wonder he'd gone. He'd tell her he didn't want a baby brother anymore – he just wanted his dad back. He'd tell her he hated her, then he'd run upstairs and cry into his pillow until he ran out of tears.

Sure enough, Jack watched his younger self bound into the kitchen. After a while, he spoke.

'Where's Dad?'

Jack's mum clutched at her stomach in desperation.

Her face broke into pieces as she tried to explain. Jack looked over at his own younger face. It was full of confusion, with anger and misery just waiting to bubble to the surface.

Jack understood every emotion that twelve-year-old boy was feeling, yet he urged him to react in a different way. He recognised the moment for what it was: the fork in the road of his and his mum's relationship. It was a lot to put on his younger self, but Jack implored him to take a different path to the one he had once chosen.

Jack watched as his younger self walked up to his mum and threw his arms around her. She held him tightly, sobbing into his neck. Jack willed words into the mouth of his younger self, and in the midst of the tears and the anguish, the boy managed to repeat them.

'I love you, Mum.'

Jack heard his mum's reply.

'I love you too.'

He watched as she squeezed the boy even tighter, and as he did, Jack felt all his knotted-up resentment ebbing away. He took deep, full breaths, exhaling pain and inhaling freedom, warming his heart and energising him right to the centre of his soul. In that moment, he resolved to turn this virtual change into something real.

Suddenly, he was back in the white room.

Jack reached up and removed the helmet. He turned it over in his hands as if he were holding a magic artefact. Tears rolled down his cheeks – but he was smiling. This technology had let him relive his own history differently – and in doing so, to experience a moment in the present that would change his future.

In that moment, Jack knew that he was going to make things better. He owed his mum the chance he never gave her at the time. Today was the start of a new path, in more ways than he could ever have realised.

'I knew it,' said a voice.

Jack looked up. Miles was standing at the door, a tablet in his hand.

'I hope you don't mind, Jack,' he said. 'I know what you just experienced was intense – and intensely personal – but I had to see what you would do with this technology.'

'What technology?' said Jack, staring at the helmet. 'What *is* this thing?'

'It is my proudest achievement; a quantum leap; a milestone of technological development. It goes way beyond simulation and virtual reality. It interfaces seamlessly with the most advanced computer in existence – the human brain.'

Miles approached Jack and took the helmet from him, looking it over as he continued.

'We have developed algorithms that map the human mind like a memory drive. Through this device, we can draw out stored memories, digitise them, and then feed them back into the user's conscious perception. People are not only allowed the chance to re-live their past experiences, but to live them *differently*, like you just did.'

Miles stopped admiring the helmet and looked straight at Jack.

'But do you know the difference, Jack? The difference between you and every other person who has tested this technology?'

Jack couldn't even begin to guess.

'Let me explain. This project is called SPOTS, which stands for "Spirit of the Staircase"; a phrase made up by a man called Denis Diderot in 1820. He used it to explain that voice that comes to you after a negative event. The one that tells you what you *should* have said, or what you *should* have done. By that point, it's too late – you're stuck with the frustration of knowing what you should have done, but you're never able to do it.'

Miles took another step towards Jack.

'Everyone else who's tried this technology used it to get back at someone. All of them. They thought about a person who's hurt them, embarrassed them, or betrayed them – and in the memory they pushed their past selves towards revenge. Even me! I went straight back to my high school canteen, where Jake Lambert, the school bully, tipped my tray up in front of everyone. And I did exactly what I wished I'd done at the time: I smacked him over the head with it.'

Miles placed his hand on Jack's shoulder, smiling now.

'You are the first person to use this technology for

good. I didn't tell you to do that, and you didn't know what was going to happen. But still you sought to heal rather than to harm. *That* is what I want for the future of this company. I want what we make to be used to connect people, or *re*connect them. To help them understand each other, and through understanding to cooperate and collaborate to steer humankind towards that future that lies at the edge of possibility. And to do all that, Jack, I need someone who has those values at their very core, to underpin decisions that could have world-changing consequences.'

Letting go of Jack's shoulder, Miles motioned for him to stand up.

'I need an apprentice, Jack. I need someone I can teach, who I can one day hand all of this over to. Someone with whom I know it will be safe. There are plenty of detractors who say that leading lives online damages human interaction and connection. But I know that you know differently. You recognise the wonder and potential of the virtual world, yet you never let go of your real-life connections – your friends, your brother ... your mum. You have seen the potential that technology has to bring people together. You can show them the way, Jack. I want you to be the future of this company.'

Miles held out his hand,

'So ... what do you say? Will you be the Luke to my Yoda?' he asked with a smile.

A universe of possibility erupted behind Jack's eyes.

Just when he thought he'd reached the top of the mountain, this revelation made him realise that the peak was merely a launch pad, and he was set to travel all the way to the stars.

Jack didn't hesitate. He took Miles's hand and shook it firmly. Then he watched as Miles, the helmet, and the entire white room began to fade, dissolving to nothing.

Within moments, everything had been replaced by blackness, and two short words:

GAME

OVER

Level 25: Memory Play

Jack opened his eyes.

As usual, everything was a blur. All he could see were cloudy shapes, vague shadows, and a light that was slightly too bright to be comfortable. He remained seated, blinking away the distortion and allowing the feeling to ebb back into his limbs as he waited patiently for the real world to return.

After a while, Jack lifted his hand and watched his fuzzy fingers coming into sharper focus. It was still weird not to be wearing the gloves, but it was way more convenient to have the upgraded RealFeel sensors embedded beneath his skin. The procedure hadn't hurt one bit, and it was so popular now that even Cameron had been brave enough to get it done. A blue light blinked on the back of Jack's hand, signalling that the sensors had disconnected from the helmet. Reaching up, he took the headgear off, then scanned the space around him.

Warm sunlight seeped through the ten-metre-tall wall of glass that lined the left-hand side of the opulent three-tiered living quarters. The white marble floor danced, refracting sunrays into rainbow shimmers. Jack's hand flicked towards a control tablet built into his plush gaming chair, and with a swipe of his finger, the glass wall tinted and the light softened. Jack still wasn't used to the after-effects of Memory Play, and the brightness didn't help his lingering headache.

Slowly, he rose from his seat. He was thirsty. He'd been in there a while, after all. Approaching a sleek drinks dispenser that had been integrated into a multifunctional gaming table, Jack mumbled, 'Tropical Storm.'

A steel cylinder descended and bubbling purple liquid began to flow. While he waited, Jack took a sideways glance at the giant screen in the centre of the living area. It was film night tonight, and the Mob were all going to be in *Ghostbusters 2*. Jack smiled. He was looking forward to seeing his friends in the real world, especially today.

As Jack took a long, quenching drink of his ShockSoda, he wondered how he'd fill the time between now and then. He scanned around the perimeter of the big screen. Housed in individual compartments was an impressive console collection that Jack had collated and curated over the last year, including everything from an ancient *Atari 2600* to the rarer *Dreamcast*, plus a first-generation *PlayStation* and all the other classic Sony and Microsoft machines. But Jack's favourite was still his LightFire Pro, complete with his old, battered controller. He was tempted to pick it up again, for old times' sake, but the remnants of the Memory Play headache pushed him past his console collection, towards a wall that was full of a different kind of nostalgia.

Jack was drawn to a framed newspaper cover. He'd looked at it countless times, yet it never failed to put a smile on his face. The picture showed the Raid Mob standing at the foot of the Hailstorm HQ building, with Miles Morgan behind them. Their unbridled grins beamed out from the page. The headline above read:

MOB RULES!

GAMERS WIN PRIZE OF A LIFETIME!

The paper was dated March 8th. One year ago to the day.

Jack had waited until the first anniversary of the Raid Mob's world-famous win to try out the latest version of the Memory Play program. Before now, users could only play their own memories, while the software used an A.I. engine to infer the actions of others. But the latest upgrade included the new "Memory Share" feature. It allowed users to share access to their memories with others. Of course, the Mob had been eager to add each other to their Memory Connekt lists, and the first memory they'd all given access to was the day that changed everything. Needless to say, for Jack, the wait had been worth it. Living out the most memorable day of his life, with access to the perspectives and emotions of all his friends, made the photograph that he was still staring at come alive in the most incredible way. *Maybe I'll do this every year*, he thought. *Make a tradition of it*. It seemed a fitting way to mark the rise of the Raid Mob.

Next to the framed newspaper, right in the centre of the wall, was another of Jack's most treasured memories. It was a photograph taken at a seaside resort. More and more people were turning to virtual tourism now – especially with VR tour companies offering trips to other planets and fictional worlds – but this photograph was taken on an actual, real-world holiday. It showed three people at an ice-cream stall. On the left was Jack, a big blob of cold ice-cream dripping off the end of his nose. In Jack's arms was Alexander, holding a flattened ice-cream cone and laughing. And on the right was Jack's mum. She wasn't smiling at the camera like the other two, but at her boys instead. It was a smile that brimmed with love and joy, both of which were reflected in Jack's face as he gazed at the picture on the wall.

Almost involuntarily, Jack's hand hovered up towards a tablet mounted beneath the frame. It washed over black as his hand approached, and a green digital icon with the word "CALL" appeared. Jack hesitated, remembering that it was Alex's nap time. He'd see them later. They lived in the same building now, after all.

Jack scanned the rest of the wall. It was a teeming testament to the craziest year of his life. There were photos of the Mob's many meetings: with royalty, tech giants, news outlets, screaming fans, and plenty of A-list celebrities – many of whom seemed more star-struck at meeting the infamous Raid Mob than the other way around. There were posters from their appearances at conferences, and endless gaming awards that the Mob had won since that fateful day, cementing their reputation as the most elite gamers on the planet.

Swigging down the last of his ShockSoda, Jack sauntered back across the living area of his penthouse, towards the wall of glass. When he'd first moved in, he'd found this view more than a little intimidating. He was *so* high up. Now, he enjoyed resting his forehead against the cool glass and looking down at the courtyard in front of Hailstorm HQ. The daily mob of fans was already there, all waiting to get their picture with the four ten-metre-tall WarMech replicas that had been installed a week after the Mob won the ultimate prize. Groups huddled around a giant Raid Mob crest mounted in the centre of the four statues, throwing up peace signs and posing for pictures that would no doubt be cropped, filtered, and posted, with Jack tagged, within the hour. Once they'd finished their selfies and stories, the crowd began to back away. Jack watched as they turned and stared up at the mechs in a moment of awe-filled reverence. He couldn't blame them. Jack enjoyed looking at them too – only to him, they were like a massive robotic family portrait.

With a widening smile, he glanced back to the memory wall, at his other family picture. He felt extremely lucky. Two whole families: one he was born into – repaired and reconciled at last; and the Raid Mob. Jack gazed upwards into a cloudless blue sky and smiled

THE RAID MOB

so widely it hurt his cheeks. It felt too good to be true. However, this time, Jack knew what was real. This time, there was no "Game Over" lurking around the corner.

With his head finally clear, Jack looked back at the big screen. The Mob wouldn't be getting together for another few hours at least. Jack glanced at the upgraded headset sitting on his gaming chair. Then he looked again at the seaside snap. What better way to fill his time than a trip down that warm, sandy, ice-cream-filled memory lane?

Jack sat in his chair and put the helmet back on. A home screen appeared with all his saved games, profiles, competition standings, and social media links laid out across various tabs. He swiped them all away without a single twitch of his hand, selecting the Memory Play app and using the search function to bring up the correct date, time, place, and set of people. Taking a long deep breath, Jack allowed himself to sink into the darkness as the menu disappeared and the Memory Play began ...

Only it didn't. There was no beach, no smell of sea air, no sensation of sand between his toes, and no coldness on the tip of his nose. There was just a single icon, floating in the middle of nothingness. It was an envelope.

'Open,' Jack said.

The icon unfolded, and a scrolling line of green text appeared.

SOME MEMORIES ARE PRICELESS.
AREN'T THEY, JACK?
WHAT WOULD YOU GIVE TO GET YOUR
MOST PRECIOUS MOMENTS BACK?

No sooner had Jack read the final word, when a blinding pain ripped through his skull. It felt like a barbed hook had been sunk into the middle of his mind, and something was dragging at it, trying to tear a part of him out. Suddenly, the words disappeared, replaced by the real world. The visor display had become transparent, allowing Jack to see his surroundings. He tumbled out of his chair to the floor, convulsing in pain. He reached up and grabbed at the helmet, but the RealFeel sensors in his arms sent a searing current through his nerves that arrested his attempts to take it off in an instant. What was happening? Had the helmet malfunctioned? Was there something wrong with the Memory Play software, or the memory he'd tried to access? Through the pain and the disorientation, Jack looked through the visor at the wall, to the frame in the centre.

Something was very wrong.

Staggering to his feet, Jack stumbled towards the photo. But the closer he got, the less sense it made. He threw his hand against the wall and pulled his face close to the image. The picture showed him at the seaside, standing in front of an ice-cream stall. He had a blob of white ice cream on his nose. He was holding a toddler, and standing next to them was a middle-aged, brown-haired woman.

Jack didn't recognise either of them.

Dazed and disconcerted, he stared at the strangers in the picture until the searing pain returned, piercing his mind and bringing him to his knees. His world went dark once more, and a new message appeared from the blackness.

WE HAVE YOUR MEMORIES.
PLAY US FOR THEM.
YOU WIN, YOU GET THEM BACK.
YOU LOSE, WE TAKE YOUR PRIZE ...
AND YOUR MIND.

The words hung, ominous and menacing. Then they dissolved. Two words took their place, glowing in the darkness ...

GAME

ON ...

GAME PROGRESS ... 100%

REWARD UNLOCKED

THE
DAUGHTER
OF
SLAUGHTER
MIX

CLocK TOWER PuBLiSHiNG

Clock Tower Publishing was launched in 2021 and is a trade imprint of Sweet Cherry Publishing. We champion new, marginalised and diverse voices in publishing, inspired by our multicultural Leicester heritage. We aim to bring our readers a range of high-quality fiction that authentically showcases the diverse and inclusive world we live in while hooking them in a compellingly great story. From fantasy fiction to future classics, we're dedicated to creating a great list of quality trade fiction that's championed by its authors and illustrators alongside a diverse team of book lovers.

www.clocktowerpublishing.com

Acknowledgements

To Claire – for your support and encouragement;
for telling me to come to bed when I was red-eyed and
weary, and for understanding when I still wouldn't give
in. Love you to the Moon. To Miles – for being the world's
best excuse to be a big kid forever. To Mum and Dad – for
all your pride and excitement, and for Christmas 1992:
the day I unwrapped my first Sega Mega Drive and this
obsession began. To Lucy – for letting me tell everyone
that I completed *Ocarina of Time* when it was really you,
and for all the two-player tail we kicked. To Atari Andy –
for being the coolest cousin and worst instigator/enabler
of all my geekiest habits. To Dave – for every time we
completed *Streets of Rage 2* before school, and for twenty-
six years of bromance. To Hera – for all the beatings you
took on *GoldenEye* only to return them on *Mario Kart*,
and for those many nights spent indulging our *Need for
Speed*. To Guy – for being in my corner and inspiring me to
be a better writer and a bigger nerd. And to Jasmine – for
discovering *Game Over* and bringing it to life, and for your
endless enthusiasm, dedication and encouragement.

Zuul's Playlist

Pre-Game

The Alan Parsons Project - *Sirius*
The Killers – *The Man*
Guns 'n' Roses – *Welcome to The Jungle*

In-Game

Dragonforce – *Through the Fire and the Flames*
Daft Punk – *Robot Rock*
Kenny Loggins – *Danger Zone*
Edwin Starr – *War*
Queen – *Another One Bites the Dust*
LL Cool J – *Mama Said Knock You Out*

Post-Game

N-Trance – *Stayin' Alive*
Orbital – *Halcyon and On and On*
The Immortals – *Techno Syndrome*

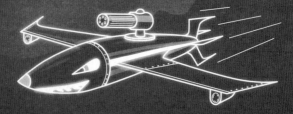